# DEATH ON THE ALDER

Jamie Tremain

**Jamie Tremain**

*PAM: The support we receive from the writing community and the encouragement from friends and family is invaluable to keep the ink flowing.*

*LIZ: This book is dedicated to all our faithful and supportive friends - many of whom are loyal fans of Jamie Tremain. We do this for you.*

# CONTENTS

# CHAPTER ONE

## *Alysha*

**Grant's Crossing Gazette**

**Drug Overdose Kills Local Man-Authorities Suspect Foul Play**

Grant's Crossing is reeling today. The body found floating in the Alder River this week, near the old sawmill property, was one of our own. Police identified Bradley McTaggart; forty-two years old, single. He worked part-time for Dr. Reid Harrison as a delivery person. Dr. Harrison is shocked by the death. Police deem McTaggart's death suspicious and are investigating. Family members were not available for comment.

McTaggart. The name rang a bell, but I had other things on my mind and dismissed the disturbing headline on my way to the lawyer's office.

Not where I really wanted to spend my time, even if the weather was stellar in this rural Ontario small town. I'd been summoned back to Grant's Crossing to meet with my late Uncle Dalton's lawyer. Seems my uncle had bequeathed me the old farmhouse. I could only imagine it stuffed to the rafters with all the god-awful stuff old people like to hang on to. And for extra fun, I'd been told livestock was included.

Do I sound ungrateful? I don't mean to be, but seriously, livestock?

Legal correspondence advised of my Great Uncle Dalton Grant's death about two months ago. I'd been unaware until the letter arrived. My fault in not keeping the post office current on my latest move. I'd been stunned to learn of my status as sole heir. Which is why I now found myself searching for the lawyer's office. Instructions had been sent requesting my presence to deal with paperwork and whatever else was necessary. While family death wasn't foreign to me its legal formalities were new territory and I wasn't sure what to expect.

I made the three-hour drive to Grant's Crossing just in time for the ten o'clock appointment. Now I wished I had taken the time to have breakfast; nerves were setting in, mixed with a dose of apprehension.

I entered the reception area and introduced myself to the no-nonsense assistant guarding the entrance to the lawyer's inner sanctum.

"Hi. Alysha Grant. I have an appointment to see Bryce Lockhart."

She barely turned her head. "Have a seat. Mr. Lockhart will be with your shortly."

She was as dry as the dust I saw layered on the

baseboards, and I wondered if the lawyer had been here since time began. Within minutes I was ushered into the great man's office. The look of surprise on his aged face bordered on comical. In hindsight, I'd say he hadn't expected to see a twenty-eight-year-old who could pass for seventeen. Envious friends say my baby face, bouncy blond curls, and waif-like figure always worked to my advantage.

Despite my business degree and real estate license, potential employers have never taken me seriously, hence the shock registering on Bryce Lockhart's face. Mr. Bryce Woodrow Lockhart (spelled out boldly on his name plaque) fell under old school, I'd say. Probably about eighty. An exaggeration perhaps, but still an old fart.

His withering gaze told me I was dressed inappropriately. Maybe my choice of denim cut-offs and Birkenstocks spoke of immaturity. But what the heck, I was between jobs, and it was summer, what'd he expect?

He adjusted his glasses and proceeded to intone details of my inheritance. His dry and pedantic voice droned on about familial responsibility. He touched on the family rift between my father and my grandparents. Thankfully he didn't mention the car crash that killed my parents. Even though it had been three years, I remained numb to the loss. I'd no desire to discuss something so personal with this dried-up shell of a man. He looked exasperated at my lack of comment.

He told me how Uncle Dalton had moved into the old farmhouse when my grandfather died. I already knew this. I admit even though he took over paying my tuition at University. I hadn't paid much attention to Uncle Dalton, or my grandmother, after my parents were gone. Too wrapped up in my own misery, concentrating on my studies, and Jeff, my boyfriend.

Mr. Lockhart's tight lips spelled out disapproval in spades. I didn't like him either. "I know Uncle Dalton moved into the farmhouse. What I need to know is how all this affects me now."

With a theatrical sigh, the lawyer paused in his ramblings and shuffled papers. I glanced around the room. For a small-town lawyer, he must have been doing quite well. Maybe he was the town's only lawyer. His large antique desk took up much of the room and comfy chairs sat beside large windows looking out onto Main Street. I gazed out on a vibrant and attractive town, not as I'd remembered it when I left. I forced myself back to matters at hand as Lockhart returned to business.

"Pertaining to the present day then, and what affects you. You've inherited the house and several acres. This includes all farm outbuildings and existing livestock."

"Define several."

Good. His reaction indicated he needn't underestimate me. He fiddled with his ear, trying to adjust a hearing aid, or playing for time?

"Ah, yes. The last survey shows just over six hectares or fifteen acres." He peered at me over his glasses. "You may not be familiar with imperial measurement."

Aaaargggh! Condescending bugger! I forced myself not to respond to the age-related dig as I struggled to envisage the size of the property.

"I remember conversations when I was a *little* girl about subdividing the property, but I never knew its exact size. When my grandfather died, Gran vowed to keep the land intact. She had vision." I smiled to myself, remembering now the sense of comfort and safety I'd enjoyed there as a child.

"Indeed. Her vision provided financial security. Her decision to open up the home to paying guests saw her through some tough times." He paused. "Which brings me to another facet of the will."

How could there possibly be more?

"Your grandmother was adamant her home provide a more personal environment for those not yet ready for assisted, or long term, care. Dalton agreed and his will provides for ongoing arrangements for the current residents."

The light bulb went on. I'd have to continue to provide a home for old people? No way. Not signing up to be a nurse. Images of lost dentures and bathroom accidents flashed through my mind. As if reading my thoughts, Lockhart carried on.

"Ms. Grant, these are not incapacitated folk. I would describe most of them as vital, young at heart, but in need of surroundings that address their social and emotional needs. Without the worries of maintaining their own home."

I broke into his endless speech. "Seriously—old people—shouldn't they be in a proper nursing home or something?"

Lockhart pinched the bridge of his nose. "If this is not for you, Ms. Grant, I can help. It's a valuable property; you would have no problem finding a buyer."

I took a deep breath. "This is overwhelming, Mr. Lockhart." Unbidden, a panicked vision of responsibilities took hold. A good time to change the topic so I asked a question. "You mentioned livestock. What kind of livestock. Horses, chickens?"

"No, three alpacas. It's a farm, there are *always* chickens."

"Right, I'd forgotten about the alpacas. Aren't they like llamas?"

"Similar. I've included information. If you recall they were pets of your grandmother's. She bought them after your grandfather died with the intention to breed them and began a business harvesting their fleece. Your grandmother came from a generation who knew how to be resourceful," he said. He sounded put out as if I should be more aware of my grandmother's abilities or was he accusing me of not being resourceful. *Really*! He knew nothing about me.

I had to bite my lip, my irritation with this whole situation had grown stronger by the minute. I wanted to escape and needed time to think.

I admit I'd been an ungrateful granddaughter and hadn't paid much attention to family matters. I hadn't even gone up to the house after Gran's funeral. Said a quick goodbye to Uncle Dalton at the cemetery and hightailed it back to Guelph. But now it had come full circle, and everything had landed on me. Karma in action.

The lawyer's lips moved, but I'd tuned him out. He must have clued in because he stopped talking and peered at me. He pushed his glasses back into position on the bridge of his nose and waited for me to respond. Was it my imagination or did his lip actually curl in a show of distaste? Or was he mirroring my feelings towards him?

He cleared his throat. "As I said, Ms. Grant. The house is in excellent shape and furnished. A complete renovation, including an addition, was done some time ago with quarters for the staff needed to run Leven Lodge. Ready to move right in, as is."

"Staff. Oh. Jan, right? She's still there?"

Another exasperated sigh. "Yes. It's what I've been trying to tell you. It may not be to your taste but, you'll have the housekeeper and a cook. A gardener is on hand a few times a week. I've reviewed the books of each business and can see your Uncle barely kept in the black with Leven Lodge's paying guests, and the alpacas. The minimal income from fleece sales goes toward their feed and vet bills. Currently, there's enough money for you to retain the cook and housekeeper for a year. Taxes and other expenses for the house are also covered—barring any major repairs."

I'd had enough. Time to take charge. "Do I have to sign these papers today? I'd like to read them and consult with my partner. It would be a huge lifestyle change but...well, I have to give this a lot of serious thought."

He started closing folders on his desk. The patronizing tone returned. "I can give you a week from today but no later." He handed me a bank manager's business card. "You'll probably want to deal with a local bank."

He held out a sheaf of paperwork. "Here's all you need, along with details of the sale of the sawmill property, if you're interested. On a side note, the sale paid for the renovations."

I took hold of the paperwork, but he wasn't finished.

"As I mentioned earlier, you may want to consider selling if you anticipate running Leven Lodge is not for you. I can negotiate for you if you decide to sell. Something to think about. However, be aware the will states any sale is on condition the new owner would continue to provide a home for any residents still there."

My brain rattled. "Thank you. You've given me a lot to consider."

"Very well, if you don't have any further questions, I do have another appointment. Call my office should you need anything."

Of course, I had a million questions. How does one go from being a graduate student coursing carefree through life, to being a landowner, a farmer? With responsibility for eight old folks in a guest house?

I stood when he did, shook his outstretched hand, and murmured a small thank you.

As I walked out into the bright sunshine clutching the folder, I felt faint. I looked for a Starbucks. No such luck. I spied a cafe sign and headed there for a fix of caffeine. My mind fell blank, allowing no room for any thoughts of antique furniture, paying guests, or animals to intrude. Where was Jeff when I needed him? His irritatingly calm demeanor, not to mention nerdy ways, was just what I needed.

Jeff Iverson and I were a couple and had been living together since grad school. He's a brilliant man but as I said, a nerd. Give him an academic journal and he's in heaven. He's attached at the hip to most computer gadgets, but bails me out when I'm stuck, which is most of the time.

The cafe was busy but I didn't pay much attention to those around me as I sat and remembered my childhood in Grant's Crossing. There were times I'd not wanted to go to school, same as any kid. But that had been the worst of my troubles. At least until Dad had that huge fight with my grandparents. Something to do with the sawmill being sold. And now I'd been handed more responsibility than I ever wanted. Maybe he was right, and I should just sell it.

I ordered a second coffee as thoughts started coming faster than I could sort them. Panic set in as I searched for my phone. I needed to hear Jeff's voice. Where was my phone? I finally found it sitting underneath my bag. Jeff answered on the first ring but didn't interrupt as I relayed the news of the farmhouse, paying guests, and alpacas.

His response was unexpected. "So what're you waiting for? You've been wanting a business of your own and now you've been handed one. And I can help you."

"But what about our life in Guelph? Won't you miss your friends, family?"

"You're my family, Alysha. Maybe, it's time to start a new life. Besides, I always wanted to hook up with an heiress."

"Funny boy. I haven't even seen the house yet. I left when I was thirteen and only had one brief visit a couple of years later. It's probably a museum. And the town itself—they don't even have a Starbucks."

"We can live without Starbucks. Why don't you go see it today and send me pics? I'm dying to see the alpacas."

"I don't know. There's so much to think about."

"Take a deep breath, I can tell you're in shock. Listen, don't make any decisions without me, right? My contract here has wrapped up. I can pack a few things and be there tomorrow."

I calmed down and said, "So you do have a spontaneous side."

I gave him directions and said goodbye. Then I finished my coffee, left the cafe and grabbed a copy of the local newspaper I'd seen earlier. Might as well start familiarizing myself with the surroundings if this was to be my new home. Headlines blared, *Drug Overdose Kills Local Man—Authorities Suspect Foul Play.*

I now had more time to read about Bradley McTaggart whose body had been discovered floating in the river near the old sawmill a few days ago. It didn't seem right that crime could be part of my old hometown, but reality told me nowhere was immune.

Main Street bustled and I enjoyed the stroll peeking into a variety of shop windows. What had made me think this was a dying town?

I passed a pub, with requisite patio, catering to locals enjoying various beverages. Colorful umbrellas advertising popular brews, and small craft ales, provided shade from the midday sun.

It made me thirsty, and I also craved a smoke after what I'd endured at the lawyer's office. I'd given up the habit a few years ago, but sometimes the urge could be overwhelming, especially when I felt stressed. I entered a convenience store to buy a pack of nicotine gum. I know everyone seems to be into vaping, but it didn't appeal to me.

"Trying to kick the habit, are you?" The clerk rang up my purchase.

"Yeah, something like that."

He handed me my change and smiled. "Not seen you around here before?"

"I'm on my way to the Grant farmhouse."

"The Grant farmhouse? You mean Leven Lodge. Estelle changed the name when she turned it into a guesthouse a few years ago. You looking for a room? Those folks are a bit old for ya."

He must be related to the lawyer. Did everyone here assume I'm too young to know anything. I declined a response, it would only lead to more questions.

He was all about being the source of tourist information. "Let's see now. Keep on walking past the square to the end of Main Street and cross at the traffic lights. Go over the bridge and keep walking. It's quite a bit further on. Sure you wanna walk that far? It's right at the edge of town—the biggest farmhouse around. Estelle and Dalton kept it looking beautiful so you can't miss it."

"Thanks, I know my way."

The shopkeeper paused. He eyed the newspaper tucked under my arm. "You're not a reporter, are you? We've had enough of them since the body was found. Terrible business. Don't know what this town is coming to. Sawmill closed years ago. Heard it got sold to some developer. Hmmph. Not sure what they'll do with it. Changes, changes, all the time."

"No, no. I used to live here, and I remember the farmhouse." I tapped the newspaper with my hand. "I've read about them finding the body though."

Maybe I shouldn't have mentioned living here before, because now he truly was interested. "You don't say. Well now you mention it, you kind of look familiar, and I 'm good at remembering. No, don't tell me." He wrinkled his brow and peered off into the distance for a moment before giving a shrug. "It'll come to me later. Now then, you'll find Leven Lodge more toward where the river is wider."

I gritted my teeth and wanted to bring this conversation to an end. I certainly wasn't going to reveal I was Estelle's granddaughter. I thanked him and made my escape to the street. I could've been trapped there all day listening to his gossip.

I decided to walk to the farmhouse and wondered what kind of reception I'd receive.

Large planters bookended convenient benches, the sidewalk shaded by trees in full leaf. I passed the town square busy with shoppers. When I reached the bridge leading to Grant Avenue, I observed and admired the mixture of architecture. Obtaining my real estate license had made me more aware of style and I was impressed by what I saw. I wondered about the housing market. If I needed a part-time job it wouldn't hurt to make contact with a local realtor.

Gazing at the river running under the bridge, I envisioned the body found floating there, and it made me shudder. I lingered for a few moments deep in thought, recalling times spent here holding my grandfather's hand when I was small. I gave myself a shake —best not go there. I still had a distance to walk so I stuffed the newspaper in my purse. It was a pleasant trek and as I rounded a corner, I could see the farmhouse situated on a small rise, the name etched into a large stone at the foot of the driveway.

Memories flooded back. Helping Gran feed chickens, picking fresh vegetables from the garden. Bedtime stories. Can you really go home again?

The house looked as if it had been there a hundred years and probably had. I started up the tree-lined driveway with well-tended lawns and flowering shrubs on either side. As I neared the house, I could make out the barn tucked in behind, and green fields spreading out in the distance.

I'd only been thirteen when I left, so I'd forgotten how big the farmhouse and property was. The realtor in me could see the obvious work gone into its upkeep. Yellow brick trimmed with dark green shutters and window frames. The windows gleamed and flower boxes welcomed me to the house.

The spacious veranda across the front and side lay in shadow. I envisioned a cool and peaceful ambience, so my return to Leven Lodge was not what I expected.

A gruff voice greeted me, "So you've arrived. We don't need you here."

# CHAPTER TWO

## *Dianne*

"Gorgeous day, don't you think?" I said.

Ty Rogers pursed his lips and cocked an eyebrow at my greeting. He put down his cup of tea. "If you like mosquitoes and spiders, then I guess, yes, it is. They're so dreadfully abundant this time of year." He gave a small, affected, shudder.

The veranda at Leven Lodge is usually in shade and a perfect place for having morning coffee or tea, but as it's edged with peony bushes and hanging floral baskets I agreed with his comment. I patted his shoulder and sat down across from him. The veranda held lots of seating, with small tables, a favourite spot with the residents.

"Guess we'll soon meet the granddaughter, right? After Jan said she'd be here checking us out today, all I can say is, I hope I don't have to move again. She might be too young and inexperienced to take over the lodge. I don't want to end up on the street."

"My, my Dianne, you'd be sure to find a bed somewhere if it happened, no worries. But Bea and Jock? At their age? Not so easy."

"Don't be jealous Ty. I'm sure I could bring you with me if need be. Now, if Rose and Lily had to find somewhere else, one of them would end up killing the other without us here to intervene. Dalton knew how to mediate with those two. Time will tell if the new owner is up to snuff. She'll have to keep an eye on Lily."

As for the rest of the group, let's just say adapting to change is not their forte. Nothing's ever constant but change and if you want to keep up, you'd best be flexible, I always say.

"Speaking of killing," Ty said, pointing a manicured finger to the newspaper beside his tea. "What do you think about Jock's nephew? Finding he's dead must have been a shock for the old guy. He's not talking much about it, is he?"

"You're right. Kind of unusual for him. He's usually the first one to comment whether it concerns him or not. I'm sure poor Bea has heard all about it though."

Bea and Jock McTaggart were Leven's original paying residents, and probably the oldest. Estelle Grant had opened her huge home to them after she was widowed. The companionship had been good for her, and for Bea. The poor woman suffered silently being Jock's wife. In my books, he's a big bully. No wonder the daughter ran away. Bradley had been their next nearest relative. And a sad case. No friends, single, couldn't hold a job until the doc offered him one, and always seemed frightened of his own shadow when he came to visit, which wasn't often.

"The police seem to think it's no suicide, or accidental overdose." Ty's comment had a gossipy overtone, and I threw him a stink eye. I put a finger to my lips and motioned to the balcony overhead.

"Shhh… Remember how voices carry. And let's not jump to conclusions, for Bea's sake, if no other reason."

"You're right, sorry." The pout was a bit over-done, but typical for Ty. "Maybe I'll learn more from Reid when I go for my next treatment. He'll have to find a new delivery person to replace Bradley I guess."

The front door opened, and I turned as Cassie DeSouza, our resident cook, stepped onto the veranda. "Everyone's seated for breakfast. You two are MIA."

I stood up. "Good morning to you as well, Cassie. We'll be right in."

"Sorry. Yes, good morning to you both. I'm a bit frazzled, trying to get breakfast ready and thinking about our new owner showing up later today. I hope I'll still have a job."

"No worries, Cassie, who else would be willing to put up with this group?" I hoped my smile would give her some encouragement. "Even with your—ah —creativity in menu planning, we certainly wouldn't want anyone else."

Pointing to the large grease stain on Cassie's shirt, Ty commented, "Just make sure you're wearing something more suitable, sweetie. I'd be glad to help you pick out something."

"Thanks, but I think I can manage. Now come on before the pancakes grow cold."

The aroma wafting from the dining room triggered growls from my stomach. I was relieved we were having a normal breakfast this morning and weren't going to be subjected to one of Cassie's new meal ideas unless of course those pancakes were made with bean sprouts and covered in chicory syrup. It's been known to happen. We all loved Cassie, but sometimes her idea of something different didn't go over too well. She needed to spend less time with the latest food fad and more time listening to what we liked. I'm just saying.

The others were already seated. We'd all been here long enough to have our own spots. Ty sits at one end of the table, which I think he's always done to annoy Jock, who sits at the other end. I'm on Ty's left. Rose sits next to me and beside her is Minnie. Now, she's a strange one, still can't get a handle on her. Been here for ages I'm told. Secretive and sarcastic. Not an easy one to like, she doesn't play well with others.

Jock, who likes to think he's the head of the table, has Bea on his left, with Lily who is Rose's twin. Looney Tunes Phil completes that side of the table. There's also room at each end for another chair. Estelle used to sit beside Jock and Dalton next to Ty. So I suppose, if she stays, Estelle's granddaughter will take one of those spots.

As Ty and I took our places, I noticed Minnie, as usual, was the first to help herself. It amazed me how she could pack the food away and still look like a praying mantis. Sorry, not nice, she's not even green. At least a healthy stack of pancakes remained dead center on the table. A platter of bacon and an assortment of fresh fruit completed the morning's offering.

Pots of coffee and tea stood on the buffet. We were all accustomed to helping ourselves. Sometimes even before breakfast, as I'd done earlier.

"Morning all," I said as I put my coffee cup on the table and settled next to Rose. "How's everyone this beautiful day."

"Might be nice to eat with some peace and quiet for once."

"Jock, please," said Bea and reached tentatively for his arm. He shrugged to one side to avoid the touch.

"These pancakes are delicious," said Rose. "Make sure you have some bacon with them."

Good deflection on Rose's part. Dalton had usually played peacekeeper when tensions between Jock and Bea ran high. He is truly missed. It'd only been a couple of months, but it seemed only yesterday he'd been found, sitting in his favourite recliner, gone.

Ty put his fork aside. "Jock, you and Bea have been here the longest. Have you ever met this granddaughter? Think she'll let us stay?"

This should be good. Jock wasn't really in a talkative mood. I wasn't the only one holding my breath.

Jock looked up from his plate and finished the mouthful of food he'd been working on. "She acted like a spoiled brat when she visited here with her folks. What I saw of her later didn't impress me. Seen her a few years ago for Estelle's funeral. Before that, only when she decided she could fit in a visit with her grandmother before heading off to some fancy school. Estelle bent over backward for that girl, especially after her parents died."

"Now Jock, the poor girl had just lost her parents." Bea tried to placate him, but he wasn't done. He must've been fuming to say so much.

"Paid for her schooling and likely sent her food money at times as well. No doubt Dalton carried on similar nonsense after Estelle passed. Couldn't even find the time to be here for his funeral. Hard to believe she's Estelle's family at all. Got some kind of degree but no real job. Waste of money. And now she thinks she can run this place. Good luck."

He threw his napkin onto his unfinished breakfast plate, pushed away from the table, and left the room.

I turned my attention to Bea. Her sad eyes glistened. "He's just upset you know. Losing Dalton after Estelle has been hard. And now the news about Brad. I thought Alysha a lovely girl. Not quite settled in her life, but young and finding her way. I'll be glad to have another Grant here running things."

I remained undecided. At sixty-something, I was the baby of the group and also the last one to take up residence. Long story about how I came to be here, but for this stage of my life it suited me fine. I'd only retired a couple of years ago, still drove and loved to socialize. Just not always with these fine folks - if you get my drift. So having someone in charge who's more in tune with today's values and trends may, or may not, work for me. She may be liberal-minded, but on the other hand if she's expecting a home full of doddering, *one foot in the grave*, inmates she'll be in for a surprise. 'cause, honey, I'm not ready to be put out to pasture just yet.

I noticed Minnie watched Jock retreating, and as

he disappeared up the stairs, she returned to her second helping of bacon, and muttered, "Nothing brightens a room like your absence, Jock."

I often wondered about Minnie's life. She landed here years ago, apparently on the advice of a local minister. She needed somewhere to convalesce after some surgery and never left. Always had her knitting bag in tow working on some project or other. Furtive too, rumor around here pegged her as a hoarder. Mind you, none of us have ever seen past the door to her room. She'll grab the vacuum from Jan, our housekeeper, and supposedly does her own cleaning. But at least she always keeps her side of the bathroom we share neat and tidy. And the door to her room always closed, too. Not just closed, but locked. I know because I had to check a couple of times. Well, why not?

The new Ms. Grant might have other ideas. Perhaps Minnie wouldn't be allowed to sequester herself as much. She'll need a backbone to stand up to Minnie, though. Dalton knew how to handle her, kid gloves over fists of steel. But even he couldn't get into her fortress, er, room.

"More pancakes, Dianne? Dianne?"

Sidetracked again. One pancake and a slice of bacon was plenty for me. I'm not much into exercise. The kind I do enjoy, well, it's better with a partner So I need to watch those calories. Kind of a mutually beneficial arrangement.

"No thanks, Cassie. I'm done. Great breakfast by the way." I hoped if I encouraged her, she might be more apt to stick to normal foods instead of her experiments.

She gave me a flustered smile.

"What time is Estelle's granddaughter showing up?" I asked.

Cassie brushed a lock of damp hair behind her ear and glanced at her watch. "Any time this afternoon, and I've got so much to do. Want everything to look just so. And Jan's in a real mood about the whole thing. She's determined not a speck of dust should be found."

I handed Cassie a stack of plates from the table. "I can lend a hand if you need help."

Another smile. "I appreciate it but we'll be okay. Just as long as all of you make sure your beds are made and dirty socks off the floor, right?"

Rose pushed her empty plate away and started to rise from the table. "Now, Cassie, dear. Don't fret, it will all be right as rain, you'll see. Lily? If you're done, let's go and make sure our room is spic and span."

As if choreographed, breakfast was done. Chairs scraped back, crumbs fell, and folks dispersed.

"Cassie?"

"Yes, Ty."

"Just a suggestion, pet, but fresh cut flowers from the garden might brighten up the rooms. The lilacs down the drive are simply stunning. I don't mind putting together some arrangements, so everything coordinates properly."

"Great idea, Ty. I'll let Jan know and she can find some vases for you."

I headed back upstairs to my room and watched

as Minnie bypassed the stairs for the elevator. That woman, who seemed as fit as anyone, never took the stairs. I'd say most of us absolutely refused to use the thing in case it was seen as a sign of growing old. Jan got the most use from it, carting laundry and cleaning supplies up and down.

Or perhaps the old crone just wanted to get upstairs ahead of me and into her room before I could sneak a peek. As if I was even interested. Well, maybe just a little.

I love my room. Except for having to share the bathroom with Minnie. My room sits between hers and the larger bedroom Rose and Lily share. When renovations were done a few years ago, bigger windows went in. I have a great view of the property. I never get direct sun, but it provides plenty of bright light. Lots of trees around, and when I need some peace and quiet, I'm content to sit in the chair by the window and take in the view. It's also a useful spot to see who's coming and going.

Ty and I are the only ones using computers and the room's spacious enough to give me a corner study of sorts. It's important to keep abreast of what's happening in the world and, in my books, even more important to stay current with the latest technology.

After checking a few emails and going through my closet to decide what I'd wear later, I grabbed a book and my cell phone and went back downstairs to find a spot on the veranda. By now there'd be a fresh pot of coffee in the kitchen as well.

I stepped out onto the veranda and noted Philip

already in his spot, nose in a book as usual. I mean, I like to read, but I can't think reading about the migratory patterns of tern gulls would be a page turner.

"Nice day to sit and read," I said as I moved towards the white wicker chair I preferred. He didn't even glance up, just muttered something that passed for agreement. The more I think about what Jan said regarding him, the more I agreed. Either he'd stopped taking his meds or his grasp on reality had shifted even further away. This might not be the best home for him much longer.

I settled back into the chair, glad of the slight breeze. I needed to run into town for some more hair spray and hadn't applied much today. I grabbed my sunglasses—no one needs to know they're prescription ones—and my book. But as I opened it up, my ears caught snippets of a conversation overhead. That would be Jock and Bea's room. I kept the book open for appearance but wondered if I'd hear something more interesting.

Voices were indistinct, but Jock's was the stronger one and I could make out the teary sound of Bea's.

"....may have to move," came from Jock followed by a plea from his wife to stay. And then something about Bradley. What good is an interesting conversation if you can't hear it properly. Still, I'm glad I reminded Ty earlier about being overheard. A door slammed and I soon heard the thump of Jock's feet coming down the stairs.

I decided it would be best if I actually was reading after all and didn't look up when Jock pushed open the door and found his way to the furthest chair from Phil and me. Judging by the furrowed brow and set lips, his shorts were really in a twist, and I wasn't about to enquire. Let him sit in the shade and cool off for a while. Poor Bea always got the brunt of her man's temper.

My book drew my attention, leaving me barely aware when the rest of the Leven gang eventually made their way to the veranda. In fact, it wasn't until Mr. Grumpy Pants made that growly sound of his and stood up, did I realize the company had arrived.

He had leaned over the railing, giving his familiar death glare to a tiny slip of a girl. Then, of course, he greeted her. "So, you've arrived. We don't need you here."

# CHAPTER THREE

## *Alysha*

I stopped dead in my tracks. Fire and brimstone would have been preferable to the antagonistic greeting. I'd been taught to respect my elders, but seriously! He may have been old, sure, but he did have a commanding presence. His hands gripping the railing were large and looked strong. The buttons on his shirt strained over his barrel chest. His whiskered face was flushed beneath a full head of white hair.

Before I could respond, he spat out, "You show up now? Where were you when Dalton was being buried? Too busy to pay respects. But now, when there's an inheritance you can find the time, eh? I know your type and I've no time for you."

My jaw dropped. I couldn't work up a retort to so much hatred. It was true, I'd missed Uncle Dalton's funeral, much to my regret now. By now, my cheeks were burning as I realized others had overheard this little speech. Great way to be introduced.

I took a step back to survey the assembled group and decided to kill 'em with kindness. I plastered a large smile on my face and with hands on hips said, "And good afternoon to you too, Mr. McTaggart. It's good to see you again." And then for the benefit of those who didn't know me. "I'm Alysha Grant. I believe you were expecting me."

Much scraping of chairs and greetings ensued when the residents came forward to meet me. All except Jock McTaggart. He'd turned on his heel and disappeared into the house.

"Don't you worry about him, dear. He's just upset about Dalton. They were quite close. Do you remember me? I'm Bea, a friend of your grandmother."

I smiled politely. "I do remember you." What a contrast to her husband! Petite, like me, and a textbook grandmother type. Sensible dress and shoes, even a pearl necklace. Her veined hands took both of mine and her voice was nothing but kind.

"Yes, of course. Let me introduce you to everyone and then I'll take you to meet our cook and the housekeeper, who can show you around. Lovely women. Oh, listen to me prattling on. I'm just so glad you're here."

Then it hit me. The body discovered—McTaggart. I wondered about a connection, but I had to focus on Mrs. McTaggart. She'd started introductions. Crap, I'd never been good with names, especially not in a bunch like this. I must have met them at my grandmother's funeral but hadn't paid much attention.

"Alysha dear, this is Philip McGee," she said and I shook hands with a dead ringer for one of my old university professors. Cardigan with patched elbows and all. Bet he'd never been married either. His expressionless face made me think he'd not an ounce of humour in him.

Next, she pulled me towards two ladies who seriously needed makeup lessons. Yikes, why did they all insist on wearing such bright red lipstick? But they were smiling at me as Bea identified them.

"Alysha, this is Rose Edwards, and Lily Courtemanche. Believe it or not, they're twins–sisters you know." They might be twins, but I had the impression one might be a little more lively, she had a warm handshake. I think that was Rose, but Lily focused on sizing me up. Kind of creepy.

From creepy to over the top. I had to take a step backward when the next resident bounded toward me. Perhaps older than he tried to portray, but he was trim, neatly dressed and his eyes twinkled.

"Hello, pet, I'm Ty Rogers. Awfully pleased to meet you. You'll be a breath of fresh air around here, I'm sure." I detected a slight British accent. He hadn't waited to be introduced, and his handshake was a little on the weak side, but I thought he might be good fun. Probably gave some of the old ones a heart attack or two. Couldn't have met him before or I'd have remembered.

Only two more to go, I hoped. Bea walked over to pull another woman forward. I got the distinct impression she wasn't a team player. Oh, boy, what a prize. She had to be older than Bea, all dry skin and shriveled.

"This is Minnie Parker."

As we drew closer, I caught a whiff of something unpleasant. I didn't even want to think about it. In fact, I began to wonder if this was all a mistake. These were all old people. What on earth could we have in common? I gave her a quick handshake and pulled away as fast I could. Too bad if it came across as rude. She didn't speak to me but turned and scurried away with a glance of annoyance at Bea. I didn't remember her. No way I'd have forgotten her. I resisted the urge to find hand sanitizer as the next person came forward.

"Alysha Grant. So pleased to meet you. I don't think we've ever met. Don't let these old farts scare you off. My name's Dianne Mitchell. I can see you're a tad overwhelmed. This must be a lot to take in."

Now, this was better, and I breathed a little easier. Dianne seemed much younger and more with it than everyone else standing around. I loved her attitude and she seemed genuinely interested in me. Her smile and hug boosted my spirits.

After the shock of my initial welcome from Jock, then trying to put names to aging faces and keep them straight, Dianne was a welcome change.

"Now don't monopolize her," Dianne told the group." I'm sure she'd like a cup of tea, or something stronger, after her walk from town."

"I guess I should have driven here, but I left my car near the town square and walked instead. Kind of anxious to see Grant's Crossing up close. It sure has changed since I was here a few years ago. I'm a coffee fiend, if that's okay."

"Of course." Bea almost tut-tutted when she talked. "Come with me, I'll take you to meet our Cassie, and dear Jan. You may remember her."

Once inside, my first impressions of the old farmhouse were of amazement. My real estate training kicked in as I glanced from left to right and peeked into a sitting room with beautiful furnishings and a large marble fireplace. Following Bea through French doors, I could see a dining room equally well furnished with a table for ten already set for dinner. The floors shone, and sweet-smelling lilacs permeated the air and mingled with the fragrance of brewed coffee. Following Bea, I reached a large country kitchen. Perfect, someone had answered my prayers. Whoever brewed a pot of coffee would be my new best friend.

This kitchen! Definitely not the kitchen of my memories. Gone was the large black cast iron stove and bleached kitchen table. Even for someone who doesn't cook, I could see this had become state of the art. From gleaming appliances to ceramic flooring, no expense had been spared.

Bea ushered me in and introduced me to my staff. "Alysha, do you remember Janelle Young, our housekeeper? She keeps us all in tiptop shape."

Yes, I thought I did remember her, but memories were vague. Now a woman of about fifty, with dark brooding eyes, she stared back at me, unsmiling. I hoped she wouldn't be a prickly one. Instinct said I'd better find her good side if we were to work together.

"How are you, Jan? I remember you from my grandmother's funeral. You were so kind to me. I have to say, the house is fabulous. And the flowers are beautiful. Are they from the driveway?" My attempt at disarming her seemed to bear fruit as her clasped hands relaxed. "I hope we'll be friends as I'm going to depend on you to keep me straight." I thought a well-placed compliment here and there might work wonders.

A small smile escaped her lips. "Welcome." After a discreet nod, she straightened her perfectly crisp apron over her slender frame.

Off to the side stood a woman not much older than me, with a bright smile, and whose dark hair was escaping its ponytail. I sensed a nervous energy about her.

"You must be Cassie. Nice to meet you." I glanced towards the coffee maker, "I'd love a cup of coffee and maybe we can chat for a minute?"

Good heavens, I thought she might curtsey. She fidgeted and twisted the tea towel she held, as she asked me to take a seat. A tray had been set with some baked goods.

"I'll be off then," said Bea. "Perhaps I'll see you at dinner, Alysha. Cassie is making her chicken casserole tonight. Nothing too exotic."

"Thanks, Bea, I think I'm in good hands."

It was awkward for a few moments as Cassie poured the coffee and tempted me with yummy squares. I drank out of a beautiful blue and white coffee cup, with a matching saucer, while Jan and Cassie had mugs. Cassie finally spoke and pointed to the cup in my hand.

"You're holding your grandmother's favourite cup. She used for her afternoon coffee. I thought you might like it."

I was touched. "How thoughtful. It's lovely. You

31

know, I really don't want to disturb your normal routine and you have to prepare dinner for.... how many? I wouldn't know where to start." Oh, man my floundering put me in danger of sounding like an idiot. So of course, I continued. "Is it possible to have a tour of the house? Oh, and I'm dying to visit the alpacas." I detected visible sighs of relief from the reserved housekeeper and the skittish cook. I continued my attempts to put them at ease. "We'll have lots of time to get to know each other."

Thanking Cassie for the coffee, I followed Jan on a tour of what could only be described as a first-rate establishment. I had a hard time recollecting how the farmhouse looked before I left for high school.

Renovations, aside from the kitchen and bathrooms, had kept in line with the period of the house. Exquisite antiques, from the same era, added to the atmosphere. The floor retained its original wide oak planks, covered in places with suitably faded Persian rugs. A minimal scattering of tasteful ornaments kept the place from feeling cluttered. Somebody obviously had a green thumb because several healthy houseplants gave the rooms a lived-in feel.

In the hallway, I stopped in front of an oil portrait. I recognized my grandfather and Uncle Dalton, impressive in their Sunday best. I recalled the portrait from when I was a child. Jan had hesitated in front of it as well.

"The Grants were handsome men," she said.

I smiled in agreement.

She didn't say much other than describing parts

of the house. Her high cheekbones and black hair, neatly tied back, suggested an aboriginal background. I doubted there'd be much gossip from her, she struck me as one who knew how to keep her own counsel. She pointed out the features of the rooms while giving me her cleaning schedule.

Oh! There it was. Memories flooded back. "I remember that piano. Gran played beautifully. Does anyone play it now?"

"Cassie and her boyfriend, Dale, play on a Friday night for entertainment. The residents make requests. He strums a guitar and Cassie's on the piano. It's alright I guess if you like that sort of thing."

Wow! The most she'd spoken since I'd arrived. It made me feel she would come around eventually. They both had to be concerned with a new owner on the premises. Maybe worried about losing their jobs. I was talking myself into taking on my inheritance and I hadn't even seen the alpacas yet. They couldn't be as complicated as the group I'd just met— could they?

"Let me take you to Dalton's rooms." She paused and looked away. "Well, of course, they're yours now."

A small elevator had been installed during renovations, but I followed Jan's lead as she took to the stairs. Jan pointed out who lived in which room on the second floor.

The tour information paused when Jan identified Dianne's room.

"What is it, Jan?"

She took a deep breath. "Perhaps I'm speaking out of turn, but I feel a word to the wise might be help-

33

ful in regard to Dianne. I'm fond of her, and because we're closest in age, we have more in common. But you may find Dianne speaks sarcasm as a second language. The words might sting at times, but her heart is in the right place." She looked contrite. "You should form your own opinion, though. Forgive me."

I was touched she felt comfortable enough with me to share the insight, so I only smiled, and indicated the tour should continue.

We continued up to the third. This had originally been a couple of large attic storage rooms. Whoever designed the addition had pushed out the roof and made a comfortable suite of rooms with a bedroom, sitting room, and bathroom, plus a small office and kitchenette. A balcony overlooked the gardens, fields, and barn. The windows provided a panoramic view of the whole property.

"It's beautiful, Jan. I can see you've put a great deal of effort into keeping this house as a home." I spoke the truth. The impressive home had been well cared for.

Her features softened with a hint of a smile. "These were your grandmother's rooms and after she died Dalton moved up here. I still miss him. Such a shock when he died. Wonderful man." Her voice grew soft, but after a moment strengthened." I hope you don't mind, but I've packed his clothes in boxes. All his personal effects I locked in his desk. The furnishings you may not want to keep, so if you want your own, I can make arrangements to have them removed."

I struggled to find the right words of empathy.

"You were obviously fond of Uncle Dalton. He was lucky to have you take care of his interests."

I was surprised to see her eyes well with tears. She turned away, fussing with her apron. Maybe more than just fond of my uncle? Before I could answer my own question, she spoke.

"Here, why don't you check out the balcony and you'll see Larry, Moe, and Curly. Our alpacas. They've not returned to the barn yet."

The names delighted me. "Who named them? Hilarious. I can't wait to meet them."

"Your grandmother named them. She loved the Three Stooges so when she decided alpacas would make great pets, she did the naming. Of course, these are descendants from the original breeding pair she bought."

I stepped onto the balcony and saw two basket chairs and a table. I took in the fields spread out in the distance. And there they were. My new livestock, and I and fell in love.

I couldn't take the smile off my face. "Is there someone who could take me to meet my new charges? I need pictures, if that's okay, to send to my boyfriend, Jeff."

Jan had loosened up and smiled. "Miss Grant, this is your home, you take as many pictures as you like. Come on, I'll walk you over to the barn and introduce you to Frank Adams, the gardener, and he can show you how to handle the alpacas. He's usually here three days a week to help with the heavy outside work."

"Perfect, and please call me Alysha."

This time we took the elevator down, walked through the kitchen and out the back door. I risked depleting my phone's battery with all the pictures I took on our way to the barn.

"Frank, meet Alysha Grant, your new boss. She's here to meet Larry, Moe, and Curly. Can you oblige?"

A sunburnt and weathered old man wearing rubber boots held out an arthritic hand for me to shake. I returned the handshake and smiled at my third employee introduction of the day.

"Glad to meet you, miss. The guys will be wandering home in a minute. They tend to be curious by nature, so a new face will bring them over."

Sure enough, still chewing, they made their way to where we stood, while Frank continued to talk. "But you're not really a new face to me, miss. I've lived here all my life and your daddy used to bring you to the municipal greenhouse when you were a wee one. Always curious about everything. You never stopped asking questions."

I laughed. "Sounds like I've never changed." We shared a smile at the memory. "So, tell me who is who? This boy is so cute with his chocolate brown coat and big eyes. Can I pet him?

"This is Larry. We have three males who are the offspring of the two originals your grandmother had. Moe is the large white one with his back to you. No, you can't pet them until they get to know you. You could try giving them a treat, some apple maybe but it's too soon. The small one is Curly for obvious reasons. Nice golden colour, and the most even-tempered of the lot."

I'd have to learn more about these creatures. Jeff wouldn't be the only expert in our relationship. "They are beauties. I look forward to getting to know them."

Jan turned to leave. "Well, I'll leave you to two to get acquainted. I'll go and make up your bed with fresh linens. I assume you are staying for the night at least?"

"Please, Jan, don't go to any trouble on my account."

She smiled. "No trouble. I'll see you back at the house after you're done here."

I realized it would be easy to become accustomed to all this pampering. I couldn't wait to share the news with Jeff. Jan strode off in the direction of the house, stopped, turned, and called out.

"Welcome home, Alysha."

# CHAPTER FOUR

### *Dianne*

Aside from Jock's *heartfelt* greeting, I think we all behaved ourselves. The poor kid seemed a bit bewildered at the start, but if she was anything like I've heard about Estelle, she'd rise to the occasion. She might be young, compared to most of us anyway, I see that as a plus. I eyed Lily and Rose, gums flapping a mile a minute. Rose tried to be the glass half full type, which means you know how Lily takes hers.

I moved over next to Ty. "So, what do you think of Alysha?"

His dark brown eyes shot me a contemplative look. "First impression? I think I like her. How about you?"

"Have to agree with you—like I usually do. She should be getting the full tour by now, which will either help to sell her on this place or scare her right off."

Minnie brushed past us, and I called after her. "Minnie. What do you think of Alysha?"

She paused and turned back to face us, scowl in full force. "An opportunist if I ever saw one, mark my words."

"She's in a good mood today, I see," said Ty as she bustled back into the house.

"I know, why do I even bother trying with her.

Let's see what the twins think, come on." I propelled Ty towards Lily and Rose, who were still deep in discussion.

"Ladies," I interrupted. "Are you talking about Alysha? Ty and I think she'll be fine here. What do you think?"

Lily beat Rose to the punch, "Kind of young don't you think? Has she got any experience with a place like this? What if she sells the place out from under us? Oh, if only Dalton were still here."

"Now, Lily, slow down. One step at a time." Rose worked to calm her sister's anxieties. "We must give her a chance and do what we can to help her. She's grown up since we saw her last. Jan and Cassie will be a big help. After all, it's to our benefit she's successful, isn't it?"

Lily chewed on her lower lip. "If you say so. I'll try."

I nodded. "You're right, Rose, we all need to be on board with doing our best to ensure Alysha doesn't fail. Philip - don't you agree?"

"What?" Of course, he retreated into his book, and I wondered if he'd heard anything we were discussing, or even gave two hoots about Alysha. As much as he loved reading, I think he's a couple chapters short a full book.

"We're talking about Alysha and how we need to stick together to ensure we don't make it difficult for her, now she's the new owner."

"Oh, right. Yes, I see what you mean. Sticking together—like glue. Mustn't sniff. I don't foresee any problems. Now if you'll excuse me...." And he followed his nose right back into his enthralling bird book.

Ty rolled his eyes at the glue comment. Another *Phillip-ism*. He had lots, most of which never made sense. We were a fun bunch. How could Alysha not love us?

I glanced at my watch. Where the heck had the afternoon gone? "I've got to run into town to pick up a few things. Anyone need anything?"

Head shakes all around. What a relief. Last time I asked, Lily wanted me to pick up those bladder control things. Beyond embarrassing. I felt like I had to explain at the store they weren't for me. "Right, should be back in about an hour, unless something catches my eye."

"Or someone," Ty teased.

I hurried back inside and up to my room to grab my handbag and car keys. I thought I heard Minnie moving around in her room, or maybe moving things around would be a better description. I'd love to know what she does in there. I don't think she has a television, and I've never seen her pick up a book, other than her knitting books. I might have to put a bug in Alysha's ear about her and see how soon she can gain access to her room.

I opened the door to leave and nearly collided with Jan and Alysha. They seemed to be getting along well, chatting about Alysha's meeting with Larry, Curly and Moe a few moments ago. "Just heading into town for a bit."

Jan switched on her motherly expression. "You

will be back for dinner?" I understood Jan needed to know where everyone was to run the place well, but it irked at times. As if we were wayward children. "Alysha has agreed to be here, and it will be a good chance to talk over any concerns amongst the group."

I smiled at Alysha. "Wouldn't miss it."

"Dianne, maybe I could bum a ride into town with you and pick up my car?"

"Be glad to. Unless Jan still needs to show you more?"

Jan nodded at her and said if they'd missed anything there'd be plenty of time to catch it later. As we walked towards my car, I couldn't help but think this would give some of the pack a thing or two to talk about. It's all about timing.

"So, what are your impressions of your family home now?"

"Honestly? It's a lot to take in. So many changes since the last time I was here. I've never had much to do with old—um—senior citizens before."

I laughed as I drove. "I hear you. I've never had much to do with old people either. Here's a word of advice. Age, as you will soon learn, isn't so much about years lived as it is about attitude. Leven isn't an old folk's home, otherwise, I sure wouldn't be here. I think your grandmother envisioned it as more of a guest home. A place for those who don't want all the headaches and responsibilities of owning a home but aren't ready for a nursing home. Anyone here is free to leave at any time, and we all have a say in how the place is run. For the most part, we all get along, but I'll leave you to sort out those dynamics and form your own opinions. I might be tempted to offer my two cents, but that wouldn't be fair."

Alysha was silent and I stole a glance. "You okay? Car sick or something?"

She licked her lips as she turned towards me. "Sorry. I've been told I'm not a good passenger." She threw a weak smile at me. "But, thanks, I appreciate your comments. For now, I'm not going to make any kind of decision. My boyfriend, Jeff, is on his way and I'll be talking things over with him. I love the house for sure. The apartment for us is better than anything I've lived in for the past few years. Definitely a plus. And I'm captivated with the alpacas. They're so cute!"

"Fair enough. For what it's worth, I'll help if you have any questions or concerns. Now, where exactly did you leave your car?"

She seemed glad to change the topic and pointed towards the location, where I pulled into the spot behind.

"Thanks again for the ride. See you later at dinner."

Maybe I should have asked her if she wanted to go for a coffee, but I knew the feeling when you want some time by yourself to sort through things. She hadn't said anything about Jock's comments on missing Dalton's funeral, but it must have bothered her.

I headed towards the pharmacy and couldn't help a sneer when I passed Dr. Reid Harrison's office —now there's a quack. He had more than a couple of my housemates bamboozled with his anti-aging gimmickry, Ty included. At least he's one person Alysha shouldn't have to worry about getting to know seeing as she's quite a few years away from age concerns. Still, it might not hurt to share some background on him. I cringe whenever he comes to the house to visit his clients. Not even a regular doctor, and he makes house calls. Apparently, Estelle had fawned all over him, too. It seemed she had a weakness for him. Slap a white coat on a person and they're like gods and everything they tell you is the truth.

I pushed those thoughts away as I walked into Taylor's Pharmacy and grabbed a couple of items I needed, especially the hair spray. It wasn't too busy, so I was out of there sooner than expected.

An idea came to me, and I crossed the street to the gift shop. If I could only find what I had in mind, that would be the first step and would require cooperation from the rest of the house. I might need to polish up my skills of persuasion.

Speak of the devil. As I entered the shop, I could see Harrison chatting with the store owner. I pretended to be interested in some chachkies on display but felt drawn to be a little closer to the conversation. He's not a bad looking sort, but nothing remarkable either and would probably disappear in a crowd. I'd put him at fifty, give or take. I must admit he always dressed smartly and stayed well groomed. And tall. Probably just over six feet. Lean build and fair skinned. Glasses were a bit out of style, or maybe those large frames were making a comeback.

I edged a little closer. He was actually holding

the store owner's hand between both of his, and the look on her face? Well let's just say I resisted the urge to change it for her.

"Bless you, Dr. Harrison. You were so right about those vitamins. Already I feel an increase in my energy level and am sleeping better. You should be marketing them on a large scale."

"Mrs. Clarke, knowing my little pills are helping you is what matters most. I'm not interested in fame or money. Love of money is the root of all evil you know, says so in the Bible."

Oh, the pious look on his face sickened me, but more galling was Mrs. Clarke falling for his pitch. Just mention anything from the Bible to her and she's sold. He could be Lucifer himself and she wouldn't see it.

"I'll have to come and see you in a few days for a refill. I'm telling all my friends how wonderful your products are."

"My pleasure, Mrs. Clarke. Phone for an appointment soon. Now, I really must be going. If you could, um, ring up my purchase?"

"Oh goodness me. Sorry. Got a little distracted, didn't I?"

He flashed her that smile—the one not quite reaching his eyes—which I'd seen numerous times at the farmhouse. And then he noticed me. Nuts.

"Ms. Mitchell, how are you this fine day?"

"No complaints, thank you."

"I've heard the new owner of Leven Lodge will be here soon. Or has she already arrived?"

I did not want to be drawn into conversation

with him. So, what a shame when my purse brushed up against a display of flowery notebooks and sent them skidding to the floor. I became overly busy cleaning up the mess I'd made while Mrs. Clarke finished ringing up his purchase.

*Hurry up and leave already.* I pushed my thoughts in his direction with some success. His focus was diverted from me, and he made his way back outside.

As I finished returning the items to the display, Mrs. Clarke turned her attention to me and for some reason, I didn't feel the same love she'd been showing the doctor. "Is there something I can help you with?"

I glanced at the last notebook in my hand. "Yes, I believe there is."

# CHAPTER FIVE

## *Alysha*

I headed straight for the coffee shop. Coffee might not be the first thing on my mind, but I needed somewhere to be alone and chill after my adventurous day. I'd called Jeff a few times and sent him pictures of the house and alpacas. He was excited for me with the turn of events and promised to join me the next day.

His last text entreated, "No decision without me."

As if I would. I can make business decisions, but this is so personal. Moving to Grant's Crossing meant a drastic change to our way of life. Then there were those old people. Jock, Bea's husband, he'd like to see me in hell, or at least out of Grant's Crossing. And Minnie whatever her name is, phew, she really did smell. But I thought of those adorable alpacas, the top floor apartment, and the staff were so nice...

I ordered green tea just to send the server away. I'd forgotten to tell Jeff there'd been a suspicious death in town. One of the resident's relatives as well. Sure to pique his interest.

I sat for another twenty minutes thinking about what our lives would be like catering to a bunch of geriatrics. In my mind, old was old. There'd be farm chores, too. Mucking out the barn? I went back to thinking about the suite of rooms Jeff and I could make our own. Much more pleasant to contemplate.

I returned to my car to be back at the lodge in time for cocktails. Cocktails! I hoped Cassie had a cold beer in the fridge. Jan said they routinely met at five for pre-dinner cocktails. Tonight would be special to mark my arrival, providing them more time to make my acquaintance. With the potential to be more like an inquisition!

Hey, grow up girl. Show them what you're worth.

I planned to have a quick shower and change clothes. I'd clean up like the best of them and then join them for cocktails. Jeff would be so proud of me.

I parked my car, grabbed my duffel bag, and entered the side door as Jan suggested. I detected goings-on in the kitchen and heard someone singing but saw no one as I stepped onto the elevator and rode to the third floor. Thirty minutes later I was showered, dressed, and after searching, I found a lipstick languishing at the bottom of my purse. I may not have been fashion magazine material, but I felt confident I'd pass inspection.

Dianne noticed me first. She stood by a bamboo bar cart, laden with a wicked selection of bottles, glasses, and a bucket of ice. I admired her make up, and bet she didn't skimp at the hairdresser either. Her short, stylish cut suited the highlights shown in her auburn hair, which framed her fair complexion. And from what I'd seen so far, she had a good wardrobe, too. No doubt these folks would have a more sophisticated taste for drinks than I did, so I decided to be grown up and have a real drink.

"Come and join us, Alysha. What can I offer you?"

Eight pairs of eyes turned toward me. No, not quite eight. Jock had positioned himself at the far end of the veranda, a large tumbler of amber liquid in his hand, which he absentmindedly swirled as he gazed off in the other direction. And the professor guy, Philip, if I remembered right, had his nose in a book. So six pairs of eyes, some with matching smiles. Can't win 'em all.

I smiled back at the assembled group and said to Dianne, "I'd love a vodka martini if it's not too much trouble."

Her smile seemed genuine. "I knew we had something in common. I'll join you. Anyone else for a martini? This is a special occasion after all," she said. "Ice or straight up? I like lots of ice myself."

Ty had a glass of white wine. Jock eyed his wife, and Rose, when they both accepted a martini from Dianne.

Jock grunted at Dianne. "You'd best make a pitcher of that stuff if you're going to pour it down their throats. You know they never touch anything stronger than sherry."

Bea and Rose pointedly ignored Jock and giggled at their first good taste of Dianne's martini, while Lily held her glass of soda and seemed content to observe the festivities.

"Time for a toast," Ty announced.

Philip closed his book and looked up. The martini drinkers were poised to raise their glasses and Jock turned slightly in his seat. Lily had a timid smile on her face, and Minnie muttered her disapproval, "Alcohol and fools are a waste of my time." She gathered her knitting, stood, and stomped off.

Dianne led the way with her toast. "Welcome to Leven Lodge, Alysha. It's wonderful to have you here. Bottoms up." She tipped her glass. We followed suit.

"Thanks for the welcome. I'm happy to be here." The words came out, but to my mind didn't sound convincing. I hoped they wouldn't notice.

We sipped our preferred drinks. Ty reached out a hand to steady Bea's arm. I'd bet a vodka martini was new territory to her. "Whoa, steady on Bea, it's an acquired taste, so just sip, like your sherry."

Bea dabbed at the corner of her mouth, "I rather like it. Nice and refreshing."

Heads turned toward Jock when we heard him grunt, "Silly old fool."

A surprise to me, but I was enjoying my first martini and sat down beside the Professor. To make conversation I started to ask him what he was reading so intently when Dianne came over to me. "Sorry, may I interrupt?" The group fell silent, all eyes were on her. Somehow, I got the impression she didn't mind being the center of attention.

"Alysha, before we head into dinner, we have a little something for you. A small token to welcome you here."

She handed me a gift bag, with coloured tissue

paper spilling out the top.

"We all had a part in this," she explained as I reached beneath the tissue and pulled out a small leather-bound notebook, with a beautiful pen attached. How on earth did they know I had a weakness for journals and pens?

"Open it," said Dianne.

The book had a perfect feel and there's nothing I love more than a brand new, unspoiled notebook. A place to record just about anything, especially for fresh starts.

On the inside cover I read:

### Welcome Home Alysha

*Home is where the heart is*
*And we hope before long*
*Your heart will be here with us*

Beneath the inscription were everyone's signatures, although I suspected Bea had signed for Jock. Cassie had pasted a recipe of the meal we were about to have, along with today's date.

From out of nowhere, someone pressed a tissue into my hand. I guess I couldn't hide the emotions the offering had produced. I was truly touched and searched for words of gratitude and thanks.

But before I could speak, our attention turned to the driveway. A silver-grey van came at breakneck speed towards us, a large logo screaming CHANNEL 22 NEWS FOR YOU stretched across the side. In unison we all stood, drinks forgotten.

Before anyone could utter a word, a young woman jumped out and with microphone in hand, literally stalked toward the veranda, scanning us each in turn.

What the hell? I didn't think my taking over Leven Lodge was newsworthy, and I chuckled to myself.

"Good evening." The woman was all business as she introduced herself. "Rachel Winters, Channel 22 news, and Gavin, my cameraman. We're here to interview Jock McTaggart and his wife about the recent death of their nephew Bradley McTaggart." She correctly zeroed in on Jock, whose expression had blanched. His hands dropped to his sides.

The young and gangly Gavin had a large camera propped on his shoulder. His skinny frame didn't seem built to carry such a piece of equipment. The camera was recording, and I felt this intrusion intolerable.

"Shut your camera off now and back away." Had I said that? I couldn't believe they'd dare even come onto the property. Thoughts of filing a trespassing charge flitted across my mind, as I stepped off the veranda and strode up to the reporter with all the anger my vertically challenged frame could muster. Dianne joined me.

The two of us stood together, hands on hips, and glared at them. Totally ignoring our demands, the camera kept rolling and Gavin appeared to be inching his way towards us while the mouthy reporter kept up a barrage of questions. The closer they got, the more my blood pressure rose. I sensed Dianne draw closer to me as if presenting a wall between them and the house.

"We need an angle for the evening news. What's going on in Grant's Crossing? Is there a drug problem here? Mr. McTaggart, had your nephew been taking drugs for long?"

Dianne drew a deep breath. "Enough lady—you need to leave. This is private property and you're not welcome." Now the camera focused on Dianne. "Unless you have an appointment with Mr. McTaggart or any of the residents here, hop back in your vehicle and head back the way you came."

Dianne turned briefly to Ty, "Grab me the phone, I'm calling the cops." She almost frothed at the mouth, and I had to struggle not to lose it myself. Jan came to the rescue and hustled Jock, Bea and the others inside. Jock had gone quite willingly.

Ty had grabbed the phone but stayed put, nursing his wine, and taking in all the excitement. Not what you'd call a take charge sort of guy. Dianne forgot about him when the reporter began her pestering.

"Listen, we're only doing our jobs," said the mouthpiece. "We're doing an expose on drugs infiltrating small towns and were told Grant's Crossing has a problem. We've spoken to Bradley McTaggart's employer, Dr. Reid Harrison. He suggested we have a word with the McTaggarts. You know, to hear it from the horse's mouth so to speak."

Right, that was the final straw. I pushed my

shoulders back and moved closer to the reporter. I made sure she turned her mic off, but I lowered my voice to a deadly whisper.

"Ms. Winter, as fascinating as a drug problem in Grant's Crossing may be to your viewers, I suggest you gather your information from the authorities. There is nothing here for your story. You have overstepped boundaries in approaching an elderly couple who are grieving. I'll give you two minutes to make yourself scarce before I call the authorities myself. And no, you may not ask my name. Now, I repeat—get lost!"

Dianne and I turned on our heels and walked back to the veranda where Ty made no effort to disguise his face splitting grin. We blatantly ignored the last sputtering comments from the newswoman as she huffed her way to the van. "You can't keep this from the public, they have a right to know!"

Ty handed us another drink while we stood and watched the retreating reporter and cameraman. I glared at them, then tossed my drink back to a round of applause.

"Marvelous performance, ladies. You were superb. Sit down, Alysha, before you fall down," said Ty.

My knees had gone weak, so I was happy to comply. Dianne rubbed my back. "Bet you didn't know you had a backbone, did you? I'm impressed. Good job."

"I hope I didn't speak out of turn. I detest pushy, rude people especially reporters. I did drama at college. Had to learn how to speak up being smaller than average, just never used it for real before." The adrenaline rush began to fade. "But surely Grant's Crossing doesn't have a drug problem?"

"I don't think any small town is immune," Ty noted. His brow wrinkled. "I'm just surprised Reid sent them here."

Dianne raised an eyebrow. "Well, I'm not. Now, I think we'd better go in and see what the others are up to."

Before we could walk into the house Cassie came through the screen door and announced, "Dinner will be ready in five…" She stopped in her tracks. "What's happened?"

She kept glancing between Dianne and me. It was a no brainer to know something significant had disrupted the party. I started to tell her. "We had some unexpected visitors. A news crew from Channel 22, and…."

"Oh! Do you mean Rachel Winters? She's always searching for stories and barges in on people unexpectedly, you know, to catch them off guard. I always get a kick out of people's reactions, and…." Her voice trailed off.

Perhaps my expression got her attention. "It might be entertaining to watch, Cassie, but not so much fun if you're one of the parties involved."

"Is that why Jan brought Jock and Bea inside?"

"Yes," said Dianne. "The news wanted an expose on Bradley's death. The poor man's not even buried yet. Some people have no class."

I nodded in agreement but thought it best to have Cassie refocused. "You said dinner's almost ready?"

"Oh, right, yes. Is everyone ready to eat, or should we hold off for a bit?"

"Jock and Bea might not be hungry right now. So how about I help you make up some cheese and crackers to tide us over," I offered. "We'd better put something in our stomachs or we'll all be wasted."

A movement off to the side of the house caught my eye. Minnie? I bet she'd been out here all along, eavesdropping. I managed to catch Dianne's attention and glanced towards Minnie. I thought I'd let her handle this.

Dianne crept over to the railing. "Boo!"

I laughed out loud at the expression on Minnie's face. Caught in the act, she didn't know where to put herself. To give her credit, she didn't attempt an excuse, just glared at Dianne as she recovered, abruptly turned and walked towards the back of the house as if she were merely out for an evening stroll.

"Let me help as well, Cassie," said Dianne, not missing a beat. She propelled us through to the kitchen. I imagined Cassie was thrown right off her routine by this turn of events, so we took over. We arranged cheese and crackers, and other munchies on some platters. I turned off all the burners on the stove. In the past, I'd only made do with a microwave, so I assumed the food could be heated later.

Dianne and I glanced through the French doors to the sitting room where Jock and Bea sat, not speaking. Dianne craned her neck to see better. The elderly couple wore solemn faces and Jan sat quietly beside them. I could see her talking to them but couldn't hear.

Dianne turned to me with a grin. "Let's serve the cheese and crackers to the starving hordes." The grin reinforced my thought we would be friends, if not kindred spirits.

Out on the veranda, others had rejoined Ty. I felt the tension right away. We placed the platters on side tables and offered napkins. No one moved to eat. Minnie, who had returned, her eavesdropping episode forgotten in favour of food, sat sullen, with her arms crossed. Sulking perhaps because she'd been busted? Before they started complaining again, I decided to assert myself.

Tread carefully, Alysha.

Adopting a reassuring voice, I added a big smile and passed around the platter of snacks, encouraging them to eat. "Let's give Jock and Bea some time to regroup, then we can have our dinner." I didn't want to downplay the events but needed to have the evening return to its purpose. "I'm looking forward to getting to know everyone. You've been kind, and welcoming. I'd like to thank you again for the thoughtful gift."

A nod of approval from Dianne relaxed me some more. Just to keep their minds off the invasion by the mouthy Ms. Winters I told them about Jeff.

Ty moved right in with the questions. "How long have you two been together? Does he work?"

So, I told them about my genius boyfriend, meeting him in graduate school, and how he takes mostly contract work until he finds his niche. "You'll be able to ask him yourself. He'll be here tomorrow."

And of course, Minnie had to put her oar in. "And just what's he going to do here? Think he'll find his *niche* with this bunch of misfits?" She burst out with a round of cackling that morphed into a coughing fit.

"Speak for yourself, Minnie Parker. If anyone is a misfit, it's you." said Rose. "I for one am thrilled to have a young man amongst us."

Thankfully no one added to the comment. Jeff was in for an enlightening time dealing with these folks. Nothing he couldn't handle.

# CHAPTER SIX

## *Dianne*

I wasn't sorry to see the news van pull away from the house, taking some of the built-up tension with it. Alysha looked shell-shocked and I wondered what she thought. She'd had quite the first day with us. I bet she hadn't expected to be involved with a possible crime investigation. Of course, neither did I. I could see the tongues were about to start wagging, so I moved closer to her. "How you doing, kiddo? Day's not exactly going as planned, is it?"

She gave me a rueful smile. "You've got that right. I've been on the phone with Jeff. I'll be glad when he arrives tomorrow."

"I look forward to meeting him."

She bit at her lower lip and looked a little distracted. Maybe she'd surprised herself at how she handled the reporter. Speaking of distractions, Minnie was wound tighter than a cobra about to strike. Hope she learned her lesson about being a snoop.

She clutched her knitting bag, stuffed with her latest project, and started to whine. "Can we eat now? I have things to do."

I don't know who she thought she was talking to, no one rushed to answer her. Behind her back, Ty shook his head and used his finger to draw a circle by his forehead. I had to bite the inside of my cheek to stop the grin. He could make me laugh, usually at the expense of others. As for Minnie, I couldn't help but wonder who benefitted from her endless knitting projects and didn't want to know what they smelled like.

But maybe she was right about eating. "C'mon on guys, let's see if dinner's ready."

As we headed indoors, the conversation halted when we saw Jock and Bea in the sitting room. The old dears didn't seem aware of their surroundings. Alysha walked over to them.

She hesitated in front of Jock but turned her attention to Bea and spoke gently. "I think dinner is ready. How about you both come and sit in the dining room. I can remember Gran telling me, no matter how bad things seem, it's always worse on an empty stomach."

Bea turned grateful eyes upward. "Thank you, dear. You know, I can hear Estelle when you said that. You're right, we need to eat. Come on Jock."

We waited silently for Jock's response. Although he looked deflated, he stood slowly when Bea did, following her and Alysha into the dining room.

Alysha might be young, but appears to have the right stuff, even if she doesn't think so herself.

Something sure smelled good, maybe Cassie's meal wouldn't be ruined by the lengthy delay. Oh, what a surprise, Minnie was already at her place, with a plateful of food from the laden buffet table.

I prodded Alysha to get in line. "Go and help yourself. This is how we do dinner—food's laid out on the sideboard. And don't be shy, Cassie always makes enough for leftovers." I lowered my voice, "But sometimes, we don't even want the first run of some of her experiments. I'll explain later."

"Can't wait to hear about it," she smiled then grabbed her plate and set about filling it. I could see she had a healthy appetite.

Everyone waited for the first comment about the reporter's arrival. Rose didn't hesitate. "Bea, I'm so sorry about this evening. This must be so upsetting to you and Jock. If there's anything I can do, let me know."

Ty chimed in next. "And these horrible allegations about Bradley's death, well, do you want to talk about it?" Damn it, Ty. Not a good question.

Jock's knife clattered to the floor. "My nephew was not a drug addict. People can go to hell if they think otherwise."

I expected him to blow a gasket, but to my astonishment, and I think everyone else's at the table, he began to cry. His shoulders heaved and tears slid down his whiskered face. Bea got up from the table, went to his side and hugged him. She stroked his hair and wiped the tears from his face with her hand. "Hush, now. We know he wasn't. The truth will come out."

I glanced around the table. Even Minnie had stopped, fork mid-way to her mouth. I couldn't speak for anyone else, but I'd never seen Jock like this. Usually, he's abrasive, sometimes rude, and generally unlikeable, but obviously Bea knew him better.

I hated awkward silences and if no one else was going to say a word I decided to jump in. "That reporter went beyond rude. I've seen her on TV before and she's even worse in person! Where on earth is she getting her information about your nephew—it's not true is it?"

Bea's lips parted, but she looked to Jock. He nodded, so she spoke. "They're still not sure how he died. The police are waiting on the results of the autopsy. We don't believe for a second drugs are involved."

"No wonder they suspect drugs, hanging around that no good snake oil salesman," spat Minnie. "I warned you no good would come of it." She peered around the table. "Same warning goes to the rest of you who think he's got the formula for the fountain of youth. Charlatan!"

I noticed Ty lowered his eyes and became seriously interested in the chicken on his plate. I might not care for Minnie, but I agreed with her. Something about Dr. Reid Harrison didn't sit well with me at all.

"Minnie!" hissed Rose. "This isn't the time."

I tried to deflect the animosity away from Minnie and turned to Bea. "Are you able to start planning a funeral yet?"

"Yes, we can make arrangements now," Bea said. "I just wish...." Her words dropped off.

I watched Jock's hands clench the arms of his chair, and he pushed himself to his feet. "She just wishes we knew where our own daughter is to let her know about her cousin. I've lost what little appetite I had. Good night. Coming Bea?"

Bea sighed. "I'll be right along. Go ahead, dear." She didn't speak again until he'd started up the stairs. "Such a sad day for us. I apologize for Jock's behavior and hope you can find it in your hearts to be patient with him. We know Bradley would never have taken drugs, but somehow, we have to get the police to understand. They didn't know him as we did."

Alysha's eyes had been on Bea for most of the conversation. Those eyes reminded me of Dalton. Taking things in and processing. She hadn't said a lot since we sat down to dinner, but I'd bet she hadn't missed much either. "Bea?"

"Yes, Alysha. I'm sorry all this has happened with your arrival."

"Nothing to be sorry about." She hesitated as if searching for the right words. "I'm wondering about the comment your husband made about your daughter. May I ask why you don't know where she is?"

"Oh, dear, it's a long story, but the thing is after a big argument Janet had with her father, she left Grant's Crossing, vowing never to return. More than twenty years now. And then just a few years ago we thought she was coming back, but we've heard nothing from her ever since."

When Alysha asked the question Rose had gone to Bea's side and put an arm around her shoulder. I didn't even know all the details of what had happened, but maybe now with Bradley's death, something would be done about healing this fractured family.

"How sad, Bea. I'm sorry. I shouldn't have asked." Alysha shifted in her seat, and looked uncomfortable, but Bea exhibited her usual warm-hearted self and tried to reassure her.

"That's not your fault, honey. Family history, as you yourself know, often has some hurtful memories in it." She managed a small smile. "Perhaps when things settle, you and I should compare notes on family issues. Now, please excuse me, I need to go and stay with Jock. Sorry if this has ruined the lovely dinner Cassie prepared."

Someone else with family skeletons? By the look on Ty's face, he'd certainly enjoyed that revelation. Another source of gossip for him. Maybe I shouldn't admit to being partial to good gossip myself, but I apologize to no one.

Cassie arrived from the kitchen with bowls of ice cream and freshly baked cupcakes to finish off our meal. Most plates on the table weren't even finished. Appetites had been quashed. But a good cup of coffee would go down well, and I filled my cup and ate a little ice cream. Others made half-hearted attempts at their dessert.

Eventually, the painful meal drew to a close. Philip retired to his room and his books. Lily and Rose would probably spend the evening watching Wheel of Fortune and Jeopardy in the front sitting room. Minnie skittered away towards the elevator, swiping two of the cupcakes on her way.

Cassie began clearing away the table, leaving Ty and me with Alysha. He was ready to fuss over her. "What are your plans for the rest of the evening, kitten?"

She gave a slight shrug. "Not sure. Should I offer to help Cassie with cleaning up?"

I nipped her suggestion in the bud. "Not this evening. In any event, Jan often lends a hand."

She nodded. "Then maybe I'll take a walk outside for a while before settling. It's been a long day and I think it's catching up with me. Plus, I have Jeff's arrival tomorrow to look forward to." She rose from the table. "Dianne, thanks for helping me feel at home today. With all that's gone on, you've been a great help."

"You're welcome. I know what it's like to be the new kid on the block, so to speak. And if there's anything Ty or I can do over the next few days to help in other ways, don't hesitate to ask, okay?"

To my surprise, she came over and gave me a hug and even planted a kiss on Ty's cheek. "Goodnight, see you tomorrow."

Ty watched her walk to the front door and out onto the veranda. Then he turned to me with a playful grin. "I'm still sticking with my first impression; I think I'm going to like having her here. Now then, girlfriend, want to come up to my room and see my ideas for a gazebo I've been thinking about?"

Seeing as no hot date loomed on the horizon, I could think of worse ways to spend a couple of hours.

But first I had to satisfy my curiosity. So, I searched on my phone for the latest broadcast from Channel 22. Sure enough, our cast of characters warranted a brief sound bite. Ms. Winters, all smooth and with fake smile in place, told of being turned away from the McTaggart home, and so had no real information on Bradley McTaggart's death. I couldn't help but grin when the camera panned in on Alysha and me—warrior women protecting the homestead. And for a brief zoom in on Ty's face. Impish look if there ever was one. I'd let him find the video clip himself.

"Sure, let's see what you've been up to."

# CHAPTER SEVEN

## *Alysha*

What a crazy day! Had it only been one day? It seemed like weeks since I'd left Guelph and came here to Grant's Crossing. I tried to comprehend all I'd learned, about having a guest house to run and being accountable for the well-being of eight seniors. Never mind the staff and the alpacas. I've only ever been responsible for myself. Jeff does the cooking and his own laundry. However, I thought the gift of a new journal might be a good way to keep track of things.

I wandered down the driveway. The heavy fragrance from the lilac bushes was somehow comforting. Honeybees droned as they flew among the blossoms; they'd soon be returning to their hives for the night. I turned to face the house, delighted to see it lit up as evening approached. Behind the farm, the sun made its way to bed, leaving the sky streaked with pink and blue. I could make out the flicker of a television in one sitting room, the other was dark. Both rooms on the second floor were lit, and as I remembered it, Jock and Bea had one, but I couldn't be sure about the other.

They must be in torment over a family member dead from a suspected overdose. Both Jock and Bea were adamant he wasn't doing drugs, but there's bound to be a connection. The police aren't stupid. I wondered if they'd be the next to show up on our doorstep.

I headed in the direction of the barn, curious to know if the alpacas needed anything at this time of night. Who looked after them since Dalton died? I soon answered my own question.

Philip dropped a bale of hay he'd been carrying. He set it just inside the barn near a feeding box. He seemed to be having a conversation with himself while he worked to fill the trough. None too tidy about it either. It was as if the conversation took all his concentration, and feeding these adorable creatures was secondary. Their cute faces, with those eyelashes, peered over the door as if to say, "Have you come to say goodnight?" Jeez, fanciful maybe, but it had been a long day.

I waited until Philip finished his chores before speaking, brushing at a swirl of gnats over my head. "Lovely evening Philip. Is this something you do every night, or do you take turns with anyone? They seem to have an attachment to you."

He started when I spoke. How could he not have noticed me? I waited and watched as Moe—I'm guessing Moe—kept looking for treats. Philip gave them all a scratch around the neck.

He turned slowly as if not sure how to speak to me. "No, I'm the only one from the house who looks after them. No fast food here. Hamburgers are no good for alpacas. Dalton and I were their primary keepers, apart from Frank. He comes in to clean up their manure."

His monotone voice put me on edge. And *hamburgers*? How to respond? "Beautiful animals. But it sounds like they take time to look after. Do you want me to find someone else to look after them or...?"

He went rigid and his words were sharp. "No! Don't! Please. Why do you have to go and change things? Dalton was my friend. He and the alpacas are the reasons I came to live here."

He finally made eye contact with me and softened his voice. "You see, I've studied alpacas for years. At my last university post I'd have taught animal husbandry, but things changed, and I had to take early retirement. They think they won, but they didn't."

I couldn't keep up with him. "Who won?" His conversation slid all over the place and again I had the feeling he was conversing with someone other than me.

"I'm not well, you know, but Dr. Harrison is trying to help."

I didn't feel comfortable making a comment about Dr. Harrison, so I tried to stay neutral and encouraging. "I'm sorry to hear you're no longer at the university. Their loss and our gain, I'd say."

As if I hadn't said a word, he carried on. "Dalton and I, we were going to add to the herd and breed them but life changes in an instant, doesn't it? Dalton's dead, and now you've arrived and will want to do this yourself. What do you know about these intelligent creatures? They're more than a hobby you know. They have feelings, too. They like me and need me." He started pacing, agitated.

I didn't know if he was speaking to me, himself, or someone imaginary, and it made me acutely uncomfortable. I'd certainly found my life changing overnight, but in a good way. I thought I'd call it a night and made a mental note to jot down some questions in my journal. I needed to find out what made this guy tick.

"Thanks for your input, Phillip. No worries, I'm not making any major changes right now. And you're right, I have a lot to learn, but for now, I'm going to turn in. Tomorrow I'll introduce you to Jeff Iverson, my boyfriend. He had an interest in animal husbandry when he studied at the University of Guelph, so you'll have a lot in common. He's looking forward to meeting Larry, Curly, and Moe. And all the residents of course."

Philip cracked a slight smile. The first I'd seen. "I hope he's wearing body armour for this bunch. Some can be so cruel. Especially Minnie. Watch out for Dianne, too"

"Sure thing, I'll warn him but I'm sure he can look after himself."

I wanted to head back to the house and away from Phillip. I turned to walk just as he called out, "The alpacas need shearing before the weather's too hot. We have a standing date in June so the shearers will be here next week."

"Understood. Go ahead with your plans, Philip. We'll talk again tomorrow." Then a thought intruded. "Oh, you mentioned Dr. Harrison. His name came up a few times today."

I had to strain to hear what he said. Philip murmured something about multi-vitamins to keep him young. I'll introduce you when he visits. You could try one of his tonics."

"Okay. Thanks, but I don't need any vitamins. G'night."

Darkness had descended as I hurried in the side door, and then over to the elevator and up to my new quarters. I felt emotional and more than a little tired but wasn't sure I'd be able to sleep. A small fridge held a jug of filtered water, so I poured a glass and sat on the balcony thinking over my encounter with Philip. Someone, Jan maybe, had left a back copy of the Gazette for me. Thinking it would help provide an interview of current events in town, perhaps

### Grant's Crossing Gazette

### Community News

Plans are being revisited to bring a long-promised Casino and Resort to Grant's Crossing. The property, part of the old sawmill, sits unused since it was sold to a developer in 1995. Town opposition kept the proposed development at bay and the land was flipped a few years later.

Are plans moving forward once again? Has the town mood changed and are we ready to consider this encroachment in our community?

A Town Hall meeting will be scheduled later this month to hear both sides

I wondered how the possibility of a casino on

the old sawmill property would go over with the residents, or if it would even matter. It was in close proximity to the lodge, so I figured there'd be comments at some point. I rested my chin on one hand and allowed my mind to wander.

Was I equipped to handle this place? And those animals, adorable as they were, had the potential to be labour-intensive. But the residents—all those different personalities. Psychology 101 hadn't prepared me for what lay ahead. I argued back and forth with myself the pros and cons of this new development in my life and hoped it might look different in the light of day.

I finally made up my mind not to make any judgments about anyone at Leven Lodge. Phillip appeared to have a few screws loose but anyone who liked alpacas was alright in my book.

I decided to open my new journal. Fresh page, fresh start.

> First full day at Leven Lodge - my potential new home? Met the residents and fended off a news crew! Friend perhaps with Dianne. I like the staff. Phillip? He seems sketchy, or not well. Who might know? Check with Jan tomorrow. Can't wait to see Jeff :-) He'll love this apartment. It's been a long day - I'll write more next time.

###

I lay listening to the morning sounds of the house waking up. I'd slept like the proverbial log and would have stayed dozing if the tantalizing smell of coffee had not teased me fully awake. I couldn't wait for Jeff to arrive, we had so much to talk about.

I didn't want to intrude on the home's routine, so until I better understood the dynamics of my role, I'd go along with what everyone else did. I had a quick shower, threw on clean shorts and a top, then followed the aroma of coffee to the kitchen.

My hair was still damp as I entered the kitchen to find Cassie busy at the stove. I also saw Jan through the window tending to some plants in a well looked after vegetable bed. "'morning Cassie. Any chance of a coffee? It smells so good."

Cassie jumped, her voice a squeak when she managed to speak. "Oh, you startled me, Alysha. Please, help yourself. It's like Grand Central Station here this morning. What with Frank showing up at the crack of dawn and Dr. Harrison arriving at seven-thirty to see Jock. Not to mention we'll have another person today to add to the menu planning and... Sorry, I tend to get flustered when my schedule is off kilter."

During her diatribe she'd been busy stirring something on the stove, then she turned away from the simmering pot. Wiping her hands on her apron she came over and stood in front of me as if about to say something. She was an attractive girl, but her looks were at odds with the constant frown on her forehead and flushed face. I wanted to put her at ease.

"Don't worry about me, Cassie. I'll take my coffee outside until breakfast. I'll stay out of your way and go say hi to the alpacas."

Cassie nodded her agreement and turned back to the stove. I picked up my steaming dark coffee and made for the kitchen door. I hesitated, turned back and asked the harried cook, "Will Dr. Harrison be joining us for breakfast? I've heard so much about him, I'd like to meet him."

"Probably not. He only came to see Jock because Bea was concerned about him last night. He'd been so upset after the news reporter left, and from the way I understand it—well, I talked to my girlfriend Gina, and she says they're talking foul play. Just who would do a thing like that. I can't..."

Jan came through the back door. She shot Cassie a stern look, and her voice sounded testy. "Cassie, stop gossiping. Alysha doesn't need to hear all this." Cassie cast her eyes downward.

Then Jan brightened her voice and turned to me. "Good morning, Alysha. I hope you slept well. Breakfast will be in the dining room at eight-thirty. Cassie's making fruit crepes with our local maple syrup."

I smiled at the housekeeper. "Sounds yummy. I love crepes."

I left the kitchen, intending to head over to the barn, but angry words between my newly acquainted staff reached my ears. Jan voicing her displeasure with Cassie, and Cassie offering excuses. I made a mental note to have a word with Dianne about their relationship.

Another beautiful summer's day in Grant's

Crossing, the air warm and fresh. I could easily make visiting the barn a morning ritual. My mind threatened to burst with everything I had to tell, and show, Jeff.

Frank, seeing me, paused in his efforts, and leaned against his well-used pitchfork. He sported a big grin. "Good morning miss. Come to help me muck out the byre, have you?"

I laughed. "Thanks, but I'll pass this morning. If you need help, I'll recruit Jeff when he arrives today. He's keenly interested in the alpacas."

The old fellow nodded. "Truthfully, Mr. McGee and I manage pretty well, but another pair of hands is always welcome."

I spotted the alpacas, busy chewing, down at the end of the pasture. "Can I go visit Larry, Moe, and Curly. I've taken quite a shine to them."

Frank looked off to where the three animals stood, and in a gentle voice said, "Estelle, your grandmother, loved them. I can see you take after her. But if you wait a few minutes they'll come to you. Look, they've spied you. Here they come."

I watched as they ambled over, heads held high as if in disdain. I went straight for Curly and offered a scratch on his head. Then Larry wanted his turn. His soft lips planted a kiss on my hand. Moe, the dark brown one, just looked as if to say, me next. I admired his long curly lashes and thick full coat.

Frank broke into my bonding time. "They like you; I can tell. I'll be going now, need to deliver this manure." His voice took on a disapproving tone. "I hope I can maneuver my truck out of the driveway. Bloody Doc Harrison parks any which way. Jeez, don't know how many times I've asked him to leave me room."

Frank started his beat-up old truck, loaded with manure, and leaned out the window. "I'll be back to meet your boyfriend, especially if he wants to help," he chuckled.

I glanced to the parking area where my own car sat and saw a late model Jaguar taking up most of the driveway. I sided with Frank. I hate inconsiderate people.

"Hey, Frank, I'm just curious, but what do you think of this Dr. Harrison? Apart from his parking skills."

The old man took a deep breath. He seemed reluctant to say, but then said, "The man's a fake. Some are taken in by it but not me. I'm too long in the tooth for his baloney. Unfortunately, Estelle and Dalton were, and bought his stupid, *I'm gonna live forever* pills. But hey, you didn't hear it from me. There are others here who also subscribe to his quackery. And that's all I'll say on the subject." He waved, then slowly drove around the Jaguar with barely an inch to spare.

### 

I enjoyed a third crepe. They were to die for and if I ate like this every day, I'd be a beach ball. Those at the table were quiet, and Jock and Bea were missing. Jan told me they were still in discussion with Dr. Harrison. Cassie had delivered a pot of coffee to them but nothing else.

Rose broke the silence with a comment about the weather, which apparently was the key to unlocking voices. Nearly all had something to add to the conversation and the atmosphere grew more inviting. Unexpectedly, the discussion took a different turn, and they directed their questions to me. What had I been doing since I left University? Had I been with my boyfriend long?

And from Rose. "So, when are you getting married dear? I'd love to help you with your dress."

They all pounced on that. I just smiled in a non-committal way and Dianne came to my rescue. "A little too personal Rose, she's only been here five minutes. I'm sure if Alysha has any plans, she'll let us know in her own time."

Whew, I didn't need to answer that one. All their questions were obviously to avoid talking about Jock and his nephew. Me, though, I was dying to ask about Dr. Harrison, the fake, to quote Frank, but could hardly do so with him still in the house.

I excused myself and went upstairs to wait for Jeff and check emails. Thankfully the house had good internet reception.

I finished unpacking what little I had with me. Jeff was bringing more of my belongings. I opened the folder from the lawyer, discarding all the legalese forms and papers I needed to sign. I settled into a comfy armchair by the window, soon absorbed in pictures and brochures of alpacas. I'd become so engrossed that the squawking noise I heard, I attributed to something outside. Then I heard my name.

A distorted voice located in the wall mounted intercom announced that a young man would like to see me. "Could this be the Jeff you're expecting?" asked Jan with a hint of amusement in her voice.

God, I liked this woman. She might come over gruff but had a sense of humour underneath.

"Thanks, Jan. Tell Mr. Iverson I'll be right down after I finish formatting my hard drive."

All I heard in return came from Jeff, "Yeah, that'll be the day."

Two minutes later I stood watching from the kitchen doorway while Jeff dramatized a story to an enraptured Cassie and an equally captivated Jan. Peals of laughter erupted at the punch line.

I couldn't resist a smart comment. "Make yourself at home, why don't you?"

Jeff stood up and I moved into his arms. He might look bookish and didn't have a body-builder physique, but for me, in his arms was a good place to be. With his arm around my shoulders, we faced the beaming cook and housekeeper. I stood on tiptoe to kiss him on the cheek. "I can see I don't have to introduce you. And apparently you've been sampling Cassie's cooking."

I hadn't seen her look so pleased with herself since I'd arrived. "He finished off the leftover crepes. Glad you liked them, Jeff."

He managed a sheepish look. "I only stopped for coffee on the way, so I was a little hungry. Being in a hurry to see my girl, you know. The weather was perfect, and…"

Oh, he made it hard to be patient, I'd missed him, so I stopped his talking with another kiss. "Jeff, there's so much I need to talk to you about. And I want to show you around, Leven Lodge."

"Sorry, just glad to be here," said Jeff. By the way, he kept glancing around, I knew his curiosity was in overdrive. I couldn't fault him there. I was still keen to explore all the lodge and town had to offer.

Cassie and Jan clucked over us like a pair of mother hens, especially Jeff, offering him more coffee and pastries. He knew how to play into the moment. "Thanks, ladies, breakfast was outstanding, but I'd better go with the boss. Hope I see you later."

Jeff knew how to charm. I maneuvered him out of the kitchen to the elevator and waited for his reaction to our suite of rooms. I kept quiet while he absorbed everything. Then I handed him water from the fridge, and we sat on the balcony where I related all that had happened since I arrived. I waited for him to comment, but at the same time, I enjoyed the way he wouldn't stop looking at me. "Say something, Jeff."

"Babe, you've been looking for the right opportunity for a long time and I think you've found it. I've not met anyone yet except the kitchen staff, but I doubt they'd be anything you can't handle."

Confidence builder, my Jeff. "Hmmn, they are different, maybe even unique, and there's a police investigation on the go with a possible murderer on the loose. They do suspect foul play, and then what do we know about alpacas, although Philip McGee, he's one of the residents, he's looking after them well, I think and..." The bemused expression on his face slowed me down. Look up the definition of long-suffering and his face will be the example. "Sorry, I'm running off at the mouth. It's so much to take in. I feel as if I've won the lottery but don't know how to spend it."

Jeff grinned." I think you've already made up your mind to give it a chance, and I'm on board if you want me."

"Of course, I want you. We're a team, although you may feel some opposition about our marital status from a few. Can you handle it? Oh, and there's also Minnie!"

"Minnie–is that a cat?"

I chuckled. "No, she's a resident. All part of the adventure, finding out where we stand with Minnie."

He raised his hands in mock surrender. "Now before I meet everyone do you think I could take a walk to the barn?"

I stood up, and held my hand out to him, "Larry, Moe, and Curly await. Let's go. To be fair I think we'll need to go out the front door. Curiosity seekers abound."

Our trek to the barn was delayed. Before we could leave the house, all and sundry stopped us, wanting introductions. Jeff resembles an overgrown schoolboy without the nervous energy most boys have. He's laid back, relaxed and I could see the women took a liking to him. As I said, he can be very charming.

"Jeff, this is Ty."

Ty had planted himself, with his iPad, on the veranda, in a comfy chair near the door. He rose, shook Jeff's hand, and without preamble, let his curiosity take over. "So, Jeff. Or is it Jeffrey? Will you be staying on as well?"

Not missing a beat, Jeff countered. "If I'm Jeffrey then you must be Tyson, Tyrone, Titus?"

Ty's eyes sparkled. "Touché, Jeff. Ty, it is."

"Well then, pleasure to meet you, Ty. As for staying on, I'll leave Alysha to keep you informed. I must say this is a beautiful house." He glanced around and smiled at the gathering group, shaking more hands. The McTaggarts and Phillip were nowhere to be seen.

Introductions complete, Jeff had a question. "I'm curious about the crest on the transom window over the front door? It's a fine piece of stained glass. Alysha?"

"I should know, but I'm afraid I don't," I said. "But maybe someone here can enlighten me. I remember it from my childhood, but I didn't pay much attention. There's an inscription but I can't make it out."

Philip had come quietly around the corner of the veranda and spoke straight to Jeff. "As a matter of fact, I'm eminently familiar with the history of the glass. Something I researched the first time I saw it. It is, of course, the Grant family crest dating back to the thirteenth century. You do know Alysha's ancestors hail from Scotland?"

Now he sounded more like a university professor. No disjointed thoughts like our previous conversation. I wondered how Jeff would react to the somewhat pompous assessment from Philip, but I needn't have worried. He had the perfect response.

"Thanks for clearing that up. And you are?"

"Philip McGee."

They shook hands, and the professor didn't let Jeff get a word in edgewise before he continued. "I understand from Alysha you're interested in the alpacas. I'd be more than happy to show them to you and answer any questions you have about their care and feeding. You probably don't need a passport."

A passport? So much for no disjointed thoughts. Glancing around the veranda I wasn't surprised no one seemed willing to participate in the conversation. Jeff sent a puzzled look my way but managed to keep the dialogue going.

"Thanks, Philip, appreciate it. But back to the inscription on the glass. In your research were you able to ascertain its meaning?"

Philip straightened his shoulders, ignored Jeff, and looked at me, but over my head. "Yes, and this is something Alysha may want to take to heart. It's the Grant family motto—Stand Fast."

I picked up on a small snicker coming from Minnie's direction and noticed Dianne's glare directed at her.

Stand Fast. I must have heard it dozens of times as a child and had completely forgotten. It made me smile when I realized how apt I am to dig in my heels. Stubborn as a mule my mother used to say. Well,

I'll have to let the residents discover that part of me themselves.

Jeff and Philip headed out back to see the alpacas. Jock and Bea had still not made an appearance. As the new landlord I wondered if I'd be expected to commiserate with them or leave them alone. I'd need to have a chat with Dianne and take her up on her offer of help. I didn't think she'd be averse to sharing a little gossip and perhaps some advice.

In the meantime, I decided to empty Jeff's pickup of my belongings. I made a move to the parking area, with both Ty and Dianne offering to help carry a few things.

Jeff's truck brought to mind photos I'd seen of Depression-era vehicles loaded to the max with personal belongings when families were displaced. Sports equipment, a guitar, fishing rods and of course boxes of books and his collection of CDs were all jumbled together with duffel bags full of clothes. Leaving heavier items for Jeff, we made our way up to the third floor and dumped everything in the bedroom. I appreciated having an elevator in the house.

"It's lovely up here," said Dianne. "I've only been once before. I'd forgotten how great the view is."

Dianne joined Ty on the balcony overlooking the back gardens, and to the left the fields where the alpacas could be seen.

I went to the fridge for something cold and offered a small prayer of thanks for Jan. She'd stocked the fridge with beer, in addition to the filtered water. I took out three beers and hoped my new friends enjoyed a cold brew.

The early afternoon sun was high and the warmth summer strong. Shading my eyes, I saw Jeff and Philip at the far end of the paddock.

"Thanks for your help." I said handing Dianne and Ty a beer.

Ty looked pleased. "Well, what have we here? Thanks, kitten."

"I think this is in order, don't you? A way to say thanks for your help."

Dianne looked at the beer as if it would bite her. Not her usual, I guess. Ty popped the beer caps and held his up for a toast. "Stand Fast Craig Elachie"

"What?" Dianne and I cried in unison. "What does that mean?"

Ty tittered with laughter and tears filled his eyes. I don't really know," he giggled and bent over double trying to contain his laughter. "I did a search on Google for the Grants and found the saying It sounded so... Oh I don't know. It sounded fitting for the occasion. No idea who or what Craig Elachie is but Stand Fast sounds good."

To myself I thought, "No more beer for you!" but aloud I said "Thanks for the sentiments, Ty, whatever it means. I can see I'll have to learn some of the family history. I do remember the sawmill and going there with my grandfather on Saturdays. Good times."

"Wasn't the sawmill bought by a developer some years ago?" asked Dianne. "When I first came I remember seeing the Grant name on the side of an old building by the river."

"Yes, that would be it. There should be an old water wheel as well, I think. Jeff and I'll take a walk tomorrow so I can reacquaint myself with it all. I understand when Uncle Dalton sold it, the proceeds went into remodeling this farmhouse."

"And we're glad he did," said Ty.

We sat quietly sipping at our beers and watched Jeff walk around the field. From this distance, he appeared to be in deep discussion with Larry, Moe, and Curly. I quipped. "Don't think I'll have far to look any time Jeff disappears."

Dianne chuckled.

I might have been dying to ask all sorts of questions of my new cohorts but held my tongue. Instead, I informed them that in honour of Jeff's first evening here we'd join them for dinner, and provide a special treat, and I hoped Jock and Bea would be able to join us.

Ty clasped his hands together. "Oh pet, I do love treats. Hints?"

I grinned at them and shook my head. "Thanks again for the help. I'm off to see what Jeff is doing and then I'll see you at dinner. Don't make your pitcher of martinis, Dianne. Tonight, I'll supply the beverages."

Ty had finished off his beer, but Dianne's bottle was only half empty when they stood and headed back downstairs. They left me contemplating my mealtime surprise. I planned to pick up a bottle or two of champagne and have Cassie prepare something special for dinner if she'd not already concocted one of her specialties.

That's when I'd tell them we're here to stay. *Stand Fast!*

I made arrangements with Cassie for dinner and to put out champagne glasses. I invited her and Jan to join us. What I had to say concerned them as well. It was Friday and Cassie reminded me of their normal evening of sing along.

"Then we'll have a party. I'm running into town later. Is there anything I can pick up for you?" I offered.

"No thanks, I have everything under control."

"Do you think you could persuade the McTaggarts to join us? They've been keeping to themselves all day, but I think everybody should be here. We could ask Frank as well?"

Cassie considered. "I'll give him a call. Not sure what I can do about Jock and Bea though. More Jan's role. I'll ask her to pop in to see them, and let's hope no uninvited guests show up and upset everyone like last night."

Leaving Cassie, I went looking for Jeff to let him know we were hosting our first dinner party. I found him in the paddock and had a hard time convincing him he needed to come to town to pick up champagne and a few other treats.

His smile said he knew me well. "I guess it's a done deal?"

I had to agree. "Yes, tonight after the party I'll read all the paperwork and sign. I'll then be the owner and operator of Leven Lodge. But babe, are you certain you want to be my partner in this. I don't want to do it without you."

"Count me in. I think we can make a life here. If we expand the herd of alpacas, we might need another barn and..."

"Stop! One deal at a time! Let's seal this one first."

We stood enjoying the early summer warmth, catching the scent of farm aromas on the gentle breeze. We were facing the back view of Leven Lodge from the paddock. Keeping us company were the three alpacas who were going to share our future, which we sealed with a kiss.

# CHAPTER EIGHT

*Dianne*

I linked arms with Ty as we headed down the stairs after leaving the third-floor apartment. "Good thing you're not driving, mister. You should see how flushed your face is right now."

He leaned into me and snickered. "Sorry, beer's not really my favourite because it goes right to my head, but I wanted to be polite. Have I mentioned I like the girl?"

"At least once or twice," I replied and gave him a poke in the ribs. We both laughed and made our way to the second-floor landing.

"Are you heading downstairs, or maybe you need a nap to sleep things off."

Ty knew how to take my teasing. Some of the others weren't quite so quick on the uptake. I thought Alysha might have a good sense of humour.

Ty's face grew serious, and he looked around as if not wanting to be overheard. "No nap. I've been working on some plans for Reid. He's asked me to re-decorate his waiting room and I'm so excited to start on it. But I want to keep it hush-hush, so I don't ruffle any feathers. I know not everyone likes him, including you."

"I wouldn't buy water from Dr. Harrison if I was

parched in the desert. I simply don't like him, and I think he's taking all of you in with his promises of staying young. Honestly, I think you looked better before you started taking those pills of his."

My friend looked crushed. I know, a cheap shot because I knew Ty's Achilles' heel was his appearance. He had no money issues especially when it came to keeping wrinkles and thinning hair away. I had to admit his hairpiece did look pretty good. I didn't think anyone else would realize he was nearly bald as an egg underneath. Might be a good time to change the subject.

"And what's your opinion of Jeff? He's easy on the eyes, and my first impression is positive."

"Funny you should say that. I think I liked Alysha right from the moment I laid eyes on her. But I can't get a feel—and don't look at me like that—for her young man. I will say he does seem taken with Alysha. And it will be good to have someone around here who's comfortable with computers. Even I might be able to learn a thing or two from him."

We stood outside his room, and I knew he was anxious to get on with his decorating plans, but I didn't want to part company with any ill feelings between us.

"Hey, you know I didn't mean to attack you about Dr. Harrison, but I can't help my feelings. And because you're my friend I worry a little about his influence on you."

"He's never done me any wrong, not that I know of anyway. But I appreciate your concern. Alysha seemed to want to know about him as well. Wonder why?"

"I imagine she's sorting us all out, but I'll try and have a word with her later; see if I can find out. We seem to have hit it off. So, go and play with your colours and drawings and I'll see you later."

He blew me an exaggerated kiss and entered his room.

I stood at the top of the stairs trying to decide whether to join whoever might be downstairs. Then I looked down the hall towards the McTaggart's room. They'd been scarce most of the day, and I knew Alysha hoped they'd be down for dinner later. I prayed Harrison hadn't meddled where it wasn't needed.

What the heck. I moved toward the door. First, I listened, but couldn't hear anything, so I tapped softly. Didn't want to wake either of them if they were resting. I didn't hear any movement, so I thought they were sleeping. After the past few days, they must have been exhausted, but I hoped the quack didn't sedate them. I stood for a couple of moments more and then made my way back downstairs.

I tried to tell myself nothing was wrong but wasn't convinced. I searched out Jan and found her in the hallway, vacuum in tow. I called out to her before she reached the on switch. "Jan!"

"Yes, Dianne. Something wrong?"

I hesitated a bit before answering. "I'm not sure. The thing is no one's seen Jock or Bea since Harrison left them this morning. I know they're really upset over Brad's death. So, I thought I'd see if they were alright. Knocked on their door, but no answer and not a sound from inside either. I assume they're still in there, but it just doesn't feel right. Do you think we should go and see?"

She pushed the vacuum aside. "Sometimes we have to trust our instincts. But I don't want to barge in needlessly. Let me grab the master key."

Vacuum forgotten, she headed towards the kitchen and returned with the key, and a pile of clean towels. "Gives me an excuse."

Outside their door, Jan knocked, and then knocked again. "I have fresh towels for you, Bea."

Still no response. She looked at me and then used the key to enter. Sunlight streamed through the windows, and all was quiet. But they were there. Bea asleep in a recliner and Jock lay stretched out on their bed. Peaceful, but too quiet.

Jan and I glanced at each other. She moved towards Jock, and I headed for Bea.

We couldn't rouse either of them. Bea's breathing was almost non-existent, and her lips had a faint bluish tinge. Jan began shaking an unresponsive Jock and at the same time reached for the bedside phone.

"I need an ambulance—now!"

Thirty minutes later I found myself at the hospital with Jan. The paramedics had arrived in record time and quickly bundled the McTaggarts onto stretchers and whisked them away. Of course, everyone at the lodge had seen the commotion—except for Alysha and Jeff, who were still in town.

I kept in touch with Ty via texts, although

there wasn't much new to report, but at least it gave some sense of being in control. Waiting is always so hard. Jan hadn't said too much since we'd arrived at the emergency room. She sat staring out the window to the parking lot. Her hands kept rubbing the tops of her legs and her brow furrowed with worry. I jumped every time the sliding doors to the patient area opened.

"Not the most comfortable chairs, are they?" I said.

"No, they never are," she agreed. "Listen, I've been thinking."

I waited for her to continue. "Thinking about what?"

She looked at me and lowered her voice. "I'm not one to spread rumours or gossip, you know that."

I whispered, "But?"

"What happened in their room when Dr. Harrison came to call?"

I knew exactly what she was thinking. That Harrison had something to do with the McTaggarts being unconscious. As soon as Jan put words to her suspicions, I realized I'd been thinking along the same lines. It raised a lot of questions. "If there was something questionable they'd find it out here, wouldn't they?"

Jan looked back at me and merely raised an eyebrow, which spoke volumes. She opened her mouth to speak, but stopped because a nurse, clipboard in hand, headed our way.

"You're here with the McTaggarts?"

We stood so fast, we bumped into each other.

Jan took charge. "Yes. How are they?"

"Much better. We had to pump their stomachs as a precaution because they couldn't tell us what they'd ingested. You don't have any idea, do you?"

We shook our heads in unison. I had no desire to offer up any information or suspicions just yet and I assumed Jan was on the same page.

The nurse looked at each of us in turn. "Are there any family members you can contact?"

"Not really," said Jan. "There is a daughter, but they've been estranged for years, and no one knows where she is."

I thought the nurse would click her tongue at us as an unmistakable look of disapproval flashed across her face, and I immediately developed a dislike of Florence Nightingale. I had more important questions for her to answer. "So, they'll recover? When can they go home?"

"They'll be admitted to stay overnight for observation." She paused to refer to her checklist. "The doctor on call wants them to be seen by a social worker before they're discharged."

Jan bristled. "What on earth for? There's nothing wrong with them. They've suffered a recent loss which is agonizing for them. But they've got a good home to return to, and supportive friends."

"It's routine in cases of suspected suicide attempts."

I angrily reacted in typical knee jerk fashion. "No way. Where's the proof? Maybe they made a mistake with some medication?"

Jan stayed tight-lipped and gave me a look that clearly said, *Shut-up Dianne.*

We watched as the nurse made a few more tick marks and notes on her clipboard. She avoided my question. I guessed she'd already made up her mind that Jock and Bea had survived a joint suicide attempt.

My phone vibrated with an incoming text and I was glad of the diversion. Ty letting me know Alysha and Jeff had heard where we were. Did we want them to come to the hospital to wait with us, or what could they do?

Jan asked the nurse if we could see Jock and Bea and was told they needed their rest and tomorrow would be soon enough. We were obviously dismissed, and she returned to her lair behind the sliding doors.

I texted Ty to tell Alysha to stay put; we were on our way back home.

# CHAPTER NINE

### *Alysha*

The celebration dinner went by the wayside. After the text from Dianne, Jeff and I headed back to the Lodge and sat in our apartment mulling over what had happened.

Jeff was about to open another beer and seemed content to sit back and relax in our new home. I, on the other hand, couldn't settle. Unpacking boxes wasn't going to cut it right now. All I could think about were the McTaggarts and hoped they'd be alright. I didn't want the residents to think we were up here hiding so when Jeff started poking about in a box I said as much.

"Leave it for now. I think I need to be with the others. Coming with me?"

We reached the main floor and found everyone had congregated in the living room. Cassie handed out napkins and had placed plates of snacks on side tables. Everyone ignored her; too busy having their opinions heard. Except... who on earth was that?

Jeff knocked on the door frame and eyes turned to us in unison. I whispered to him, "Who's the guy wolfing down Cassie's sandwiches?"

"I bet he's with Cassie. See the guitar?"

"Good going, Sherlock." I raised my voice, "Hi.

Hope we're not interrupting anything?"

Rose's face lit up when she spied us. "Oh no dear, come right in."

Ty clarified for us. "We've just been discussing Jock and Bea and wondering what we can do to help."

Lily added to the drama, weeping and wringing her handkerchief. "Tragic, tragic."

Rose sighed, moved next to her sister, and tried to console her. The mood here didn't call for champagne. I needed to introduce myself to the boyfriend before he finished all the sandwiches. I caught Cassie's eye and nodded toward him. She understood and moved to my side. She steered me away from Lily and Rose, and over to the piano where she made the introductions.

"Alysha, this is Dale Scott. He's my friend and our Friday night guitarist. Dale, this is Alysha Grant, our, er, my new boss."

Wow, I couldn't imagine where she'd found him. Long stringy hair, wimpy mustache, and a muscle shirt, which seemed two sizes too big. Not the type to fit with these folks. Maybe he had something else going for him. His plate was empty, while sandwiches lay untouched on others. I had to focus on Dale; Minnie's incessant clucking drove up the excitement on faces eager for news. Did she find this funny?

"Nice to meet you, Dale." I glanced around the room, "But I don't think anyone's in the mood for a sing song tonight."

His face fell, as he shook my hand. "Not the best way to start out here, Alysha. But pleased to meet you, too."

"I think I have to agree with you, Alysha." Cassie turned to her boyfriend. "Here, have another sandwich, Dale. Looks like you're the only one enjoying them."

I looked on in amazement as he continued eating. Life goes on I suppose. I turned and found the whole group staring at me. "Has there been any word from the hospital yet?" I said to no one in particular. "I know you're all worried about Jock and Bea."

As if on cue, the front door opened. Had to admit my relief at seeing Jan and Dianne. "Perfect, here they come now. I'm sure they'll have news."

Before I could even say hello, questions were fired as others moved to surround them.

"How are they? What happened? When will they be home?"

My relief gave way to impatience. "Let's at least let them get in the door." Jan looked spent and Dianne shot daggers at Minnie, who tut-tutted at the back of the pack. The two women settled themselves. Dianne's mascara had smudged a bit, and worry lines creased her forehead. Jan, anxiety etched on her face as well, appeared ready to speak. Have I mentioned I liked this woman? No nonsense about her, but then she needed it with this crew.

Lily tried to rush in with questions between her tears.

Jan raised her hands. "Now hold on a minute, please, we need to catch our breath." The chatter continued, and she tried to make herself heard. "To answer the most important question, they're going to be fine."

Before more questions were thrown at Jan, Dianne stepped in. Raising her voice, she hollered "Enough already. Don't all talk at once. We'll tell you what we know."

Jan nodded her head to Dianne to go ahead. "Unfortunately, we weren't able to see Jock or Bea. The staff at the hospital feel they need their rest. But they might be back with us tomorrow after they've been seen by a social worker."

Rose looked lost. "But what happened exactly, and why do they need a social worker? We can look after them perfectly well right here."

I noticed the looks passing between Jan and Dianne as Jan coughed and continued with the story. I watched, impressed with how she made eye contact with each person in turn. "The doctor suspects a suicide attempt on their part but until Jock and Bea can tell them what they ingested, and toxicology results are back, they feel a social worker should talk to them."

A clamour arose, adding to extended crying on Lily's part. Jeff and I said not a word. We wouldn't have been heard anyway. I noticed Jan move over to Philip's side to help him stand. He seemed extremely agitated, his eyes darting back and forth. Mumbling nonsense and trying to brush Jan's hands away, he looked about to bolt. It made me appreciate Jan's leadership. This was not something I'd ever dealt with. She took him by the arm and led him out saying she'd make him a cup of tea.

Ty, the only one who seemed aware of Philip's distress, shook his head from side to side as they walked away. Dianne continued to deal with questions bombarding her. My ears pricked up at one comment she did make, and I filed it away. "Doc Harrison has a lot to answer for in my opinion."

So many negative opinions around here about him—I must speak with Dianne later. I took Jeff aside and asked him to check on Philip. He seemed to have developed more of a rapport with him than I had. I'd hold the fort here until they'd settled down. Rose tried to comfort Lily and dry her tears. Ty's attention had turned from concern over Philip to being up in arms at Dianne for berating Dr. Harrison yet again.

And Minnie. She sat in a corner, cocooned in a beat-up old cardigan that had seen better days. Bright rouge on her cheeks like red polka dots and her wiry hair put me in mind of a cartoon character. I couldn't tell if she was upset, or pleased, at the outcome. She was far enough away I didn't need to worry about any unpleasant odours. My bad!

I did my best to encourage them to eat Cassie's sandwiches, or what was left of them, but no one had an appetite. Cassie and Dale sat in another corner oblivious to everyone, or not sure how to interact. Before I could ask Cassie if she'd refresh the coffee pot Jeff tapped on the door and indicated for me to come with him.

When I reached the kitchen I saw Jan on the phone, while Phillip sat motionless at the kitchen table. A blank stare greeted me. He was miles away and seemed unresponsive to anything around him. Jan pointed at the chair next to him. I sat.

"What's going on?" I really felt helpless and out of my depth. And I'd bet Jeff felt much the same.

He looked at me and shrugged. "I'm not quite sure," he said. "Phillip is not feeling well. Jan called his doctor and they're making arrangements."

"Arrangements for what?" Oh boy, a little more information would be helpful. I turned to Philip. "Can I get you something? Would you like to lie down?"

Jeff touched my arm. "Babe, he can't hear you. Jan explained he's in a catatonic state and has probably had a breakdown. She says he'd been diagnosed with autism spectrum condition a long time ago, but lately hasn't been doing well. She told the doctor she's concerned about any non-prescribed medications he might be taking in addition to what he'd described for anxiety. The ambulance will be here soon to take him to the hospital."

Jan must have seen the shock on my face because when she finished her call, she came over to me and took both my hands in hers. "I'm so sorry Alysha, I've not had the time to tell you. His doctor couldn't predict when this would happen, but it's been building up for some time."

I wasn't sure what to say other than, "Poor guy, what can I do?"

"If you and Jeff could just sit quietly with him, I'll tell the others to stay where they are. I'll go wait for the ambulance."

Jeff and I looked at each other as if to say, "What have we gotten ourselves into?"

And so, for the second time in one day, an ambulance arrived at Leven Lodge. Jan once again found herself making the trek into town, this time accompanied by Ty who'd packed an overnight bag for Phillip.

We closed the door and watched as the ambulance pulled away. Dianne had waited to fill me in and pulled me to one side.

"I think seeing an ambulance here again has finally put the brakes on all their chatter," she said in a hushed tone. "Lily's waterworks have dried up and Minnie seems to have found the off button, thank goodness, but she is enough to send *me* to the nuthouse." She immediately sounded contrite. "Oh, I didn't really mean that. I do feel bad for Phillip, poor man."

"Dianne, I think I know what you mean. Listen, Jan says Phillip's doctor will be waiting at the hospital to admit him, so they probably won't be long. Do you want to wait here with me till they come back? Convince the others the party's over. Poor Jan doesn't need to be pestered for a second time this evening whenever they get back."

With only another potential long wait for news ahead, Rose and Lily went off to the sitting room to watch Jeopardy. I reminded them to take some of the remaining sandwiches with them if they were hungry. Who knew where Minnie had scuttled off to. I hoped I wouldn't be expected to be their keeper all the time.

Dianne and I settled into a couple of wingback chairs by the fireplace with coffee. My mind jumped ahead to a cold winter's night and how comforting it would be to sit here with logs burning and a mug of hot chocolate. But for now, dusk had fallen and looking out onto the front of Leven Lodge, I thought the light seemed magical. The soft swish of the fan overhead kept us cool. Dianne moved across the room and closed the French doors. "The walls have ears and now might be a good time to have a chat if you want."

"Sure. You read my mind. I have a million questions but don't answer anything unless you want to."

She shot me a wicked grin. "Oh, don't you worry. If it's not worth sharing, then I don't know enough. When Jan returns, I thought we might offer to help her put the dinner away. The poor woman must be exhausted. She is so loyal to the Grants." She reached for another biscuit.

Her suggestion to help Jan reminded me of my freshman status here. "Yes of course. I should have thought of that myself."

She brushed away crumbs from her mouth. "Now, you said you had questions?"

Where to start? "Without sounding rude I'd love to know what you think about your housemates. It may be a while before they feel comfortable with me, and I think I have a handle on some, but I'd appreciate knowing what you think."

Dianne proceeded to give me her version of Leven Lodge and its inhabitants. She came across as funny and irreverent, but I liked her take on things. She seemed especially fond of Ty and was concerned about his relationship with Dr. Harrison. We were just getting around to the twins when Jan and Ty returned.

His predictable eagerness to provide all the latest on Phillip was undercut by Jan. She gave us the facts while Dianne and I helped clear the dinner table. Then the four of us sat at the kitchen table where finally, Ty put his spin on Phillip.

"He didn't recognize Jan or me, poor soul. It came on so fast. We all knew he had a few screws loose but..." Ty's woeful look was touching, but it made me wonder if any progress would ever be made accepting mental disorders as being just as real as a physical ailment. Or maybe it was his generation. Sad

We fell silent thinking about Phillip. "I guess he's in the right place to get help," I said uselessly.

Jeff had gone to look after the alpacas and Cassie and Dale were nowhere to be seen. Our cook had earlier informed me this was her weekend off so maybe she'd left the lodge. If they were expecting me to take over cooking meals, they'd be going hungry.

The evening had fallen flat, the party forgotten. Leaving Jan to shut things down for the night, I headed upstairs where I sifted through more of Uncle Dalton's paperwork while waiting for Jeff to finish putting the alpacas to bed. Finally, we were able to sit on the balcony sipping beers as we looked over the fields and enjoyed the late evening warmth.

"So, Ms. landlord, landowner, and farmer, after

all this drama, are you ready to throw in the towel?"

"Not so fast partner. I have no intention of quitting at the first sign of, what shall I say, the tribulations of the guests. In fact, I'm ready to sign on the dotted line."

Jeff added a note of concern. "Not afraid of any more guests being carted off to hospital? You've only been here two days and you've lost three already."

I flicked my beer at his grinning face. He loves teasing me. "Farmer Iverson. Do I assume you will take over the care of the alpacas?"

"Love to. It's just as well Phillip filled me in. I knew he wasn't firing on all cylinders but, events tonight were a surprise."

I had more news for him. "Did he tell you the shearers are coming next week?"

"Er, no he didn't. I'm sure I can handle them. I can always check with google for some enlightenment."

"Frank Adams, he's our part-time gardener, can help you there. He'll be back in the next day or two. As for me, I'll have to wait until Monday to take the paperwork back to the lawyer. I have some more reading to do and I'll have a lot of questions for him."

We sat chatting for a long time going over everything that had happened in the last—was it only two days?

I still hadn't told everyone our decision to stay and Stand Fast and decided to wait until the McTaggarts were back home and inform them all together.

I remember my grandmother saying *And tomor-*

*row is another day.* I couldn't agree more.

# CHAPTER TEN

*Dianne*

What a night! I'd be just as happy to never see another ambulance on the premises again. And talk about a baptism by fire for Alysha. If the past couple of days didn't scare her and Jeff away, then she might make it here after all. I enjoyed our chat and hoped I hadn't said the wrong things about Harrison, but she did ask. Pretty sure I'd have to smooth Ty's ruffled feathers at some point.

With thoughts of what I'd say to Ty running through my head, I headed off for a morning shower before breakfast. As I entered the bathroom my nose detected something unpleasant. It had to be coming from Minnie's room. A shame it hadn't been *her* carted away last night instead of Phillip. I reached for a can of air freshener and gave the room a couple of squirts, and for good measure I aimed another spray at the bottom of the connecting door to Minnie's room. First on my list would be to have Alysha do something about my neighbour, who'd been at the lodge since before dirt and heaven only knew what she had going on in her room.

Even with the exhaust fan running and my continued spritzes of air spray, eau de Minnie lingered. I rushed through my makeup and dressed for breakfast.

Coffee beckoned, and it was the only fragrance I cared for first thing in the morning.

Voices drifted up from the dining room as I neared the bottom step. The empty chairs gave me pause. No Jock, Bea, or Phillip. Who could Minnie pick on?

The smaller crowd made it a bit easier on Jan. She provided meals on Cassie's weekends off. Secretly I think we're all glad when Jan's in charge of the meals—no culinary surprises. I'd almost expected Alysha and Jeff to be sleeping in, but there they were. Fitting in like they'd been here for some time. I smiled to myself until I looked at Ty. Oh, brother, he looked to be in a sulk. He threw me a cursory glance and returned to work on his waffle.

"Good morning, Dianne," said Alysha. Jeff nodded a greeting, his mouth too full to speak. "You haven't missed much. I think we're all making up for lost appetites from last night."

I sat myself down with a coffee and debated whether I'd have more than one waffle. They were working hard to tempt me. "Any more news on Phillip, or the McTaggarts?"

Alysha had the update. "Jan's going to call the hospital in a little while."

"Phillip should fit right in with the rest of the wingnuts," muttered Minnie between mouthfuls of bacon.

Rose couldn't abide unpleasantness, but she had her limits. "Minnie, don't be unkind."

But Minnie didn't care. "I call it as I see it. He

should have been locked up months ago. Didn't belong here with normal folks."

Rose's voice rose in exasperation. "Normal? That's rich, coming from you. You certainly know how to drag out a temporary stay."

This was more fun than a tennis match. Minnie wound up for the next serve. "Brought your extra-large spoon to stir up trouble today, I see." I wondered if laser beams would flash out of her squinched up eyes.

"Now ladies," said Alysha. "Let's not say things we might regret later." It pleased me to see how she jumped right in before things turned nastier. Rose pinched her lips together. Her nudge to Minnie's shoulder was no accident as she got up from the table for a coffee refill. Another forkful of food kept me from laughing out loud.

Minnie had to score the final point. "Even that Harrison wouldn't have a pill to make me change my mind. Crazy is as crazy does." She scraped her chair back, swiped at her mouth with a napkin, and left the room. Alysha had a puzzled look on her face and glanced at Ty. What did I miss?

So now there were only six of us having break-fast, and the mood needed to be lighter. I figured I'd better start with Ty and get it out of the way. "Ty, I guess I have to apologize for my comments about Dr. Harrison last night. I can only put it down to concern for the McTaggarts. I'm not going to change my opinion of the man, but he is your friend, and I should be more respectful of your feelings."

The focus was on him, and Alysha had turned to see how he'd respond. Funny how a few seconds can seem so long. Finally, he looked up from his breakfast. "Sounds like an apology, girlfriend?"

"Close as you'll get from me, and you know it," I teased back.

"Aw, go on. Kiss and make up, you two. Life's too short to hold grudges." Jan had walked in at the tail end of our exchange to start clearing the table.

Ty reached over and patted my hand, "All's forgiven."

After breakfast, I wandered down to the barn where I found Alysha and Jeff. With Phillip gone, Jeff volunteered to take over the care and feeding of the alpacas. I wasn't overly fond of them myself. I understand their cute appeal, but I'd rather enjoy the finished product of their coats. Last Christmas, Ty gave me a gorgeous cream coloured sweater made from alpaca yarn.

Never mind Christmas; we were enjoying a beautiful, early summer day. The sun was warm and not a cloud in the sky. If I owned a convertible, I'd be on the road to somewhere. But I felt it better to stick around to wait for news on the McTaggarts. Like everyone else, I hoped they'd not have to spend another night at the hospital. It gave me chills when I thought what might have happened if I hadn't trusted my instincts that something was wrong.

I felt a small twinge of something—envy, regret —when I saw Alysha standing so close to Jeff, her arm about his waist as they discussed the woolly creatures before them. They made a good couple, and I genuinely hoped this place would work out for them. "Hey. How are the four-footed children today? Think they miss Phillip?"

Jeff's smile made me think of a little boy who'd just received the best present. "I think they'll survive. I never would have thought I'd be taking care of animals this big, but I've been doing some research, and Phillip did manage to give me a good overview of their care. I'm sure Alysha will be just as glad I have something to do that will force me to stay off the computer at times." He gave her such a tender look; I knew they were meant for each other.

Right, enough about the woolly things. I turned to Alysha. "Something I wanted to ask you. This morning at breakfast when Minnie went on about Reid Harrison. I thought she was talking to Rose, but then I noticed you were looking at Ty and it seemed I missed something in the conversation."

She furrowed her brow for a moment. "Oh, right. I remember. I thought she was talking to Rose too, but she seemed to make the comments about Dr. Harrison to Ty, which I thought a bit odd. Ty likes the doctor, right?"

"Yes, he does. I can't talk him out of seeing him either. Between you and me I think Ty may have a little thing for the doc."

It took a moment for that nugget to make a connection in Jeff's mind and when it did, it was almost comical to see the expression on his face. I guess because I've known Ty for so long and his, um, preferences, I tend to forget not everyone may have caught on. While Ty has always been discreet, he never hides things either. Knowing a little about his early years in England, I wondered at times how much it affected him. It might account for his petty, and sometimes mean, comments at times, and his lack of close friends. And yet, he could be thoughtful and kind. In other words, complicated, just like the rest of us.

Leaving the lovebirds to their own devices I wandered back to the house and decided I needed some me time. I settled in the shade with my book and waited on word from the hospital.

Ty woke me from a deep sleep, where I'd nestled in a lounge chair. I'd dropped my book and my sunglasses had slipped down my nose. I hoped I hadn't had my mouth open as well. Thank goodness it was only Ty.

"Sorry to wake you, Sleeping Beauty, but Jan would like you to go with her to the hospital to pick up Jock and Bea. She says there's a social worker on duty today who wants to have a word about their care. I think Jan would rather you go with her than ask Alysha."

I shook myself awake and stretched. "Thanks. Do I have time to freshen up?"

"The meeting's at two, and the hospital is less than fifteen minutes away. Don't worry, you look perfect as usual, so you've loads of time."

Good for my ego as always, that's Ty.

I gathered up my stuff. "Wonder what they want to talk about. Any idea?"

"Sorry, I've no idea what they want. Jan might know more, I'm just the messenger."

I should mention we don't really have a set lunch at Leven Lodge unless you specifically ask for one. A large breakfast takes most of us through the day until we have dinner at six. And we're all free to make a bite to eat in between. But for some inexplicable reason, I found myself hungry.

"I could do with a snack before leaving."

"Jan was rustling up something for you. Should be ready by the time you are."

I made a quick change out of my lounging-in-the garden clothes and dabbed on some lipstick. Jan would expect it of me. I know she'd say, "You never knew when you might bump into some nice available doctor." Other than Harrison, of course.

Jan had set a plate of sandwiches and a pot of tea in the kitchen. Ty sat with us and for a few moments, we were quiet. I didn't know about them, but I wondered what we would hear at the hospital. I noticed Jan had spruced herself up as if she wanted to put on a good front for the McTaggarts. She really was a handsome woman. Her black hair showed some grey but pulled back it really emphasized her killer cheekbones. Funny, I always sensed a sadness about her which she generally hid well. I supposed she had secrets like everyone else.

She focused on Ty. "Can I ask you to keep an eye on things until we get back? There's nothing to do, but with everything that's happened, there's no telling how the others might be feeling. Alysha and Jeff thought they should stay here but I suggested they take off and see the town."

"No problem Jan, I'll hold the fort until you return. Maybe some fresh flowers would be nice in Jock and Bea's room. I'll see what the gardens can offer."

Typical of my buddy, always thinking ahead.

### 

Once at the hospital, we made our way to the social worker's office. I should know better, but I expected a kindly older woman to greet us. Instead, a barely thirty-something male, who looked straight out of university, asked us to take a seat after shaking hands. His spartan desk had only an open file folder and pen on its surface. A laptop sat to one side, screen saver in place. *Matthew Hall* read his nameplate.

On the drive over, Jan and I had agreed to present a united front and wanted to reassure the authorities that Leven Lodge should be the only home Jock and Bea needed. We would convince him the residents and staff there were every bit as meaningful and supportive as family.

He glanced at the folder. "Mr. and Mrs. McTaggart are anxious to return to their home and medically they are cleared to be discharged. However, after a conversation with them this morning, I'm prone to think there are some serious family issues they need to deal with. Especially if we are to prevent any future incidents."

Jan tensed beside me. "Mr. Hall, I'm the first to agree with you that the McTaggarts have had more than their share of family sadness, and their well-being is of utmost importance to all of us back at the lodge. What do you suggest? Counseling perhaps?"

Oh boy, what a self-righteous smile on his face, but Jan played her cards right. We needed to keep on the right side of Junior if Jock and Bea were to come back home with us.

"I'm going to set up a meeting with a counselor and would ask your assistance to ensure they keep the appointment, Mrs. Young."

She bristled. "It's not Mrs."

He never even blinked but kept right on as if Jan's correction hadn't been heard. "Their first appointment is scheduled for Tuesday. Here are the details."

He pushed a small card towards Jan but looked at me. And I mean he was *looking* at me. I wasn't in the mood, and besides he probably still lived with his mother. "So, Mr. Hall, what you're saying, to Ms. Young and me, is, if we ensure the McTaggarts see this counselor, you'll allow them to be released back into our care today? And we can take them back to the home, where I live, with all the other seniors? We might all be drawing pensions, but we do care about one another and offer as much support as any family. I'd be proud to have a son as concerned about their welfare as you are."

I was gratified to see some colour rise in his cheeks and he turned his eyes away. "Yes, good. Um, another condition to their discharge, is that you allow for a follow-up visit by a special community officer from the local police detachment. As a result of our aging population, several communities have established an informal program with local police agencies to make certain our senior citizens are not being taken advantage of, and that their environments are healthy and safe."

Oh, oh. Junior had just stepped onto incredibly thin ice. Jan pushed her knees together and tightened her grip on the handbag on her lap.

"Excuse me young man, but I resent any implication that Leven Lodge is an unsafe home for anyone. I have overseen the care of several older guests over the years, and not once has there been a complaint or even a hint of anything out of line."

I touched her shoulder. "Jan, I'm sure he doesn't mean anything personal by it, more a matter of routine procedures. Am I right, Mr. Hall?"

His eyes darted between us. "Correct Ms. Mitchell. And if, as you say, all is in order where you live, then there is no need to be concerned. In fact, I'd hope you, and your fellow residents would take comfort in knowing you're not being brushed aside in your golden years. That the government is concerned for your well-being."

Oh, fine. The government's concerned, is it? Well, maybe they could show more concern by upping my pension cheque. With effort I made myself refocus on the real reason for this meeting – springing Jock and Bea from this place. "Not an unreasonable request, and we'll be glad to comply. Won't we Jan?"

"If it's required, of course. Now, can we take

them home? I have some folks back at the lodge who are anxious to see their friends again."

His pen scratched across a piece of paper, and he closed the folder. "My office will arrange for a visiting nurse to see the McTaggarts over the next few weeks. Save them from having to make the trip into town. Their medications will be monitored, as well as their general health."

Jan put the card into her bag and stood. "Can we see them now?"

I rose beside her and swallowed my pride, holding out my hand to shake Junior's hand as we left, and thanked him for his time.

"I'll call the floor nurse and let them know you're on your way to take them home. Pleasure meeting you both."

Jan's determined footsteps down the tiled hallway left no doubt of her mood. And I knew she had felt it a personal attack on the reputation of Leven Lodge.

"Hey," I said. "Let's take a breath before we see Jock and Bea. You look so nice today, you don't want to spoil the effect."

My well-intentioned remark resulted in a raised eyebrow, daring me to go on. So, I did. "Just let it go, Jan. You and I both know Leven Lodge is still being run the way Estelle and Dalton wanted. You do them proud, and I'm happy to call it my home. But there is one thing."

Jan turned to me; her face still tense. "I'm not the complaints department, Dianne."

I put on my serious face, "What are we having

for supper?"

"Oh, you…" But at least she managed a smile and her shoulders relaxed, so by the time we reached Jock and Bea, she'd calmed down and was genuinely happy to see her friends.

They looked older and tired, but Bea's eyes lit up when she saw us. "Are you taking us home?"

"We are. Unless you want to stay another night? I hear they're having gruel with real flavour for breakfast tomorrow. Or would you prefer Jan's coffee and scrambled eggs?"

I gave Bea a heart-felt hug and looked at Jock over her shoulder. He wasn't saying much but seemed anxious to be on the move.

"You two gave us a scare you know," said Jan. She moved toward Jock and offered her arm. He took it without hesitation.

"Let's get the hell out of here," he said.

# CHAPTER ELEVEN

*Alysha*

Jeff and I'd been dismissed from the lodge by Jan, whom I had quickly learned was a capable woman. Not long after breakfast, she'd given us a list of things to see and visit in the area. She promised she'd see to the McTaggarts with Dianne and bring them home.

We set off with maps and brochures of various Grant's Crossing tourist attractions and advice about where to have our lunch. "They make a nice shepherd's pie at the Crossings Tavern, and don't forget to visit the Y." She informed us she hit the swimming pool twice a week.

It was market day in Grant's Crossing and the town square, and a side street were cordoned off to traffic. Local farmers with fresh produce and baked goods lined the street shaded by colourful canvas awnings sprouting from store fronts. Tables were set up with local preserves and assorted pickles.

Other vendors caught my eye, food wasn't one of my interests. When I stopped to examine hand crafted silver rings Jeff wandered off. After trying a few I settled on a beauty. A girl couldn't have too many rings, and I wore my new thumb ring with pride.

The warmth of the day helped me decide to wait for Jeff and people watch at the same time. I shared a bench, bathed in bright sunshine, with an elderly woman. Judging by the bags she'd collected, her shopping day must be done. I could easily commiserate with her when she said shopping was hard on her feet, and she, in turn, admired my new thumb ring.

She soon departed, and I sat in silence, eyes shut, while my mind sifted through the changes in my life in such a short time. Thoughts raced around my mind.

Is this my future? Can I make a success of the Lodge? They say you can't go home again. Not sure who *they* are but it feels right to me. I've come back home but not as I remember it. I needed to let go of sad memories of Dad and Grandad always shouting. And then when Mum and Dad were killed. Never having made up with Gran, never saying goodbye. This could be a wonderful chance to...

"Aly, Aly are you ok?" Jeff nudged my shoulder. I blinked and worked to get my eyes in focus.

"Sorry, I'd been reminiscing, and the sun was so relaxing I nearly dozed off."

He laughed. "I think you were past the *nearly* stage – looked like you'd gone to sleep. Listen, I want you to meet someone." He pointed behind us to a vendor down the street. "The stall down there sells everything alpaca. The farmer, his name is Rick, says he'll help and give me advice and he has some alpacas ready to breed and..."

I put my hand up. "Whoa, I can see you're excited. Slow down. Get your questions answered first so you're well informed and then we can discuss it together."

I'd learned how to reign in his impetuous side when it surfaced. I loved the silly grin he wore as he pulled me up from my comfy perch.

"You're right, but just keep an open mind. This guy has loads of experience and they have a three-year-old alpaca for sale, and he can put me in touch with other breeders and..." He reminded me of a child who's just been given the latest action figure.

"Jeff, I've not even signed the papers yet. Grab the info and keep it until after I meet with Bryce Lockhart on Monday if I can get an appointment. Which reminds me, I'd like you to be there to meet this character. He's not my favourite person."

"Sorry, babe, guess I'm excited to finally find something I'm interested in that doesn't deal with motherboards and terabytes. At least, let me introduce you to Rick, and then we can talk over lunch at the tavern. I feel the need for a brew, and we can try the shepherd's pie Jan raved about." I gave in.

After meeting Rick Murdock and his family at their booth we headed for the pub. Jeff was enamoured with all the possibilities of breeding and raising alpacas. Including the use of their fleece to make yarn. He'd better not expect me to take up knitting. Although as a potential business I could see the possibilities. It didn't hurt that Rick and his wife, Amelia, were not much older than us, and seemed like people we'd enjoying getting to know.

He went inside to order two shepherd's pies, a large frothing ale and a half-pint of something light for me while I snagged the last table on the patio. We faced the main street, crowded with market shoppers.

We sat quietly eating our lunch, enjoying the weather and activity around us. The alpacas were forgotten for the moment. Jan hadn't been wrong with her recommendations, and I could envision this being a Saturday ritual.

Between mouthfuls of a delicious meal, Jeff asked, "What's the name of the girl who cooks at Leven Lodge, Cassie is it? She just served me at the bar."

"Cassie, here?"

"Yea, she introduced me to her dad. He owns the place, and she helps in the bar on her weekends off. This is where she met the boyfriend."

"Oh, the charming Dale. He must be an asset to the business."

"Now, Aly, don't be catty. He plays guitar here on a regular basis as well."

"Right, we have a *real* professional playing at the Lodge Friday nights." I smiled at Jeff to assure him I was only having fun. "I'd rather listen to you on guitar any day."

"I can see it now. A moonlight serenade on our balcony, right?" He left no time for a reply and continued. "Cassie said she'd come by and see you. Oh, here she comes now."

She approached our table and smiled hello. "Nice to see you here. Hope you like the food."

I could only speak the truth. "The shepherd's pie was excellent—is it one of your creations?"

She appeared more relaxed here than she did at Leven Lodge. Not quite so frazzled, but obviously bursting to tell us something. "No, but thanks. I don't cook here. My dad's in charge of the kitchen. I prefer to work the bar."

She took a seat at the table and leaned forward. She lowered her voice to a whisper. "I'm going to point out someone. Just in case you want to meet him."

I was confused. "Who? We met Dale last night. Jeff says he works here as well."

"No, not Dale. Doc Harrison. He eats here most days, him being a bachelor. Never drinks but likes the bar food we serve. Probably our most regular customer. Always alone, you know, never with a friend."

"Well, it takes all kinds," said Jeff." Some are just loners by nature."

"Perhaps, but he still manages to sell his pills and tonics to loads of people around here. Do you want to meet him? He's almost finished eating, so you won't be interrupting his lunch."

I hesitated. "We're just about to leave. More to see around town because I'm dying to see how much I remember." Curiosity won out. "Still, it's an opportunity to meet him isn't it."

"I don't think you should bother him," said Jeff.

"Right, but I do have to go to the ladies before we get back to our adventuring. Perhaps Cassie can introduce me as we pass him."

Jeff smiled at me. "You are a devious one. I'll wait here, don't be long."

Cassie and I headed for the doors leading to the

tavern's darkened interior. She stopped me inside the doors. "Shoot, I'm sorry but I'd forgotten about the poor McTaggarts. Any news?"

"They should be home today if Jan and Dianne have anything to do with it."

"What a relief."

I decided not to tell her about Phillip. Jan could provide details.

"There he is. The one with the newspaper. Oh, he's signaling for his check. Let's go."

My first impression let me think Cassie had it all wrong. In my mind, Dr. Harrison represented the devil incarnate doling out pills to all and sundry with never a thought to the consequences of his actions. The man before me, while not dark and handsome, was easy on the eyes.

Polite and charming, he smiled when introduced. "I wondered when I'd meet you, Ms. Grant. I'm sorry I missed you yesterday. I hope you'll be happy at Leven Lodge."

Eyes as blue as the summer sky grabbed my attention, but I did notice the absence of warmth in them. "Call me Alysha. Glad to meet you, Dr. Harrison. I've heard a lot about you."

He'd risen when I came to the table, and we shook hands. Then he indicated the seat across from him.

"Thank you, no. My boyfriend and I are exploring the town this afternoon and we have lots of ground to cover."

Cassie had returned to the bar where customers

waited. I wondered if he knew about the McTaggarts. "Perhaps we'll meet up again if you visit the McTaggarts when they return from the hospital later today."

Guess he didn't. "They're in hospital? *Both* of them?" His brows furrowed and the piercing look he gave me bordered on intimidation. I felt like I'd done something wrong in his books. "What happened? When I saw them yesterday they were fine. Depressed over Bradley's death, yes, but I wasn't overly concerned."

"Obviously no one called you. They were admitted for observation yesterday after a suspected suicide attempt."

"No, impossible. They may have been depressed but certainly not suicidal. This is terrible. If you'll excuse me. I must make sense of this to understand what went wrong. This wasn't what I thought would happen."

What an odd reaction to the news. *This wasn't what he thought would happen*? He dropped money on the table and hustled out the door before I could say anything else. I stood for a minute, unsure of exactly what had just been said. I shook my head and waved to Cassie as I left. I rejoined Jeff who waited for me in the sunshine.

"Did you learn anything, nosey parker?"

"It's strange, every comment I've heard about him since I arrived has been negative. But he seemed charming and concerned for the McTaggarts. Maybe I shouldn't have mentioned them."

Jeff's face broke into a grin. "Ah, he was good

looking then. Should I be jealous?"

"Oh, you. Let's go. We'll find out more if he turns up later." I grabbed his arm and pulled him along the street. The day had grown hot, and we had loads to see. We walked in the direction of the old sawmill at the other end of town. Although the area had seen many changes and had obviously grown, I could still see traces of the town as I remembered it. Older buildings were mixed with new but somehow, they'd kept its small-town vibe.

"I think if we walk past St Andrew's Church and the graveyard we'll eventually arrive at the sawmill. I attended Sunday school there for a time and of course played in the graveyard with my school friends when we felt especially brave."

"I think you were a rebel." Then in a more serious tone, he said, "What else haven't you told me about your past."

I giggled and wrapped my arm around his waist. I snuggled closer to him, and he leaned down to kiss me. I appreciated my good fortune to have him in my life as we started on this new adventure together.

We lingered a while at the river's edge near the sawmill. Situated on a large property, the building itself was in disrepair. You could still make out the faded stencil sign identifying Grant's Sawmill on one side. The huge water wheel had long since ceased to turn. As a kid, it had fascinated me to watch the water flowing over the wheel. "I loved to come here and daydream when I was little."

He teased me. "Never had anything like that in

my old neighbourhood."

I gave him a brief history, telling him how the sawmill had been the largest employer in Grant's Crossing after the woolen mill closed. "My mind's playing tricks on me, I can almost smell the sawdust. Look there! Something I never thought I'd see here."

A large colourful billboard proclaimed a developer's name and proposed casino to be built in the near future. It was a jarring contrast to the peaceful setting.

"Could be an interesting development for the town," said Jeff. "Busloads of tourists and the penny slot ladies might like to buy yarn from our alpacas. Don't you think?"

"You're jumping ahead again. Let's live here at least a week before we make any big decisions."

"Lighten up Aly, I'm only teasing you."

"I know." I glanced at my watch. "Okay, let's check out the Y and then head back home. We should make an appearance to check on the McTaggarts. If everyone is at dinner this evening, I'll let them know we're here to stay."

It was past three o'clock by the time we straggled up the driveway in the scorching heat. Too hot for a June day, I hoped it didn't mean we'd be in for a blistering summer. But maybe it would be easier to take the heat here, rather than in the city.

Rose knelt in the shade tending to bushes on the front pathway. We waved but didn't stop. Sweat trickled down my back. "I guess it's too hot for the others. I don't see another soul."

Jeff pointed off into the distance. "Except for someone sitting out in the field."

I peered ahead, shading my eyes from the bright sun. Ty sat at an easel. Painting the alpacas, I assumed. He wore a large straw hat and appeared totally engrossed in his pursuit. The alpacas ignored him. But as soon as Jeff approached the fence their heads bobbed up and they ambled slowly over to meet him. Maybe they disliked the heat as well.

Jeff gave me a look as if to say, "Shall we?"

We headed in the direction where Ty sat. I was curious to see what he'd done. The shaggy trio stopped as one and sauntered back to where they'd been chewing the grass.

"How strange is that? Don't they like him?" asked Jeff under his breath.

I announced our arrival to the artist. "Hey, we're being nosey and want to see what you're doing, I hope you don't mind."

Dabbing at his neck and forehead with a huge colourful handkerchief he looked away from his painting. "Not at all. These fellows are a constant wonder to me. People love paintings of them. They're so appealing. Don't you think?"

Jeff laughed out loud. "I don't think the feeling's mutual. They're keeping their distance."

"Yes, I see what you mean but that works in my favour today because I want to capture them a little removed. Maybe it's the smell of the oils or the cleaner I'm using. I can't think what else it could be. Never seems to be a problem in the barn. I can pet them all I want in there."

In addition to the work in progress on the easel, there were two more nearly complete canvasses leaning against his folding stool and I acknowledged his talent. "These are very good. Do you sell many?"

"I've sold one or two with the connections I still have in Toronto. I try to get there once or twice a month. Now, what have you two been doing?"

We gave him a report of our day in town, and he gave us a rundown of the McTaggarts' return a few hours earlier. According to him, both were quite subdued and resting. I don't know why but I didn't relay my bumping into Dr. Harrison to him.

Ty gathered up his gear. "This is good timing. I needed an excuse to stop for the day."

We strolled back to the barn together. Not until we reached the other side of the fence did the alpacas return for some attention. Jeff reached for a shovel leaning against the fence. "I guess I'd better earn my bread and butter and clean up after these boys. Then it'll be time for a few beers. Who wants to join me?"

"Mucking stalls or drinking beer?" I laughed, "Get to work and we'll see you at cocktail hour."

"Never had a cocktail in my life," muttered Jeff as he turned away into the barn to put the shovel to use.

Ty and I headed for the house. "Thanks for showing us your paintings. And now, if you'll excuse me, I've some reading to do. See you later."

Back in our apartment, I wasted no time showering and changing into something cooler. I wanted to make notes while thoughts were still fresh. Opened my journal and began.

> *Day three at Leven Lodge. Interesting day in town. Met the famous, or infamous, Dr. Harrison. I found it strange his comment regarding the McTaggarts. something like, 'not what he was expecting'?*
> *Let's see what the evening will bring. Oops, I forgot to tell Harrison about Phillip being carted off to the hospital. I think he's also one of his pill popping customers.. Details later*

# CHAPTER TWELVE

*Dianne*

I looked at Jan across the kitchen table. "They're sure not saying much, are they?"

We'd only been home about half an hour and had seen Jock and Bea up to their room. Jock was taciturn but compliant with Jan's attention. Bea seemed in a daze. I wished they'd open up to someone about what happened. But not a word, just *'Don't want to talk about it'* from Jock. Not much help there.

Jan rubbed her hand over her forehead. "I think Bea might say something away from Jock. We may have to bide our time. But I tell you, Dianne, I'm going to do everything I can to keep Harrison away from them. I don't trust him."

I thought back on our meeting with the social worker. "Do you think we should have said anything to Junior?"

She sighed. "We only have suspicions right now. And if Harrison is up to something, I don't want to warn him off before we can prove it. Let's keep our eyes and ears open for a while, and if we do get some proof we can go straight to the police."

I wasn't entirely convinced we should wait, but I trusted Jan's instinct.

She got up from the table. "Time to get dinner

ready. Life goes on and the last thing I need right now are complaints about not being fed."

"Need any help?"

She tied on her apron and set about opening cupboards. "Thanks, but I'll probably do better by myself. Why don't you search out Alysha and Jeff and see how their day went. They'd probably like an update on our patients as well."

Good idea. Both their vehicles were parked, but I knew they'd walked to town, so I couldn't be sure they were back. I decided I'd wait a while out front and watch for their return. The house was peaceful, and I guessed the day's heat had sent most to their rooms for a nap. I thought about Phillip and wondered if he was getting the treatment he needed.

No one could say the past few days had been boring around here. I glanced at the liquor cart in the hall and debated about having the usual Happy Hour this afternoon when all were not happy around here. Well, I couldn't make the decision for others, but I wasn't in the mood. I was in the mood for information though. Ah, perfect timing. My reliable source of information had come down the stairs.

Ty's nose had definitely been out in the sun, so I assumed the rest of him had been as well. He seemed glad to see me. "I came to find you, pet. How are the McTaggarts?"

"Join me out front and I'll fill you in."

We found a shady corner of the veranda and settled ourselves. I smiled at him. "You missed a spot." The tip of his left ear retained a faint smear of green.

"Painting, were you?"

"I couldn't waste such a glorious afternoon and headed out to pasture, so to speak. I almost finished another piece. The kids arrived as I was wrapping up."

"The kids? Oh...Alysha and Jeff. They're home, then?"

He wrinkled his nose. "Jeff's up to his waist in alpaca stuff, and I think Alysha headed upstairs. She quite liked my paintings by the way."

"Well, they are first-rate Ty, you have definite talent. Alysha obviously has good taste."

"I have good taste for what?"

I hadn't heard Alysha arrive. "Oh, there you are. Ty said you liked his paintings."

"Yes, I think they're super. Why aren't any on display here in the house?"

Ty sported a naughty grin. "Now that is a very good question, pet. I've never been asked and have to admit some of my earlier works were, perhaps, amateurish. But maybe now's the time to have the new owner see if one strikes her fancy?"

"As long as it features Leven Lodge, or has some connection to it, I think it would be great to have an original piece of art on display. I'll have to see what you've created so far."

"Oh good. Then you'll come up to my room to see my etchings—I mean my paintings?"

I groaned. "Could you be any more cliché?" Thankfully, Alysha got the joke.

Now she was here, I could update them both. "Jock and Bea are in their room. They've not said

131

a word about what happened, although I think Bea might talk out of his earshot. They need to have follow up counseling and at some point, we'll be having a visiting nurse come by to check up on them. Otherwise, there's not much else to say."

I hesitated to mention Jan's and my concern about Dr. Harrison with Ty on hand. Like Bea, I'd have to wait until my partner was out of earshot also.

A cloud passed over Alysha's face. "I hope they're glad to be home? Any suggestions on what I need to do for them? You both know them a whole lot better than I do."

Ty offered, "I'd bet it wouldn't hurt for Reid to see if he's got a pick-me-up for them. I should give him a call to let him know what's happened. He'll want to come and see them."

Alysha's revelation came as a surprise. "Actually, I met him in town today, and mentioned to him they'd been in hospital, so he does know now."

Before Ty could react, I put my two cents in, "I think we should wait until the nurse has come to see them. After all, they are under supervised care for a while." Perfect excuse to keep Harrison away from them. "We don't want to get on the wrong side of the authorities, this being a business as well as our home. And none of us want to jeopardize the Lodge. So, let's stick with the prescribed visits for now. Sound good?"

Reid Harrison was a sensitive subject where Ty was concerned, so I prepared for a rebuff. Instead, he agreed. "Yes, maybe you're right. I'd hate for us to lose our home here because of some… infraction."

That was too easy. He must have been out in the sun too long. I turned to Alysha. "Did you enjoy your visit to town? See all the highlights?"

Ty stood abruptly. "I'm not being rude, but as Alysha and Jeff told me all about it earlier, I think I'll go and get ready for dinner." He rubbed his ear. "And I need some more cleaning up apparently. You girls have a nice chat now."

I shot him a reminder. "Dinner should be soon, don't be late. Especially if you want a drink before?"

He called over his shoulder. "I'll be back shortly. Don't let the ice melt."

As he entered the house, Alysha started to fill me in on the day. It sounded like she and Jeff enjoyed themselves and were considering putting down roots. I truly liked them and offered encouragement as a means to entice them. "It's a nice town and I'm sure you'll make some friends your own age in no time."

Alysha laughed. "I think Jeff might already have a friend with the alpaca farmer he met."

I nodded, gathering my thoughts. "Before the others come down for dinner, I've something to share with you. I didn't want to say anything in front of Ty because he's so pro Harrison. But Jan and I have concerns about his dealings with the McTaggarts and we want to keep Harrison away from them. You met him today, what are your impressions?"

She nibbled at her lower lip before speaking. "I'd only heard negative things about him, and I guess I had preconceived ideas. Truthfully when I met him, I was surprised. He's polite, charming even." She hesitated as if thinking. "But you know, when I told him about the McTaggarts, he didn't react the way I'd expected. Upset and concerned, yes. But then took off, saying he didn't believe they'd be a suicide risk and that he had to look into things. Then I thought about Phillip. How both he and the McTaggarts use his tonics or vitamins, or whatever it is he sells."

"And you're wondering if there's a connection?"

She nodded, "I think so, but..."

"Shhhh...I hear someone coming. Let's take this up later, with Jan perhaps."

"Got it,' she said as Rose and Lily arrived on the scene.

Where on earth had Rose found that garish shade of lipstick? Ye gawds, it was intense, to say the least. Or maybe only because poor Lily looked so drab in comparison. "Evening ladies. I haven't brought out the trolley—not sure if anyone wanted a drink this evening?'

"I'm still breathing, aren't I?" laughed Rose. "I'll get the cart and some ice."

She went back inside. Lily quietly made her way to a chair near the railing and gave Alysha a tentative smile. For a moment I thought she might speak, but then Minnie arrived.

"So, they're back, old fools. Don't know what's wrong with them, but I'm hungry. Maybe there'll be more helpings with Phillip gone."

What a ray of sunshine. I leaned over to Alysha and whispered, "Remind me to talk to you about Minnie later as well." I lightly pinched my nose together and saw her smile.

Jeff arrived on the scene. Freshly showered by the look of things. He might qualify as cradle robbing status, but I appreciated a healthy-looking young man. He came straight over to Alysha and gave her a kiss.

"The children are fed and will need to be told good night in a little while. Now, where's that beer I've been looking for."

Last but not least, Ty returned behind Rose and the cart. He looked a little flushed. I guessed he must have become sidetracked with something because he'd still forgotten to clean the dab of paint on his ear.

He chose a bottle of red wine and raised it. "Drinks are on me."

His smile faded a little as the door opened and the McTaggarts joined us.

# CHAPTER THIRTEEN

*Alysha*

Even Minnie remained silent while the elderly couple found basket chairs on the veranda. Jock positioned himself at the far end and Bea sat beside him. She looked tired and wan but Jock, for once, looked in fine spirits, whistling a tune. He'd shaved and I caught the scent of a clean aftershave.

Before anyone could say a word of welcome Jock jumped up, hands deep in his pockets, and stood by the railing much like he did when he welcomed me to Leven Lodge. Was he going to say something?

Then my Jeff, with beer in hand walked up to Jock and introduced himself. Much to everyone's surprise Jock shook hands with him and grunted a hrmph. "This is my wife, Bea. Suppose you've heard all about this commotion yesterday. Well, don't believe a word of it. Fuss about nothing."

A statement that tolerated no discussion, but Jeff had successfully made an impression. He smiled warmly at Bea. She nodded and gave him a smile back. Another conquest.

Jock turned to face all of us. "And before you all start haranguing Bea and me, I'll tell you what we told them at the hospital." His jaw clenched as he took a deep breath and sat down again. The jovial mood had gone. "We've been upset over the allegations about Bradley taking drugs. Load of crap. Someone murdered our boy and if I ever get my hands on him..."

The vehemence in his voice mesmerized me. No one touched a drink except Ty, who managed to pour himself another glass of red wine. But who's counting.

Bea stretched out her hand to calm her husband. "Remember your blood pressure."

"My blood pressure's fine. What I want to tell you folks is," he paused, and the fervour of his words diminished as he continued. "I guess you could say everything caught up to us. First, we lost Dalton, and a better friend a man never had. Then Bradley being murdered, our Janet missing and now we may get turfed out of our home. Bea's not been sleeping, and we were both exhausted."

"So why couldn't we wake you?" asked Dianne. "We were so worried. Did Dr. Harrison give you something to help you sleep?"

I wasn't the only one sitting on the edge of a seat waiting for the revelation. Only the click-click of Minnie's knitting needles broke the silence.

"No, he did not! Reid offered us grief counseling but after he left, we stupidly took some over the counter sleep aid because we wanted to get a decent rest. Guess we took too much. The doc at the hospital said it probably interfered with Bea's heart meds and my blood pressure pills so they're doing some tests to find out how they interacted. So now you know, and the case is closed."

No one commented—perhaps afraid to—and

the silence grew awkward. Jock took a breath, "So, are we ever going to eat around here?"

A choking sound diverted our attention. I watched as Dianne thumped Ty on the back. It looked like he'd swallowed his wine the wrong way and he gasped for breath.

He soon got himself under control, and Dianne moved away. The poor guy looked suitably embarrassed and waved away any other attention. Like a flock of birds, the group moved together on to the next item at hand. No one seemed willing to say much to Jock or Bea. I couldn't ignore the events. This might be a chance to gain a better footing with Jock. I walked over to them. No need for others to overhear, so I kept my voice low.

"For what it's worth, I'm so glad you're both okay and are home. I may not know you as well as the others here, but I am equally concerned. If there is anything I can do to help you, please let me know?" I waited on a reaction from Jock. While he didn't offer to hug me, his thank you seemed genuine.

Bea visibly relaxed. "We will, dear. You're all so kind." She turned an eye in Rose's direction. "She seems het up over something in the newspaper."

Rose tapped her finger on the paper. "Casino. Here in Grant's Crossing. Whatever for? It'll bring criminals. People can't afford to gamble. Can they, Lily?"

Dianne had mentioned to me that Lily enjoyed playing the lotteries and placing bets now and then. I glanced over at her. She wouldn't meet her sister's eyes.

Minnie muttered a casino would be a non-issue if we didn't have a home. Good point. I made up my mind to tell them our news after dinner and put them out of their misery. I doubted there'd ever be a dull moment around here.

I made to go find Jan, but she already stood at the door and poked her head out. "Come and get it. I'm cooking tonight so no surprises. I grilled a few steaks on the barbecue with fresh veggies."

Everyone moved to the dining room except Ty and Jeff. Ty seemed determined to finish all the red wine. I noticed Dianne glanced his way as she continued into the dining room. Jeff had hung around to roll the cart inside and smiled at me as if to say, *Aren't I a good boy*. Men!

The dinner conversation was subdued as if no one wanted to say the wrong thing to Jock or Bea. I served Bea a cup of tea and she thanked me quietly. Poor woman looked done in. Rose continued to chatter on with talk of the casino. She fervently opposed it.

"Ty, how about some coffee?" offered Dianne." I'll get it for you."

Ty had brought the wine bottle, with its last dregs, to the table. To my eye, he was wasted, and dismissed the offer of coffee. Was he upset with Dianne for mentioning Harrison?

Something had got him going.

Jan served a wonderful fruit tart for dessert. I couldn't resist, and told myself I'd better get back to running or I'd need new clothes if I kept eating like this. When each had a coffee or tea in front of them, I felt it time to tell them our decision.

I got up and stood behind Jeff. The room fell quiet. All eyes were on me except for Ty. He'd fallen asleep, his head bobbing onto his chest. Dianne leaned over. I nearly laughed out loud when I realized he wore a hairpiece, and it had slipped! Dianne quickly made an adjustment and he never stirred.

Oh, he won't like that. But the tension let up and a few were smiling. Minnie would be sure to tell him about it later.

Before she could make a comment, I tapped my spoon against a glass. "I'd like to say a few words." I had their attention, and suddenly had butterflies. "I would have waited until we were all here but under the circumstances, I feel I owe you our decision. It didn't come lightly because it's been pointed out how we're young and inexperienced. True enough, but with your help, and the wonderful staff here, we're sure Leven Lodge can thrive."

I detected a smile on Minnie's face, but it might have been a grimace. Lily cried and Rose patted her hand and looked relieved. Dianne beamed at me with approval from where she sat beside buddy Ty, still out for the count. I could see a big hangover coming tomorrow. Jeff might come in handy later if Ty needed escorting to bed.

I did a double take as I watched Jock take his wife's hand and smile at her. Would wonders never cease?

"I appreciate you all miss my Uncle Dalton, and I

can't take his place but we'll keep things as they are for now. Jeff has agreed to take on the alpacas and plans to breed them once he's learned the ropes."

Amid applause, Jeff got up and took a bow. That was Jan's cue to bring out a tray of champagne. She came in smiling and told them to go easy on the bubbly as she didn't want to tuck everyone in tonight, referring to Ty who gently snored.

The champagne went down a treat with Rose, and Jan handed Minnie and Lily a soda. Jan raised her glass to me and smiled as if to say, "Well done."

The evening began to wind down, and Jeff left for a final tour of the barn, to tend to his boys. I looked around at the others. They were my family now and I was glad to be here.

Ty snored on, evidently comfortable so, except for Dianne, we ignored him. With her set jaw, she had more colour than usual in her cheeks. The looks she shot him did nothing to hide her disapproval, bordering on anger. I looked on benevolently as I'd seen enough overindulgence in university. I never would have pegged him as a drinker. Had something triggered it, or was it a regular occurrence? He'd pay for it tomorrow.

Jock and Bea declined the champagne and stood to leave but then turned, walked back, and took me aside. Jock wouldn't look me in the eye, but Bea smiled. When I'm her age I want to look just like her. Classy lady.

"Alysha dear, Jock has something he wants to say to you."

"Oh?" I moved to put my back between myself and Dianne. If she'd craned her neck anymore trying to listen in, she'd be needing traction.

"I ah, I need to say, er, well what I wanted to say was..."

"Spit it out, Jock," said Bea, not unkindly.

"Give me a minute woman. I'll say it in my own time." He cleared his throat and mumbled quietly, "I apologize for my behaviour when you first arrived. Only..."

My heart melted. "I understand. You've both been through a lot and change is always hard. I'm glad to be here. As I said before, you can count on me to help in any way."

Bea looked on indulgently at her husband. "I told you she takes after Estelle."

Jock had teared up and looked older to my young eyes. An expression came to mind. He'd lost all his piss and vinegar.

Bea would have made a good diplomat. "Thank you, dear. I think we'll go off to our room now. Goodnight."

I watched them walk slowly out of the dining room and from the corner of my eye I saw Dianne studiously pretend not to have been listening. She and Ty were the only two left in the dining room. She patted a chair beside her. "What'd they say?" she asked while Ty snored on. I had nothing else to add to Jock and Bea's chat.

So, I smiled at her. "You mean you didn't catch all of it?" I glanced at Ty. "I'll call Jeff to help move

Ty to his room. We can't have Jan stepping around a drunk when she clears the table."

The grim line of her mouth let me know Ty wasn't her favourite at the moment. "I'm not impressed with him. And I'm not apologizing for him even though I've never seen him like this before. Something's not right. I'll have a word with him tomorrow. Headache or not."

I could see Dianne owned a cruel streak and hoped it would never be aimed at me. Best not to make a comment, so I texted Jeff to come help with Ty.

He soon arrived. Between the three of us, we had Ty on his feet and half dragged him to the elevator and then stumbled our way to his room. Dianne held the door open while we propped him against the wall. He came to with a silly grin and unintelligible nonsense about Reid and his great ideas and then blanked out.

Ty's snoring kicked in again before Jeff had removed his shoes and managed to lay him on his bed. Dianne threw a cover over him, and I left a glass of water at his bedside. He'd be in need of more than water when he woke up. I have to admit to some experience in this area. Thankfully those days are done.

Jeff went off to hook up his computer in our apartment and Dianne and I helped Jan clear away the dinner dishes. What a tireless worker. No wonder the lodge ran so well. More dishes were stacked, waiting for the dishwasher's next round. Jan decided to call it a day.

She removed her apron. "Thanks, the rest can

wait, and I'll finish up later. We need a tete a tete to discuss a few things. Why don't you ladies be my guests in Cassie's and my sitting room? We'll be away from prying eyes and ears."

Dianne grabbed a half-full bottle of champagne off the counter. "Bring the glasses, Alysha, we'll finish this off. Doesn't make sense to try and save it."

Jan had a fan running but she'd also opened the windows wide to capture a soft breeze coming from the north. In the distance, I recognized the sound of frogs courting in the warmth of early summer. The best time of evening when the sky shows the promise of tomorrow. Dianne and I settled in an ample sofa and Jan sat opposite in what looked to be a favourite chair, with a matching footstool.

I relaxed and had another glass of the bubbly, but the energy thrown out by my new friends was palpable.

Dianne raised her glass. "What shall we drink to?"

"How about friendship?" I offered, trying to read the mood of these new friends.

"I think we should drink to the truth. Finding out the truth," said Jan in a quiet voice.

I had an inkling where this we might be headed. "The truth? What do you mean?

"What I have to share with you both is confidential." She looked at each of us. "Are we all on the same page about trying to help the McTaggarts?"

Dianne and I nodded.

I needed more. "So, fill me in on them. What

144

exactly did you hear at the hospital?"

I learned they appeared to have made a recovery, but this had to be hard at their age. Not that I had any experience. Jan relayed what the social worker had told them and what to expect with the visiting nurse and social worker checking up. I understood the advantage of a nurse's visit, but not so sure the McTaggarts would agree.

Jan had more to add. "I for one will be most interested in what the toxicology reports show. Something feels off. When you think about it, anyone in this house who has been taking Harrison's pills and potions has been adversely affected in one way or another."

Uneasiness replaced the pleasant feeling I'd had. "What do you mean? Who else has been ill after taking medicine from him? I'm still in the dark here but I get the feeling he's not on your Christmas list. Dianne, do you feel the same?"

They looked at one another, and then Dianne busied herself pouring us another drink. Who'd go first? They were making me nervous as I looked from one to the other. Jan shifted in her comfy chair and crossed her arms and began.

What I heard made my hair curl more than usual.

# CHAPTER FOURTEEN

*Dianne*

We settled in Jan's comfortable sitting room. I hoped our talk wouldn't overwhelm Alysha, and I let Jan take the lead. While she talked, I kept an eye on our young friend.

And so, Jan began. "A little history is probably in order. I've been here for about fifteen years—not long after you and your family left Grant's Crossing. Dalton, as you know, had already been here a few years by then. He was such a great help to your grandmother and Leven Lodge wouldn't be the place it is now without his vision."

Her voice always grew wistful when talking about Dalton. It didn't get talked about, but we all knew their relationship existed. For now, though, I needed to concentrate on what she told Alysha. "The place kept us busy. We had a lot of temporary guests for about ten years. Eventually the residents settled into the group we have now. We haven't had a new face since...well, since you, Dianne."

I gave her a mock bow to acknowledge my rank in the pecking order.

"After losing your grandmother, I'm glad Dianne came to us the following year and decided to stay. Which is why I feel she and I are best suited to bring you up to speed on our concerns."

She smiled at me, "Do you agree?"

Knock me over with a feather. I honestly didn't know Jan felt so comfortable with me. But I guess maybe because we're closer in age than the rest it makes sense, although we certainly don't have much more in common as far as I knew. Guess it's true what they say about still waters running deep.

"Sounds good so far, Jan. Carry on."

"Right. So, as I said, we had many guests and now we have our family. All seemed pretty routine until Reid Harrison arrived on the scene a few years after I came on board."

"What happened to change things?" asked Alysha. "Maybe it was only a coincidence?"

"Over the years, I've thought about it at times, but this latest incident with Jock and Bea has pushed things beyond mere coincidence—at least in my books. What do you say, Dianne?"

I hesitated a bit, trying to be diplomatic I guess, out of loyalty to Ty's friendship, even though I didn't like the doctor. "Up until the McTaggarts went to the hospital I never connected the dots, but in hindsight, I'm beginning to have my suspicions about Dr. Harrison. I'll admit I don't like him, but I'm trying to be objective here."

Alysha reached for an open notebook on the coffee table and glanced at Jan, "May I?"

The beginnings of a grocery list were bypassed, and a fresh page appeared. "Alright. I know you both have history, but I'm still finding my way so it might be helpful to make some notes. Easier to connect those dots, Dianne." She shot me a smile and I began to feel like one of three new musketeers.

"How about I ask questions about the good doctor because I think that will help me get a better picture. For instance, who here consults with him?"

She made two columns and wrote as we filled her in. Then she wanted to know when he'd arrived in Grant's Crossing in relation to the later guests of Leven Lodge. I had to hand it to her, she soon put an orderly and logical history down. When she showed Jan and me the end result, we could see in black and white there were concerns.

The McTaggarts, Phillip, and Rose were all fans of Reid Harrison. With Ty in the running as his biggest supporter around here. Plus, Estelle and Dalton had also been partakers of his various tonics and therapies.

Jan and I exchanged a light bulb moment, which I vocalized. "Do you realize Rose, and Ty appear to be the only ones not ill, or dead, out of everyone connected with him?"

Alysha said, almost to herself, "I'm not much of a believer in coincidences."

Jan looked thoughtful. "You know, when Estelle and Dalton passed, no autopsies were done. Natural causes went on both their death certificates."

"But there's no real proof of anything is there?" I said. "I mean it's easy to jump to conclusions. And as much as I dislike the quack, you can't spread rumours."

"Oh, I'll spread no rumours, Dianne," said Jan with a lift of her shoulders. "It will only be facts. Which means we have to find the facts to give us the proof."

Alysha seemed taken aback at the determination in Jan's voice. "Um, we're not detectives you know. Maybe we should take our suspicions to the police?"

She'd touched a nerve with Jan. "And have them do what exactly? I know how they work; they need to catch a murderer red-handed before they'll believe someone could be guilty. Everyone's so afraid of lawsuits these days...chickens."

I had a feeling where this was leading and braced myself as Alysha responded.

"Jan's right, we do need some kind of proof. Dianne, do you think Ty would be willing to help us if we—you—could get him to see this as more than coincidence?"

I don't think I successfully hid my distaste at the thought. "I don't know. Ty is so into Harrison, he thinks the man can do no wrong. If I even hint at a criticism of him, he's up in arms. And to suggest to him we suspect Harrison, of what, murder? Well, I can only imagine where that would go. Straight down the toilet, along with my friendship."

I heard the frustration in Alysha's voice. "But what's more important? Friendship, or getting to the truth about murder?"

Nuts, I hate questions like that. As if I'm supposed to show I have a higher moral code or something. I aimed for a conciliatory tone. "I get what you're saying Alysha, but it makes me uncomfortable."

Jan crossed her arms. "And how uncomfortable would you feel if Rose, or Ty, falls victim."

Oh sheesh, the guilt card now. But she had a point and I needed to clarify. "Do you think Harrison might have murdered Estelle or Dalton? And had something to do with the McTaggarts' close call?"

Alysha doodled on the notepad. "What about Bradley McTaggart?"

Both Jan and I snapped to attention. "What about him?"

"Well, he worked for Harrison, didn't he? Maybe he found out something and threatened to report Harrison to the police."

I had to admit that piece of the puzzle had me thinking. "If, and I say, if Harrison is somehow linked to all these deaths, then we need to be cautious, don't you think? Say I talk to Ty, but if he doesn't side with us, he may tip off Harrison."

"True," said Jan. "Now I don't know a lot about computers, but I do know you can find out almost anything about anybody if you know what you're doing."

Alysha jumped in. "Leave that to me, if I can't find information, I know Jeff will help."

Jan sat back, visibly relieved. "Right, you can be in charge of information searching. Something else we need to consider is what happened to Phillip. I'd bet it's no coincidence the downturn in his health is connected with Harrison's tonics."

I jumped on the opening to deflect any more thought of me talking to Ty. "Have you ever mentioned this to Philips's doctor?"

"No, Diane, I haven't, but if the opportunity arises, I will be sure to let his doctor know. Although I doubt his doctor would be willing to betray client confidentiality."

Great, she has an excuse to be let off the hook about awkward questions. Wish I had one and was about to say so, when she continued.

"Well, ladies, I think we each have our work cut out for us."

She tilted her head and gave me a look that was not unsympathetic. "Dianne, I know it will be awkward to approach Ty on this, but it has to be done, don't you see?"

On some level, I agreed with her, but I dreaded the outcome if Ty's loyalty stayed with Harrison above all. "I know you're right Jan. Let me sleep on it and I'll figure it out."

Alysha closed the notebook and rose to her feet. "I have to say this chat didn't turn out as I'd expected, but if Leven Lodge is to be my home, I'm responsible for what goes on here, so thanks for including me. I think we can all work together and gather evidence, or at least more substantial suspicions, to take to the police. We'll make them listen."

And then I remembered. "Oh, and I want to talk about Minnie."

Alysha opened her mouth to speak, but Jan was

quicker. "Why don't we leave Minnie for another day. We've bombarded this poor girl with quite enough for one evening, don't you think?"

I glanced at Alysha and by the look on her face, I think she welcomed the suggestion. Jan was right, Minnie could wait. After all, we've waited this long, a few more days wouldn't hurt. I'd be sleeping with my window open for a while longer.

"Thanks for the drinks, Jan. And now I think Dianne and I will head our separate ways."

To my surprise, Jan held open her arms and with no hesitation, Alysha went forward for a hug. "Dalton would be so proud of you, little one."

I'm not prone to tears, so I must have been over-tired. At least that's what I told myself as I searched my pockets for a tissue.

Time to call it a night.

# CHAPTER FIFTEEN

### *Alysha*

Exhaustion dogged me when I left Jan and Dianne to make my way upstairs. I found Jeff sitting at the desk surrounded by all his gadgets. He'd successfully accessed the Wi-Fi, so we were in business.

"Great internet strength here, Aly. I just have a few things to set up and then you can tell me what the ladies wanted to talk about. Give me five minutes."

"Okay," I said and moved into the small kitchenette, where I made a cup of tea in hopes it would counteract the lethargy washing over me. Everything I'd heard, and considered, earlier seemed in gigantic proportions to what I was capable of. I stood behind Jeff, and I laid my hands on his shoulders, giving them a squeeze. "Can you finish that later please. What I have to tell you has me anxious and I'm wondering what I should do about it."

We wandered out to the balcony. If the chairs had been any comfier I would have fallen asleep, instead, they were firm enough to keep me awake. We gazed over the fields and barn. Night had arrived and with it a few stars in the clear sky. Temperatures thankfully had dropped.

Jeff put my thoughts into words. "This is a great house, I think we can be happy here, don't you?"

"I agree, but you might change your mind after I tell you what Jan and Dianne had to say." I proceeded to recap their suspicions concerning Dr. Harrison. Jeff sat quietly and listened with growing disbelief.

"Babe, they can't be serious. They can't go around accusing people of murder with absolutely no proof. You'll get nowhere with the police either. Just because he sells alternative medicine does not make him a murderer. What's his motive? What does he gain by it? I think you should leave it alone."

"Maybe, but I find it intriguing. I wonder if the lawyer could tell me something about him. Perhaps I'll ask him on Monday."

Jeff shifted in his chair. "Right, the lawyer. Listen, I think I'll pass on going with you. I have to set up a day with the shearers and arrange to have the rest of our stuff brought from Guelph. Think you can handle him yourself?"

I looked at him sweetly, "If I can handle you, I can handle an old duffer like Bryce Lockhart."

Jeff grinned, "You like them young; you like them old. I'll have to keep an eye on you, Alysha Grant."

I stretched, then rose to go inside when I remembered. "If my laptop is ready, I need to do some research. I want to find out a few things about this man they either love or hate. No in-between with him."

He grew serious. "You have Wi-Fi now, but you're on your own with this. For the record, I don`t think you should be meddling."

"I just need to clarify a few things to help me

understand who or what I'm dealing with." I left him sucking on his beer and went into the bedroom. I could sleuth on my own. Journaling would have to wait.

###

Except for Phillip's empty chair we had a full house for breakfast on Sunday. Jan had outdone herself with a fry up of all Jock's favourites. Sausages, and bacon with fried bread. I noticed Dianne hardly touched it, but Jeff wasn't shy about digging in. Ty was quiet and not eating much either, which might have something to do with the greyish tinge of his complexion.

Jan bustled in with more coffee for the sideboard. "I'll be glad when Cassie gets back tonight. You can look forward to her cuisine selections for the next couple of weeks. I'm hanging up my chef's hat for a while."

Funny she hadn't mentioned anything last night about taking a break. I brushed the thought aside when she warned Jeff. "Don't be surprised if Cassie makes you something exotic, Jeff. She loves to try her creations on unsuspecting victims."

Jeff, who would eat anything put in front of him, said, "I look forward to it."

Minnie finished a big plate of Jan's breakfast and left the table. She wasn't one for small talk apparently. I still needed Dianne to give me the rundown on her later.

155

Rose, Lily, and Bea left to dress for church, their usual Sunday morning ritual. The day was overcast and threatened rain, so I decided to read through more of the paperwork from the lawyer and search through Uncle Dalton's desk. I had no idea what I searched for.

I'd begun to grow familiar with the house routine. Jeff and I decided we wouldn't take all our meals with the residents. We'd like to pick up a burger or fish and chips occasionally. We still needed our quota of fast food, and I was anxious to try out various pubs in the area.

Dianne and I followed Jock and Jeff as they wandered out to the veranda, Jock with his newspaper. It heartened me to hear Jock discuss world events with Jeff as they walked. Ty scowled at us and quietly left the room, leaving Dianne with me.

"We've been abandoned," said Dianne chuckling. "Unfortunately, I'm going to do the same to you. I'm off to see a friend who lives about an hour away, so I need to head out."

I ventured a bold question. "And is this friend male or female?"

"That's for me to know and not to tell, Miss Nosey." A reprimand softened with a smile.

"I've been called worse. Have a safe trip and maybe we can discuss that other issue when you return."

"Other issue? Oh, you mean she who knits. Yes, we need to deal with that. See you later."

She left and I went to do research and read dry old lawyer stuff. I anticipated spending the day ensconced in our new apartment. I set up my laptop and went through the files from the lawyer. I decided to use my business degree and added all the numbers Lockhart had provided onto a new spreadsheet. Leven Lodge struggled to make ends meet from the guests and even less from the alpacas. In fact, they barely broke even.

I'd have to talk to Jeff about budgeting until we started to see some revenue increase. There had to be a way to save a few bucks. I'd remain positive and hope for clarification, or suggestions when I next met with Lockhart.

After creating my files, I decided to dig through the boxes of Uncle Dalton's personal papers. It felt intrusive, but someone had to do it, or significant papers could be thrown away. There were boxes of files from his ownership of the sawmill. Those had also belonged to my grandfather. A book on the history of the Grants. Oh! I unfolded a set of original house plans of the Grant farmhouse before it became known as Leven Lodge. I set this aside to read later and do it justice.

I kept digging not knowing what I was looking for. So far, no real surprises. Another box held records of all the births, marriages, and deaths of the Grants since 1858 when the original founder of Grant's Crossing arrived from Scotland. Dalton had put the most recent on their own, all bundled neatly together. Uncle Dalton's birth certificate I also found but no death certificate. Made sense if he had been the one organizing the papers.

Under some tissue, I found a beautiful carved wooden box. I hesitated to open it. For some reason, I wanted Jeff with me when I did. I carefully laid it to one side. Time for a break anyway.

I went in search of him. It must be hard work cleaning up after the alpacas. Seriously? I found him sitting on a hay bale, reading a book. "The minute my back is turned you're slacking off."

Jeff cracked a smile, "I'm enjoying a few minutes rest. Look, I found this paperback on the bookshelf in the front room. It must be Phillip's. All about how to care for young alpacas."

"Sounds interesting but I could use your help sifting through boxes. Then I thought we could go for a run."

He stood and stretched. "Sure, all's under control here. Find anything interesting in your digging?"

"Lots of reading material but I also found some photo albums I'd like you to look at with me."

Jeff slipped the paperback into his back pocket. "Why do you need my help?"

"I feel weird, as if I'm intruding, looking at my uncle's personal stuff so I'd like company. And you're elected."

"Let's go and have a look and then we can get in a few kilometers before I need to put out hay for the boys." He slipped his arm around me and pulled me close. I guessed I'd better get used to the smell of alpaca because I love being close to him.

We spent so much time going through my uncle's effects we never did go for a run. By the time we decided to take a break, clouds had rolled in, and a summer storm was in full force. Rain battered on the windows and lights were needed when the sky grew dark.

But as fast as it had come over the rain stopped, and a brilliant rainbow stretched the length of the meadows. We watched from the rain-soaked balcony where the alpacas had sheltered under a wooden structure built to hold their hay. The air was fresh and sweet after the cleansing rain.

Jeff held me, gave me a kiss, and said, "Leave the rest for now and we'll check it later."

"Are you off to watch over your babies? You know, I'm so proud of how seriously you're taking this."

He beamed. "I'm loving it and can't wait to get going with the breeding and increasing the herd. I'll get in touch with Rick and see what we need in the way of equipment."

Which reminded me. "Hey, I don't want to burst your bubble, but after looking at the finances of the Lodge, we need to have a better understanding of how much to invest and what our return will be."

He looked suitably contrite. "I'm sorry if I get carried away. Lots going on here to sort out before we go big time. I'll be back in half an hour."

I gave him a kiss and sent him on his way.

I surveyed all the boxes we'd opened, some we'd closed up, and put back in the closet. The foraging around in my uncle's affairs had made me uncomfortable. There were pictures of weddings and parties obviously taken in the farmhouse as I remembered it. Pictures of my parents I had never seen and of myself as an infant. And on through the years of me growing up and remembering how my blond curls had to be tamed with bows and barrettes. I could still feel the hair pulled tight on my scalp when my mother did her best to keep my hair in check.

A beautifully carved box with DG engraved on its lid caught my eye. Inside I found more pictures and letters. To me, the letters were private and not for my eyes.

One set of photos stood out.

A beautiful, dark-haired woman, about my age, looked straight at the camera. Uncle Dalton had his arm around her and in many of them she smiled and looked up at him. They appeared so happy. The date on the back said 1990. The woman was Jan.

I wondered if we should invite her up here and hand over these mementos of their life. They must have meant a great deal to Uncle Dalton, but then again I'm a sucker for a romantic love story. I let out a sigh.

Needless to say, all thoughts of researching Harrison had vanished. I hoped I'd have more to go on when I spoke with old Lockhart.

# CHAPTER SIXTEEN

*Dianne*

I'd hoped the afternoon away would have provided a diversion from the niggling thoughts at the back of my mind. No such luck. Jan's comments earlier about Reid Harrison troubled me. Well not so much about Harrison, I've no time for him, but more for the fact Ty puts so much stock in him. As his friend, I knew if a connection existed between Harrison and what he dispensed, then Ty might be at risk. But how on earth could I broach the subject and avoid him getting all defensive? Still, better offended than sick, or worse, I supposed. I'd have to find a way.

Dusk triggered the streetlights as I drove by. I'd taken Gordon Lightfoot along for the drive, but now it was time to put my favourite music away. The house appeared quiet as I came up the driveway. Appearances could be deceiving, but it seemed odd no one was outside enjoying a perfect evening.

I spoke too soon. No sooner had I left the car than Ty came flying down the front steps. Had he been watching and waiting? He practically skidded to a stop in front of me.

I held up a hand to slow him down. "Whoa... what's the rush? And before you say a word, I think you'd better catch your breath."

Unusual for Ty, his eyes flashed, his lips pressed tight. Something, or someone, had set him off. He took a deep breath. "I wish people would learn to mind their own business around here."

Red alert. "What happened?"

"They wouldn't let Reid in to see the McTaggarts."

"And who are *they*?"

"Jan and Alysha, that's who. They have no right. This is the McTaggart's home as much as anyone's and if they want Reid to see them, they should be allowed."

I mentally winced and prayed for Solomon's wisdom. "We covered this before, remember? Because the McTaggarts are under medical supervision, we felt it best to not have Dr. Harrison offer conflicting advice—at least for the time being. Did anyone ask the McTaggarts if they wanted to see him?"

Ty looked down at his feet and mumbled something I couldn't make out.

"Well, did they?"

"Not exactly."

I suppressed a sigh of frustration and wished I'd kept on driving. "So, what happened? And just the facts. I'm tired and not much in the mood for drama."

"Drama? Me? I'm crushed."

I almost smiled. "Oh brother, get on with it already!"

He glanced over each shoulder. "Just after you left this morning, Reid drove up. I was out front and saw him arrive. He told me he wanted to come and visit the McTaggarts and see how they were doing, so

I started to lead the way inside. Well." He paused for effect, but I made no comment, so he continued. "Before we got up the steps, Jan opened the door. Stood there with her arms crossed like some kind of guardian and asked if she could help him."

I pictured Jan in my mind's eye and added a rolling pin in her hands for good measure. Ty couldn't spit the words out fast enough. "Reid said he'd like to see the McTaggarts. Oh, and get this. They were out on their balcony and could see everything, but they didn't say a word."

Ever seen a grown man throw a temper tantrum? Ty was almost there. "Jan basically told him, no, and not overly polite about it either. She didn't even offer to go and ask the McTaggarts."

My mind blitzed through lightning-fast scenarios. In the blink of an eye, I considered if I should tell my friend our concerns about Harrison and my sincere fear for his own safety, or should I let sleeping dogs lie, for now.

"Ty, listen, Jan's first priority is the well-being of the McTaggart's, and she made the judgment call to not ask them. Whether she should have, I don't know. I wasn't there so perhaps there's more to what went on than I know. You said the McTaggarts knew he was there? So, they had their chance to say something, right?"

"I suppose, but Reid's concerned for them as well. And he got a little, well I'll just say he got a little testy when he wasn't allowed inside. Voices raised and the next thing you know, Alysha shows up. Of course, she's siding with Jan and now the two of them are barring any entrance to the house. It felt like a standoff. I still don't see what harm it would have done to have let him in."

Without tipping my hand I didn't want to say too much, although from where he stood, he did have a point. No wonder I felt a headache brewing. I didn't much like being put in the middle of all this. "What if I talk with Jan and Alysha about what happened? Likely, in another day or two, Dr. Harrison could come and see the McTaggarts. And in the meantime, I'm sure you told him how they were doing."

He could act like a petulant child at times, but it didn't sway me. "If you say so. I just don't know why you're so against Reid. He's never done me any harm."

Not that we know about, yet. "Not to change the subject, but I've had a long drive and I need to use the washroom, so if you don't mind, I'm going to head upstairs. Coming?"

We walked inside and started up the stairs. Boy, it was quiet inside with no one in sight, and I figured all were in their own rooms for the night. As we passed Phillip's door, I wondered about him and if he'd ever be coming back.

Ty must have read my thoughts. "Looks like Alysha will have to find another guest now Phillip's gone. Not likely he'll be back."

"You're quick to write him off."

He tapped the side of his head. "You didn't see him at the hospital like I did when they admitted him. Didn't seem to be much of Phillip left in there, you know."

I'd had enough of hearing about people's problems for one day and decided to ignore him. "Whatever, Ty. Good night. See you in the morning."

We parted ways and I went on to my room, where I closed the door behind me with a sigh, glad to be in my own sanctuary, away from the gossip and trials of the day.

Then I glanced down at my feet. A folded piece of paper had been pushed under my door. Opening it up, Alysha had written:

*I'm going to see Bryce Lockhart tomorrow and will ask about Reid Harrison. If you have any questions you want me to ask let me know.*

So much for closing out the rest of the world from my room.

# CHAPTER SEVENTEEN

### *Alysha*

Jeff and I agreed to wait for an appropriate time to hand over Uncle Dalton's box of mementos to Jan. We decided to leave it up to her if she wanted to divulge any more of her relationship with him.

Our first full week at Leven Lodge had begun and routine settled in. Cassie arrived back the previous night, annoyed she'd missed the drama of Phillip being taken to hospital. She had tried to give us her two cents worth about the professor, but Jan would hear none of it and made it clear to her that Phillip was not to be discussed with the others.

I'd made an appointment to see Bryce Lockhart later, so I had a few hours to kill. I wandered out back of the farmhouse and went exploring. There were a couple of old outbuildings that had seen better days but with a good cleaning and minor repair, I'm sure they could be put to use again.

Shrubbery and hedges behind them had been left to grow wild. But on the other side of them was an overgrown and neglected garden. A partial brick wall, in need of repair, sported deteriorating trellises. Memories stirred. Gran had looked after me during the day while my mother worked, and I spent many hours at her side. As the sun warmed my face, I could almost hear her voice, talking about her roses, and how to care for them. In hindsight, I knew she'd loved this spot. Now, I could only see thorny, overgrown shrubs, and wondered if they were the remnants of her garden. Another cause for curiosity – why had the garden gone wild? Roses out in front of the house were well tended. Still, I felt a sense of purpose but knew I'd have to enlist Frank's help with any gardening before I could return her roses to their former glory. I would do it in her honour.

Satisfied with my plan, I mentally ticked things off in my mind as I wandered to the edge of the property. It ended on a rise, and I stood leaning against a waist-high stone wall where the view gave me a glimpse of the river Alder and the old sawmill which I'd never noticed before. Perhaps there'd been trees hiding it. Another question for Frank.

How fortunate to have this beautiful place to call my own. Lost in a daydream about the gardens, the animals, and the residents, Jeff startled me when he came up behind me.

"You're deep in thought," he said. "And this is the perfect place to do it."

I smiled as I turned to him. "Isn't this view awesome? I love how the water rushes by on its way to the water wheel. I never knew you could see all of this from here. Look, we can see the mill where we sat by the river on Saturday."

Ideas flew into my mind.

"What a shame if this gets demolished for a casino. It looks to be in good shape. Maybe it could be converted into a restaurant, or spa?"

"And you accuse *me* of daydreaming?"

We stood close enjoying the warmth and the view. Jeff interrupted my reverie. I knew that excited tone in his voice. "But did you notice these old buildings? I'm sure they could be restored. Once I know what we need to expand the herd and start breeding we can look at having them repaired."

He had a one-track mind where the alpacas were concerned, but I agreed with him on the buildings. "My thoughts as well. I want to talk to Frank about a rose garden behind them. It's a perfect spot, don't you think?"

He obliged me with a noncommittal shrug. His head could only fathom alpacas.

We wandered back past the rose garden wall I envisioned and entered a broken-down stone barn. It was more or less a shell of a building. Shattered windows, old farm implements, and an assortment of building materials lay scattered about. I didn't want to think about how many spiders lurked, cobwebs draped everything.

"This looks like a money pit." I didn't want to entirely discourage Jeff, but I could see the dollar signs.

"Yes, it does need quite a bit of work to make it habitable for livestock. But I'll have a chat with the farmer I met at the market. You remember, Rick Murdock. I'll see what he suggests."

"Good idea. I've been wondering if there are any survey plans for this property in those boxes of Uncle

Dalton's. I'll also ask the lawyer when I see him later. He may have a better idea."

"Never hurts to ask. Sorry, I can't come with you, babe, but Frank said the shearers will be here about two."

"That's okay. I think I'm up for the task now and it won't be all surprises today. I'll dress up like the businesswoman I am. Maybe then he'll take me seriously."

### 

Thank goodness Jeff had brought more of my clothes. I selected a lightweight navy dress with a grey linen blazer. Low heeled navy sandals and the usual spritz of cologne, some gel on my unruly curls, and a dab of a sheer lipstick ensured I left for my appointment suitably dressed for a business meeting with Lockhart. I hadn't changed my mind about him but better he be friend than an enemy because I needed information. I could play it two ways, but I'd have to see how he reacted to my business self before deciding how to handle him.

The old guy would never know what hit him.

I slipped my notebook into my small portfolio, along with a copy of the spreadsheet and all the numbers. Proof of my organizational skills and that I understood what we were about to discuss.

I planned to be in control of the financial part of the proceedings. I'd been dismayed to see the price Uncle Dalton received for the sawmill property. In my view, he'd been shortchanged. I know real estate and looked up the price of properties fifteen, twenty years ago in the area. In my opinion, the developer stole it from them. I'd see how Lockhart answered these questions before I made any comments.

When I'd prepared the spreadsheets, I realized the monthly income from the residents barely covered the expenses of running Leven Lodge so I needed his input. Where did he think any money could be saved? I'd hastily scribbled some last-minute notes.

*Can the alpacas be more profitable with breeding and adding to the herd? Do I raise the rents? Do we sell any produce? Perhaps a stall at the market on Saturdays.*

My mind raced a mile a minute. Although I had all these questions written down, I needed to have them quite clear in my mind for this meeting. I also needed answers about Harrison. I knew I'd have to carefully word my questions here in case they were friends or business acquaintances. I determined to put Lockhart at east and assure him all was in good hands.

It was a short drive to his office, and I managed to park in the same spot as I had last time. The warmth of the day meant the outdoor cafes and pubs were busy. Moms with strollers and shoppers laden with bags made for tricky maneuvering on the pavement. Early summer cottagers were getting in their supplies at the corner supermarket. I took a deep breath and checked my reflection in a shop window.

Good to go. If I do say so myself.

I thought I looked professional and competent. Right on time. I let the receptionist know I was there to see her boss. I waited, and I waited. Ten minutes passed. I began to wonder if this might be an intimidation tactic.

"Could you please inform Mr. Lockhart again I'm here, waiting. I do have another appointment today." Maybe a little white lie, but really.

Stay cool Alysha. Don't get off on the wrong foot.

On the verge of asking her again how long I'd have to wait the door flew open, and Dr. Harrison swept past me. His face was like thunder. He didn't see me as he banged the door on his way out. Thank goodness, because I'd had enough of him yesterday when he tried to visit the McTaggarts. Jan and I had stood our ground and sent him packing. Ty's displeasure at our stance may have ticked him off at the time, but he'd get over it.

I heard a *hmm, hmm* followed by throat clearing. My summons. "Ms. Grant, please come in."

I extended my hand in as professional a manner as I could muster. "Good afternoon, Mr. Lockhart."

"I'm sorry I kept you waiting but I had to attend to an upset client. Please take a seat."

"Yes, Dr. Harrison did seem to be angry about something."

Lockhart raised a bushy eyebrow. "I believe you

had a run-in with him yesterday?"

I needed to be diplomatic until I knew what he thought of Harrison. "Not as nice as our first meeting. Yesterday he wasn't at all pleased when I wouldn't let him visit the McTaggarts. You are aware they'd just come home from the hospital?"

"Yes, Reid has informed me." He hesitated. "I don't think this will breach client confidentiality, but he feels you've overstepped your authority. Which is why he came to see me, upset and seeking any kind of legal recourse, and sympathy."

"And did he find any?"

In answer, I received a noncommittal *hmmm*. For a lawyer, his vocabulary didn't impress me.

Lockhart sat back in his chair and tried to look relaxed. To my eyes, he was anything but. Would his judgmental assessment of me never end? Hell would freeze over before I'd get his approval apparently.

He didn't waste any time. "Have you come to any decisions about Leven Lodge? You must have found it quite overwhelming. The number of people and personalities and what with the McTaggarts taken off to the hospital. I wouldn't blame you if you decide to sell."

While he talked and assumed, I took out my notebook and set it on his desk. An action met with a disapproving look.

"On the contrary Mr. Lockhart. We, that is my partner, Jeff Iverson, and I have decided to stay. He would have come today but he's busy with the shearers and the alpacas. He's had to take over from

Phillip McGee now, as he is ill and in hospital."

Lockhart's eyes widened in shock. "Mr. McGee's in the hospital? When - what happened?"

"I thought maybe Dr. Harrison would have told you because Phillip is also his patient." I ventured to press on for another reaction. "Did he also tell you the doctors suspected a suicide attempt with the McTaggarts?"

He dropped the pen he'd been fiddling with. Had I rattled him?

"Harrison did tell me he was providing grief counselling to them. And now you say something's happened to Mr. McGee? Are you implying there's a connection?"

He seemed legitimately surprised at the news, so I offered a little more. "I understand from Jan Young, Phillip has been under a legitimate doctor's care for some time. But he took a turn for the worse, perhaps not unexpectedly. And yes, I do wonder about a connection. Both Phillip and the McTaggarts are known to have supplies of Harrison's pills on hand."

He picked up the pen again and made notes as he talked. "Surely, just a coincidence. You don't know exactly whether Phillip and the McTaggarts were taking the same type of supplements from Harrison?"

"Correct. I didn't get much of a chance to know him. The little I saw of his behaviour bordered on erratic, but on Friday night he just flipped and lapsed into a catatonic state. Jan called his doctor and he admitted him to the hospital. I'm not sure of the prognosis yet. He may never return. Depending on toxicology reports they may be able to treat him."

I sat in silence and waited. Lockhart was visibly upset. He mumbled to himself, and I strained to hear him. "Silly fool. I warned him many times."

Which fool—Philip or Harrison? I leaned forward. "I hope you don't take any of Dr. Harrison's medicine, Mr. Lockhart? From where I sit, his track record is disturbing. Everyone taking his pills gets sick." I'd gone out on a limb but needed to take the chance he wouldn't tell Harrison I had concerns.

I was rewarded with a slight smile. "No, I don't. I don't believe in alternative medicines. You never know what you're ingesting. I told Reid as much only last week when he tried to ply me with one of his tonics. Now the police are checking into his background. One more thing he was so angry about this morning. Bradley McTaggart worked for him you know. Hope the poor fellow didn't have some of his supplements either."

He paused as if he realized he may have spoken out of turn. "Can I count on your discretion to not divulge anything to Harrison about what I've told you today."

"I should probably ask you the same thing, now I've raised some questions about the doctor as well."

The stern look made a comeback. "Harrison may be a client, Ms. Grant, but I believe he is not a person to befriend in other than business matters."

I needed to backtrack and have him on my side. "Of course not. I just needed to know if you were friends and shared confidences. You know, client -

lawyer privileges."

"Reid Harrison, as far as I can tell, is not an accredited MD."

"And that brings me to my next question. Everyone calls him Doctor and I'm not adverse to alternative medicine, but those products need to be regulated before I would ever take any. How did he ever get a license?"

"Good point Ms. Grant. I'll have my assistant research the industry. Let's hope all is above board."

Better, much better. I smiled. "Nice to know we're on the same page now. Please let me know if you find something?"

"Of course. Now then, I'm happy you've made the decision to stay at Leven Lodge. I've been associated with it from the start. It needs a Grant to steer the ship. Let's have a look at the numbers, shall we?" This smile had warmth.

I relaxed and felt we could now get down to business. That's two old men I've tamed this week. Jock first and now Bryce. Perhaps I've found my forte.

We poured over the finances. Incoming money and outgoing expenditure. He liked my ideas concerning a market garden and a future alpaca herd increase to make us solvent. He suggested an accountant would be the best person to answer those questions.

Now we were getting somewhere. He was being helpful, perhaps I'd misjudged him. He handed me a card with the name of an accountant he highly recommended. My next business move.

He suggested other sources of income for the

home. It had been set in stone how much the current guests were paying. Both my uncle and grandmother were kind and soft-hearted people. But, if anyone new took up residence then we could ask for more. Encouraging.

I signed the papers, and we shook hands again on working together. He promised to advise me on any information regarding Harrison as it became available.

"I'm impressed with the way you have handled your inheritance, Ms. Grant. Yes, you're definitely a Grant. They're like a dog with a bone and never give up."

My opinion of the fussy old coot had done a one hundred eighty degree turn and I was sure we'd do business agreeably. "Thank you."

"Good day, Ms. Grant."

"Why don't you call me Alysha, Mr. Lockhart."

We weren't at hugging status, but I knew I'd gained ground when he said, "And my name's Bryce."

# CHAPTER EIGHTEEN

*Dianne*

I'd wandered into the kitchen in search of coffee and found Jan and Alysha deep in conversation. I apologized for interrupting.

Alysha welcomed me into the discussion. "I'm glad you're here. I'm starting to tell Jan about my visit with Bryce Lockhart."

"Dianne, perfect timing," said Jan. "I'd advised Alysha that Lockhart had never been one of my favourite people, but after what she's told me, he's moved up a notch in my estimation."

I didn't know the lawyer, but trusted Jan's assessment. Alysha provided a recap, bringing Jan and I both up to speed. "I may have been too quick to judge when we first met last week. He assured me he'd investigate and forward any information my way. I see no reason to distrust him."

Alysha and Jan bounced back and forth about Bryce Lockhart. When Cassie entered the kitchen, Alysha suggested we go for a walk.

Jan did away with her apron. "Laundry's doing its thing, I'm ready for a break."

Alysha led us to a spot she said she'd discovered. I had to agree, the view was splendid. We availed ourselves of an old bench and chairs, recently retrieved from the barn.

We sat in the shade of an aged chestnut tree, and Alysha had brought a notebook with her. The air felt muggy when we left the house, but up here I swore it was cooler.

Jan contemplated the scenery, her voice taking on a nostalgic and stirring tone. "It's a long time since I've been here. If you lean over the wall you can see the old sawmill's water wheel."

Alysha and I glanced at one another. I'd bet there's a story there, maybe her placid manner concealed a passionate nature. The three of us sat quietly enjoying the peace and quiet.

Another beautiful June day and all was right with the world—at least for the moment.

Jan broke the silence, turning to me. "Where's your right hand man today? He usually shadows you everywhere."

I shrugged. "He's not happy with me at the moment. I didn't take his side after the run in with Harrison so he's sulking. He left early today to drive to Toronto. Business, he said."

Alysha nodded. "Just as well. It's better we discuss this on our own. I wonder if Ty would change his mind about Harrison if he might not be a legitimate doctor. Bryce will look into the industry as well, but we might be able to check into Harrison himself and then compare against what Bryce uncovers."

Jan's protective side flared. "If I learn he's not legit and has been pulling the wool over our eyes, I'll take care of him myself! Seniors like the McTaggarts wouldn't think to question his credentials. And poor Philip. Making house calls was just the icing on the cake to con them."

Jan had her dander up, not a surprise. The idea he might not be legit had thrown me as well and added to my general dislike of him.

"It does put him in a different light, doesn't it?" said Alysha. "We can't blacklist the naturopathic community as a whole just because of one rotten apple. I'm sure the industry is regulated. I don't know enough about natural medicines, so no idea if it's normal practice for them to create their own supplements."

Jan's frown deepened, and I questioned her. "What else, Jan?"

She hesitated. "You know that I've some knowledge of the medicinal qualities of plants and herbs. You may think it cliché, but it is my heritage."

I nodded and waited. She wasn't finished. Her hands had balled into fists and her voice was sharp. "For the record, I have nothing against their use, or of anyone who understands how to properly use them. It's just Harrison I have issues with—him and his claims to eternal youth."

The colour had risen in her cheeks and her eyes flashed. Unusual for her to show that kind of emotion, and I reached out a hand to touch her knee.

Alysha sat for a few minutes not saying anything. I wondered if Jan's outburst had disturbed her, or how she might react. Her open notebook lay untouched on her knee. She tapped her pen against her lower lip and then put the pen down. "I'm sorry, Jan, if this is upsetting to you. Over the short time I've been here, I can tell you care a great deal about everyone here. I totally get you're pissed off about Harrison. All the more reason we need to work together, right?"

I looked over at Jan. She rubbed her forehead. "No, I should be the one to apologize. When anger fills the mind, common sense leaves." She smiled at us, and the moment passed. I picked up where Alysha left off.

"Can we find out if there've been complaints?" I asked. "He has a big following in town, but we can't be the only people who mistrust him. And maybe there's a history of what he did before he arrived here."

Alysha picked up the thread. "Right, ladies, we need a plan. I'll do some research. Checking for complaints is a good idea. Dianne, without question, you need to speak with Ty about Harrison."

I winced because I dreaded the task and kept procrastinating. "I know, I need the right opportunity."

Jan reached over and patted my arm. "You are his best friend, just keep his welfare as your motivation. Surely he will understand you're only concerned about him."

"If you say so, but I have my doubts."

Jan added a suggestion. "What if I try and question the McTaggarts, to see if I can gather anything useful?"

"Good idea, Jan." Alysha paused, and tapped her pen against the book. "You know, it might be wise to keep Ty in the dark a little longer until we know for sure he's on our side."

Again, I was caught in the middle, although a little relieved at the reprieve. "I can't say I'm comfortable keeping things from him. It feels like a betrayal. If he asks me directly, I can't lie to him."

"It's only a suggestion, Dianne," Alysha said. "I guess we'll have to let you handle him the way you think best."

Jan glanced at her watch. "Sorry, but I need to get on with some chores. This place doesn't keep itself clean." She stood and smoothed her shirt. "I think Cassie's going to experiment with dinner this evening, so just a head's up."

I laughed. "Ah, she means well, Jan. And sometimes the meals aren't bad. But I won't throw away my antacids just yet."

Alysha piped up. "Jeff loves to barbecue. I'll see if he could make a few suggestions to her and perhaps provide one or two of the main meals during the week. Would she be offended?"

Jan reassured Alysha. "If I say it's a good idea, she'll go along with it. Might be nice to have a change. I'm comfortable with doing up hamburgers and steaks, but that's about it. Tell Jeff it's fine with me."

Jan headed back to the house and a comfortable silence fell between Alysha and me. My eyes grew heavy with the warmth of the morning. Just as I was about to give in, a voice brought me back.

"Anyone here want to help tidy up the alpacas' pen with me?" Jeff may have asked the question to both of us, but he only had eyes for Alysha, and I didn't want to be a third wheel. Besides, I really wasn't interested.

"You know, if I didn't have to go and sort my shoes, I'd be right there with you, Jeff. I think I'll let you and Alysha take care of things. If you can manage without me."

He chuckled. I could see Alysha's attraction for him. Easy going, good sense of humour and not hard on the eyes. Lucky girl. I stood to leave. "See you two later and stay out of trouble. I hear those alpacas just cannot keep a secret."

Lighthearted, I walked away from the lovebirds and headed back to the house. I'd need another cup of coffee to prepare for the serious thinking I had in store concerning Ty.

He'd left quite early, not stopping for breakfast. I knew he'd kept in contact with several former clients in Toronto and often drove in to see them. To me it seemed as if they said *jump* he would. Maybe he'd retired too soon and still missed the big city. Even though we were the best of friends, there remained a lot about him I still didn't know. But I guess he'd say the same about me.

If I didn't care as much about him, I would care less about his relationship with Harrison. But evidence seemed to suggest anyone being seen by him didn't always have a healthy outcome. Maybe I'd wait till Alysha had gathered information about him from Bryce Lockhart and whatever she could find online. I thought the more ammunition I had the better I'd be able to convince him to be careful. Then again, if there's one thing I am good at, it's procrastinating.

"Dianne?"

Oh crap. Minnie. She beelined it down the hallway straight toward me. Instinctively I pulled my mug of coffee closer. "Hi. Did you need something?"

She drew herself right up to my face and I found myself holding my breath. Her bulging bag of yarn hung on her arm. If wool had weight, she'd have muscles in those spindly arms.

"Dr. Harrison," she whispered.

"What about him?"

"I know things."

"What kind of things, Minnie? What are you talking about?" I needed an excuse to get away from her.

She looked behind her. "I can't talk about it here. But I know young Ms. Grant has concerns about him, along with you and Jan."

Right, she'd been eavesdropping again. A collar with a bell might make a good Christmas present. I forced myself to pay attention to her.

Her eyes narrowed. "And I know things about Ty as well."

Hold on, now that got my attention. I made myself react with a calmness I didn't really feel. "Do you want me to get Jan or Alysha?"

"No, not yet. I wanted to talk to you first. But not here in the hallway."

For the briefest of moments, I actually thought she was going to invite me into her room. Silly me. She inclined her head toward the TV room. "No one's in there right now. Come."

Who could resist such a warm invite?

We moved into what I liked to call the media room and seated ourselves. I looked longingly towards the veranda and hoped this would be quick.

"Ty likes Dr. Harrison, you know."

Not a news flash. "Yes, that's a given. What else?"

"The last two times he came here, I saw Ty give him small packages. Heard him say it was from the garden. Harrison all smiles when he tucked them into his doctor bag, or whatever he wants to call that purse thing he carries. How foolish for a man."

Curious, I had to admit I wanted to know more. "Did Harrison say anything?"

"Something like he was glad to have Ty as his supplier. Made me think of a police show."

Ty did spend a lot of time puttering in the gardens. Was he growing something Harrison used in his supplements? Jan was knowledgeable when it came to plants and herbs. I made a mental note to ask her.

Minnie sat with a satisfied look on her face. Was that it?

"Is there more? Did Harrison give Ty anything in return?" I worried Minnie might reveal something about Ty I wasn't ready to learn, but she only shook her head.

"No, but I'm watching them. That Harrison is a no-good con man. Anyone who spends time with him might be cut from the same cloth."

Enough was enough. "Hold on Minnie. You're

talking about my friend. Unless you've something concrete, I'd be careful what you say."

She smugly leaned back against the chair and began to show a keen interest in the contents of her knitting bag. Guess there'd be no more conversation. No kidding, she was likely exhausted. I'd rarely seen her engage in more than a sentence or two with anyone. My allegiance to Ty struggled with the obligation to share this news—even if insignificant—with Jan and Alysha.

The information well had run dry, so I took my coffee and headed to the veranda, hoping I'd have some quiet time to mull things over.

My monkey brain grew tired with all the thoughts swirling around in there and I finally gave in and dozed for a while. I woke feeling hungry and realized it was past noon so went in search of something quick to eat. As had everyone else, so no chance to get Alysha or Jan aside and tell them what I'd heard from Minnie.

Alysha and Jeff planned to head into town, another opportunity lost. Jan was busy cleaning and the others had their own interests to occupy them for the rest of the day.

I was antsy. Which provided all the excuse I needed to head into town and drop into the Legion for a while. It would get my mind off things and fill in some time before Ty returned. I scouted out a potential companion.

"Rose! I'm heading into town and thought I'd pop into the Legion for a bit. Interested in coming along? We might find a euchre game, or bingo?"

Without skipping a beat, she responded. "Let me grab my purse."

As we pulled out of the driveway, Ty's car peeled off the main road and roared past us. He didn't even glance in our direction but seemed hell-bent on reaching the house.

# CHAPTER NINETEEN

*Alysha*

I settled at my laptop to research Harrison. Sitting at the small balcony table in the shade was ideal for my work. I brought my to-do list up to date although I hadn't learned much more from Jan or Dianne. Plus, I needed some reminders. I needed to meet with Frank and draw up plans to enlarge the vegetable garden. Jan would need to be consulted; the plants are her territory. Maybe it would be a good chance to ask her about the rose garden. And I needed to make an appointment with the accountant.

I'd helped Jeff in the barn, and we'd enjoyed making plans. Then we discussed a concern of mine. Had I neglected the other guests by focusing so much on the McTaggarts and Phillip? Rose and Lily were a pair; needed to know them a little better. And of course, Minnie. I had to agree with Dianne about her pungent personality, but at least I had her on my radar, and so I returned to my research.

So far, I'd not found much. I confirmed through the registry he was a bona fide accredited naturopath, entitled to be called Doctor. He could put ND after his name on business cards if nothing else.

Had he practiced somewhere else? If so, there might be more to learn about him. I'd have to wait until I heard from Lockhart.

Satisfied with my notes, I changed into my running gear and waited for Jeff to finish his chores. We'd decided to run the short distance into town and reward ourselves at the pub. Maybe I could persuade him to stay there for supper. I wasn't sure I wanted to taste any of Cassie's concoctions.

I heard the metallic click of the elevator door opening, and then Jeff bounded into our suite, full of energy.

We snuggled for a bit until my nose twitched. Was that alpaca I smelled or just a hard day's work? "Off to the showers with you if you even *think* we can have a date running this afternoon."

"But, then I'll just need to shower again?" My *are you serious?* look hit home. He saluted me and laughed. "Give me ten minutes and we're off."

True to his word we soon sprinted from the side door. I waved to the McTaggarts, seated on their balcony overhead, and was pleased to have my wave returned. Except for the occasional appearance, they'd been keeping to themselves.

With a slight change of plans we decided to head in the direction of the sawmill first, located on the outskirts of town. We ran at an even pace, finding a path which meandered by the river. Arriving near the old mill, we took a breather. Then turned and headed back to town.

We stopped briefly to drink from our water bottles. A couple of friendly dogs demanded our attention, and then we were off again, but cooled the run down to a stroll in order to enjoy the town's busy atmosphere. Not a market day but still busy. Cars packed the library parking lot, and we passed the school yard during recess where exuberant children played. No wonder they were excited. Summer vacation was just around the corner.

We found a shaded bench and rested a while. I glanced at Jeff, he seemed deep in thought. "Something on your mind, sweetheart?"

He blinked a couple of times. "No, I mean yes. It's not important but I'll tell you anyway."

"Tell me what?" He had a tendency to drag things out, so I waited.

"It's probably nothing, babe, but you and I both are beginning to realize Leven Lodge is full of personalities."

"And? Don't keep me in suspense!"

"Well, earlier today as I came from the barn to the side of the house, I saw Dianne, with Rose, in her car heading down the driveway. At the same time Ty came screeching around the bend and parked his car. He acted like he didn't see anyone. Didn't wave to Dianne or Rose and slammed his car door. He looked furious, and didn't acknowledge Jan, who was watering the flower baskets. He just stormed into the house."

"According to Dianne he can be a real prima donna. If there's anything to it, I'm sure we'll hear all about it later." I wasn't much in the mood to discuss the residents. "For now, can we forget about Leven Lodge? I'm sure there are people under thirty at the pub we can chat with and catch some music."

"Sure, but I have no one to check on the alpacas, so just for a while?"

I smiled at his new-found devotion. We found a handful of locals nearer our age to share in a game of darts and whiled away a couple of hours before heading back. We'd have to assign someone to give Jeff a break now and then, especially if we added more animals.

He managed to talk non-stop all the way home about—guess what—the alpacas. There wasn't much else on his mind. Which worked for me as I didn't want to discuss Harrison or our theories about him. We'd have to be pretty sure of our facts before taking them to the authorities. If I was barking up the wrong tree I'd need to wait until I had something definite.

These were my thoughts on the way home. But Jeff's running commentary of the alpacas reminded me about their shearing. I reminded myself to check on this potential income later.

At the house, I popped my head into the kitchen to tell Cassie we wouldn't be joining them for dinner because we'd made other plans. She asked what they were but I deflected her questions with a vague shrug.

Then I managed to have a word with Jan before heading up the stairs. "Jeff and I are ordering pizza tonight. Wanna join us? We've found something we want your opinion on."

"I'll pass on the pizza, thanks, but I'm curious about what you've found. I could come up at seven, when things have settled for the night." She hesitated,

"Will it take long though? There's a movie I'm dying to see at eight."

I smiled at her, "I promise you'll be back in time for your movie."

"See you later then," she said, starting to move away.

"Jan, before you go. Do you know of any young person looking for a part time job? Jeff needs some help in the barn. After school, that sort of thing. Maybe the odd day on the weekend."

"Okay I'll give it some thought and get back to you."

### 

Wiping a streak of tomato sauce from his chin, Jeff said, "Great pizza babe, we'll order from there again."

"Yes, it was delicious, and I'm stuffed. Help me clean up before Jan gets here. I don't want her to think I'm a messy housekeeper even if it's true."

I fussed around and cleared the table while Jeff left with the pizza box and other garbage.

As I waited for Jan to arrive, I set out coffee mugs and brewed a fresh pot. Jan didn't seem like the beer type. I hoped she'd be able to shed light on why Ty had been in such a snit today. Jeff would tell me not to stick my nose in, but shouldn't I know what's going on with my guests? I was determined, though, to avoid discussing Harrison with Jan, I wanted to focus on her and Uncle Dalton.

I decided the balcony might not be the best

place to hand over my uncle's wooden box. It had taken on mythical powers with me, and I was eager to know what it represented in their lives. The Grants' history had held no interest for me growing up but now I hungered to learn every detail.

When Jan entered the apartment, with Jeff following right behind, she took my breath away. She was of average height but at the moment she appeared much taller and so handsome. Her black hair, normally swept off her face, cascaded down her back. She wore a multi coloured flowing skirt and a sleeveless fine suede leather top. Beautiful native beaded earrings completed the outfit.

Jeff poked me in the arm. "Alysha, close your mouth."

"Sorry. Jan, you look wonderful. Please, come and sit down."

She bestowed us an unassuming smile and sat opposite me. Jeff served the coffee. "I don't always look like a dowdy housekeeper. When I go home on weekends to be with my family it's like shedding a skin. I must show you the dresses I wear for the pow wow. I'm a dancer, you know."

"I'd love to see them, and those earrings are lovely. Not sure I could wear something as long as those. Being vertically challenged has its limitations."

She brushed away the compliment as if uncomfortable with the attention. "Here, I brought you both a welcome present."

She handed me a parcel wrapped with pale green paper and darker green ribbon. "How kind.

Thank you."

I took my time untying the ribbon and releasing the gift from the paper. I couldn't believe what I saw. It was a smaller replica of the box we were going to give her.

Her smile warmed my heart. "I had one of the elders carve both your initials on the top. See, you're now together for eternity. On the reserve where my family lives, he creates these boxes for a living. He uses Black Oak from the savannah nearby. I hope you like it and know how happy I am to have you both here."

I couldn't speak so Jeff jumped in. "It appears Alysha is at a loss for words and trust me that rarely happens. So let me thank you on behalf of us both, your gift means a lot."

I sat nodding my head like one of those irritating dogs they have in the back of cars, not trusting myself to speak.

Jeff continued. "We both love it here. You being at the helm, so to speak, influenced our decision to stay." He glanced at me, and I let him continue. "And now, we'd like to give you something in return. If Alysha will allow me the honours?"

Jan and I exchanged smiles while Jeff rummaged in the closet.

Then she, with a gasp of surprise, became the speechless one. Jeff lay the carved box on the table next to the one she'd given us. Apparently crafted by the same artist.

"Oh, my. You found it! I searched everywhere after Dalton died, but obviously missed it. Wherever did you find it?" She began to dab at her eyes.

I finally found my voice and said quietly, "The boxes you'd set aside of Uncle Dalton's were a treasure trove of history, and it was at the bottom of one of them, under some albums. We feel you should have it. The letters are yours and the pretty woman is either you or your sister."

"Oh, that's definitely me in those pictures." She turned her bright eyes toward me. "I'm guessing you want an explanation?"

"Only if you want to. Of course, my natural curiosity is begging to hear the story now I've found a new interest in my family history."

Her fingers rested lightly atop the treasured container. "I think I need a moment to catch my breath, then I'll tell you of my love for your uncle. I'm sure you've guessed already we meant a great deal to each other."

Slowly, and reverently, she opened the memento filled box and lifted out a packet of letters. We stayed silent as she pored over pictures and opened a few of the letters written many years ago.

When we'd found the pictures and personal letters earlier, obviously written by Jan, we put them back trying to keep the contents undisturbed. But now, I watched in surprise as she extracted a small jewelry box. She held it, unopened, in her hand, tracing the jeweler's name, then laid it gently on the table. Her gaze lingered on it for a moment.

Then she settled herself on the sofa and flipped through a handful of pictures until she came to a specific one. She handed it to me, and Jeff leaned over to have a look. "Taken the year we met. I was only twenty-five and Dalton fifty-seven. He'd come to the pow wow with a group from the sawmill. We literally bumped into each other after I'd finished dancing. One of the young men who worked at the mill introduced us. I was shy and awkward. I hadn't encountered many boys, or men, outside of the reserve but when I met this handsome older man, I soon found my voice."

She closed her eyes for a moment. "The attraction was immediate, and the others eventually left us alone to talk—well into the evening. I never did show up for the dances."

A tender smile softened her features. I could only assume memories were flooding back. Jan grew quiet and I felt the need to say something. "And I would have only been a child. Sorry, I don't mean to interrupt you."

"I don't mind. I'll jump ahead a few years now, to when most of the letters were sent. At the time, Dalton often travelled on business for the mill. He'd inherited full ownership when your grandfather died." She paused and held my eye. "This is where the rift started, did you know?"

My stomach lurched. My parents never spoke of the reason we left Grant's Crossing when I was thirteen. Did I want to know? I met her gaze and took the leap. "I never knew the details. Please."

"Well, little one, I will tell you what I know. Dalton and his brother Wilf—your grandfather—held joint title to the land we are now on. By the time your father, Benjamin, was born, Dalton and Wilf also held joint ownership of the sawmill. When Wilf died, ownership of both transferred to Dalton's name alone. Your father always believed he would inherit the sawmill and the property. Or at the very least he would share equally with Dalton. However, your grandfather had his reasons—unknown to Dalton—for excluding Benjamin from any ownership. And as long as your grandmother lived, the farmhouse belonged to her."

Snippets of conversation came to mind that I'd overheard as a child, pieces falling into place. "Go on."

She nodded. "Over time, tension between your father, Dalton and Estelle grew. I didn't know your father well, but I know it grieved Estelle, and Dalton. Anyway, then Dalton moved into the farmhouse, which further annoyed your father. He was already displeased that the McTaggarts had come on board. Couldn't, or didn't want to, understand your grandmother needed the companionship and financial help. But then Dalton decided to sell the mill and it was the final straw. Your parents took you and left Grant's Crossing. Estelle never saw them again."

My heart ached for the lives forever changed and lost chances for reconciliation. My parents had been killed in the car crash years later. No doubt the tragedy hastened Gran's own death. I couldn't stop the tears, sobs broke through.

Jan came over, tissue in hand. She stroked the side of my face. "Hush now, little one. The past can't be changed, but you are here now, and healing can take place—for you."

Jeff had come alongside me as well. I took comfort in their presence even as more tears flowed. They provided time to collect myself, and few minutes later I trusted myself to speak. "Jan. Thank you. So much makes sense now." I made a final dab at my eyes and got us back on track.

"Can we hear more about your letters now?"

Jan squeezed my shoulder and settled back on the sofa. "His letters brought me joy. Imagine back in the day of no instant email. How I waited for them! I worked in a housekeeping capacity for a couple of families near the reserve. I was of an age where I had a duty to help my parents financially. I still do, but that's not the story."

I thought she might shed tears as she closed her eyes in remembrance, but I had no words to offer. We waited, and when she opened them, they were bright, but her face was peaceful and she continued.

"Yes. We had a passionate affair which lasted until his death. The community, out of respect for Dalton, never talked about it, at least to our faces. Back then an affair of our nature—an older non-native and an Aboriginal girl—was not condoned. Certainly not in my family. Once I'd started supporting my parents who were ill, I decided early on I wouldn't have children."

I had empathy but couldn't express it. Neither Jeff nor I made any comment while she finished her coffee. Then she continued but looked so wistful I could have cried. But there'd been enough tears for one day.

"Around 1990, he began thinking about selling the mill. He wanted to settle down and proposed. I, to my everlasting regret, turned him down. And that's when he moved into the farmhouse to help your grandmother. The McTaggarts had come in, as paying lodgers, a year before. Your grandmother and Dalton then decided they would have more paying guests. When Dalton sold the mill a few years later, the renovations began."

She looked at us. "You must be wondering about the age difference."

Jeff opened his mouth to speak, but I nudged him into silence.

"Our age was never a problem, and even as Dalton grew older he stayed in shape, kept young at heart, and was so handsome. I hated being apart from him and missed him so much. Then he suggested a way we could see each other daily—if I became the housekeeper at the farm. It was a wrench to leave my parents, but I wanted to be near the man I loved. I still visit them every other weekend but now my home is here."

"What about the guests? Did they know about you and Dalton?" My romantic side drank in her story.

Jan nodded. "Estelle knew of course and stayed incredibly kind and supportive to us and the situation. She regularly urged us to marry but I'd made up my mind. When I had a weekend off Dalton was usually absent as well. We found the time to be together as often as we could.

Jock and Bea accepted the situation. Jock and Dalton became great friends. Which is why his death has been so hard on him." She leaned back against the cushions. Her face looked tired, but peaceful. She'd relived a lifetime of memories in a short time.

I had one more question. "And Minnie? She's been here a long time. From what I've seen of her so far, I can't see her being understanding."

"Ah, Minnie. She always suspected and, in the beginning made remarks but Dalton could always deflect her questions or hurtful innuendos. We never discussed it with any of the other residents although I suppose they had their suspicions. We felt it wasn't their business."

I was overcome with emotion. "Oh, Jan, such a beautiful, but bittersweet, story. I wish you two could have married. You would have been my aunt and this house would have been yours."

She bit her lower lip. "I'm still not over his death. It was so sudden. To have him go so quickly. Not even a goodbye." She took a deep breath before saying more. "And as to the house belonging to me. *Pfft*. It's with the rightful owner now, a Grant. You and Jeff will be happy here." Her face brightened. "Listen, I tell you what. You've no relatives now, so when you two decide to get married your Auntie Jan will walk you down the aisle. If you want." Her heartfelt smile soothed my bruised heart.

She reached for the jewelry box. Nestled in white satin, lay a gold wedding band set low with an exquisite emerald and two diamonds. Stunning. Once again I was speechless.

Jan explained. "This ring originally belonged to your great-great grandmother. The first Grant who came from Scotland gave it to his bride, which was then passed on to future Grant women. Eventually to Estelle. When your father and mother married, your mother refused the ring preferring something more modern. Because your mother turned it down, Wilf and Estelle gave it to Dalton, for a *someday*."

I tried to remember what my mother had worn. I'd not paid much attention. "Yes, after my parents were killed I had her jewelry box. I've never looked inside, it's still too painful."

Jeff reached his arm round me, and said. "Perhaps it's time to open it. It can't be good to hang on to bad memories."

"Jeff's right. The only way I've been able to go on after Dalton died is to keep the good memories and let go of the bad. Having this box and all the things he kept will help me treasure the good times."

Sighing, I smiled at them both. "This has been some week. Emotionally I feel drained, but not in a bad way."

Jan reached over and patted my knee. "There's more. Let me tell you the rest of the story. After your mother refused the ring, your grandmother kept it for you some day. But when she knew Dalton was hell bent on marrying me, she decided he should have it. The proviso would be to pass it on to you when you married. It's all written down somewhere amongst those papers. So, as we never married, it legally belongs to you. And is yours for when you marry."

"Nothing like pressure put on a guy," laughed Jeff.

Jan took the ring from its nesting place and handed it to me. The ring had been fitted for Estelle, yet it slipped on my finger easily. I removed my many silver rings and admired the gems.

Jan prompted me. "If you look on the inside there's an inscription."

I took the ring off and tilted it to read. Of course, the Grant motto *Stand Fast*. Handing it back to Jan, I said, "It's beautiful. Please, Jan, you keep it for now. If we decide to tie the knot, we can talk about it again."

She returned the ring to the box and gathered up the pictures and letters and placed them in Dalton's box of treasures. The visit was done—almost. I had one more question for Jan. She knew so much about Leven Lodge; she'd have to know.

"Jan, one more thing. Why did Gran's rose garden fall into neglect?"

A pensive look passed over her face, and she took hold of my hands. "Little one, all I can tell you is that Estelle wished for the garden to return to its natural state after she passed. And while we have honoured that, I believe she'd be happy for you to bring the garden back to life."

How could I say no. I merely nodded in agreement, and looked to Jeff.

"Let me carry that back downstairs for you," said Jeff.

After hugs, I said goodnight to her, and she followed Jeff out the door. I wandered onto our balcony, my new place of refuge. I enjoyed its peaceful solitude while contemplating all I'd heard tonight. I picked up my journal and scribbled my thoughts.

> *Jan reveals all— finally understand what happened with family. But beautiful ring found, exciting and an emerald ring to boot. (So romantic) I wonder if Jeff felt the same.*
>
> *I need to meet with Dianne and Jan before Thursday's appointment with accountant. And I'm dying to hear all about Ty and any updates on Harrison. Oh, Jan has this weekend off. Wonder if I'm expected to clean the bathrooms.*

I came back inside to open the windows for the night. The apartment tended to hold the heat of the day. As I opened the last one, I saw headlights approaching the front of the lodge. I wondered who on earth had come to call at this time of night and decided to head downstairs to find out.

# CHAPTER TWENTY

*Dianne*

Rose and I passed a couple of hours at the local Legion. We'd coerced a pair of proud veterans into a game of euchre. Not my favourite, but it ensured a lively conversation, and both Rose and I did our flirty best to bring a smile to the gents' faces.

But all the while in the back of my mind I kept replaying Ty's face when he'd flashed by us returning to the lodge. He'd not been himself lately, and I wondered what Harrison had to do with it. Ty never really talked about it, but I think he had a hard time accepting the fact Harrison wasn't interested in him that way.

In addition, the extra pressure I started to feel from Jan and Alysha to talk to him about Harrison weighed on my mind. I still didn't have a clue how I would broach the subject. Somehow I knew I'd have to be motivated by my concern for him. And I was concerned. Ty's usually even keeled, but lately something had really been setting him on edge. I determined the first time an opportunity presented itself, I'd take it. I hoped.

We left the Legion and decided to pick up a coffee and enjoy a stroll down the main street. A little window shopping wouldn't hurt either. Stalling, because I wasn't in a hurry to return home. Fortunately, Rose was happy to follow my lead.

"Oh look," she said as we neared Wilson's Dress Shop, "What a beautiful dress. Mind you, I'd have used a tighter stitch on the hem. And the jacket's not a good fit for that style."

She sipped at her coffee and ogled all the window displays. I made the effort to tune out her opinions on fashion that didn't measure up to her standards. I let her prattle on and only half-listened.

Eventually I couldn't put it off any longer. "Hey Rose, look at the time. Guess we should head back and see what culinary creation Cassie has in store for us."

She laughed. "Sometimes it's really hard to be polite, isn't it? And please slap me if I ever get to be like Minnie. At least we have some barbecues to look forward to. That'll make a nice change."

"Think Alysha and Jeff will be able to manage running the lodge, and dealing with the likes of Minnie? "I asked as we drove back.

"At first I didn't think so. She's such a young thing isn't she? Could use some fashion advice too. Still, she seems to have hit it off with Jan. Long as she backs them up, I'm sure Alysha and Jeff will do just fine."

"You're right. And I'm relieved to know we still have a home. Other than Minnie, I don't really have anything to complain about."

"Oh yuck. I hope she's not knitting us all scarves for Christmas or something. I've no desire to touch anything that comes out of that knitting bag."

"Agreed, but let's change the subject, it's almost dinner time," I said, and we had a chuckle.

I pulled into my parking spot and saw Ty's car still there. I half formulated a plan to try and talk to him before dinner. And then I berated myself for being such a chicken over this Harrison thing.

Rose undid her seatbelt and opened the door. "Thanks for the invite, Dianne. I enjoyed myself and it's nice to have a break from Lily at times. She's so dependent on me you know. Just one of the crosses I must bear in this life."

Before I could comment she'd shut the car door and headed to the house. Probably just as well because I didn't feel sociable anymore. Knowing I'd have to talk to Ty had deflated me.

Turned out to be a small group for dinner. The kids had decided to have a pizza in their own place, and I applauded their decision to make time for themselves. They were far too young to feel they had to spend all their time with us. And the McTaggarts were once again taking a meal in their room. I hoped this wouldn't go on for long. Jock's *genteel* repartee kept meals lively if nothing else.

Then as I looked at the offering Cassie had prepared; I began to think a pizza would have been a better choice for me as well. Oh dear, a huge casserole with a lot of beans and greenery. Healthy I'm sure, but not so appetizing. Minnie picked through hers as if looking for something, then shrugged and started shoveling it down her throat.

Rose kept busy between mouthfuls describing

the window displays in town to Lily. And Ty? Well, I couldn't figure out what kind of mood he was in. I decided to play devil's advocate. "You seemed to be in a bit of a rush when you came home earlier. Did you not have a good trip into the big city?"

"What?"

"You barreled right past Rose and I in the driveway, not even a wave. To put it mildly, you looked ticked off."

He threw me a puzzled look. "Sorry, I must have been concentrating. I don't remember seeing you."

"That kind of concentration isn't so good when you're behind the wheel," I said. "So, what were you concentrating on?"

He opened his mouth, glanced around at the other diners and said, "A lot on my mind, that's all. But the trip to Toronto went well. Had to help a couple of friends planning a big soiree."

"Sounds like fun. Anyone I'd know from back in the day?"

"No, sweetie. I do have friends outside our circle you know."

Ouch. What had I done to deserve that dig? "Right. Well, let me know if you need an extra set of hands for the big event. I'd be glad to help out. Anything for a friend you know."

He smiled at me. "I'll let you know. I value your input and if it's needed, you'll be the first I'll ask."

I pounced. "Speaking of input, there's something I'd like to talk to you about after dinner. Care to take a stroll 'round the estate with me in a bit?"

"My pleasure, darlin'."

I smiled back at him, but the butterflies had begun to take flight in my stomach.

Dinner ended and as Cassie began clearing away less than empty plates, Ty and I headed outside. We passed Jan starting up the stairs with a small package.

"You two going for a walk?" I didn't miss the direct look she gave me.

"Yes, it's too nice of an evening to stay inside. And how about you? You're looking quite dressed up for an evening indoors?"

"And a pretty present, too. Who's the lucky giftee?" asked Ty

A bemused look crossed Jan's face and she glanced down towards her feet. "I'm having a visit with Alysha and Jeff in their apartment. Brought them a little housewarming gift, so thought I'd clean up a bit for the occasion." As if uncomfortable with the attention she took another step up, "Enjoy your stroll, and stay out of trouble."

"Always," I promised.

Robins offered up their evening choruses and the aroma of freshly mowed grass drifted on the gentlest of breezes. I wished I could feel as relaxed as the atmosphere warranted. We sauntered across the lawns and settled in a couple of lawn chairs by a lush weeping willow. I loved how Frank had thought to place random seating areas about the property.

"Have you talked to Jock or Bea today?" asked Ty.

"No, they've been keeping a low profile. I'm

thinking Jock is more than a little embarrassed by the whole episode and this is his way of dealing with it. But they can't stay shut away forever. Otherwise, Minnie will think she's ruling the roost, especially at meal times."

Ty snorted. "Did you see how she attacked the casserole tonight? The way she dived right in, you'd think it was her last meal or something. Wish I had her metabolism. She never seems to gain an ounce." Ty patted his slight paunch.

"And without any of Dr. Harrison's magic pills either." Crap, that had slipped out without thinking. Or maybe, as Freud might say, it was my subconscious doing the dirty work for me. I waited. He didn't respond, which puzzled me. I looked at my friend. "Are you alright? You usually come right back at me if I say something against him."

He produced a big sigh. "I managed some serious thinking today, while driving. About Reid."

Tread carefully, I admonished myself. "Oh yeah, what about?"

"I don't think I'll be taking advantage of his, um, services anymore."

"Did something happen?"

"No, not really. I've, ah, found a replacement, shall I say. Unfortunately, he's in Newmarket, but no doubt it will be worth the drive."

"Newmarket! But what happened with Harrison? You've always been so keen on him."

He raised a hand. "Nothing really happened, sweetie. I just feel it's time to move on. When I started thinking about all you'd been saying about him, I began to wonder if it's more than a coincidence that Jock, Bea, and Phillip, who are his customers, have had some problems."

Stunned, my jaw must have dropped judging by the reaction on Ty's face.

"Oh, but I certainly don't think any harm was done intentionally," he hastened to add. "Although lately he's seemed a little, um, distracted. So, better safe than sorry for moi."

"I'm relieved to hear you say this." Truthfully, I was very relieved, and I only hesitated a moment before taking him into my confidence.

"Believe it or not, it's what I had wanted to talk to you about. But as you're not seeing him anymore, now I can fill you in on what we think of him."

He cocked his head to one side. "And who is *we*?"

"Jan, Alysha and me."

He raised an eyebrow, but didn't comment, so I brought him up to date on our concerns and suspicions. When I finished, he sat silent for a minute and then spoke. "Well, pet, thank you for sharing. It seems as if all the pieces fit now, don't they? You'll have to keep me in the loop."

"Can I ask you a question though?" I risked the fragile truce we'd established over Dr. Harrison.

"About what?"

"About those packages you gave to him the other day? It was Minnie who'd commented she'd seen you handing him something. Of course, you know her, she had to dramatize it and said you looked like a drug dealer making a sale." I laughed, trying to make light of the incident.

He waved his hand as if brushing away a fly. "Oh, Minnie. Trust her to make a big deal out of nothing. Reid knows we have some Horse Chestnut trees here and he asked me to gather a few of the chestnuts for him. I think he wanted it for some new concoction or the other. Yes, big market in illicit chestnut dealing here in Grant's Crossing." He rolled his eyes, stretched, and stifled a yawn. "It's been a long day and a boy needs his beauty sleep. Ready to head back?"

Twilight spread over us, and a bat or nighthawk dove past me as we made our way back.

I pulled up short as we rounded the corner of the house. A large and unfamiliar vehicle sat parked out front. No hubcaps, and an extra antenna were the hallmarks of an unmarked patrol car. Even Ty caught on, judging by the change in his demeanour. He didn't seem sleepy anymore. We looked at each other and headed up the veranda steps.

# CHAPTER TWENTY-ONE

*Alysha*

Jan and I rushed to the front door at the same time.

This place saw more activity than a day at the fair. Even during my university days, with all the usual hustle and parties, I'd never seen so much coming and going. What with television crews and ambulances, and now we had the cops paying a visit.

Never a dull moment. I left it to her to do the talking because her manner spoke of a familiarity with one of the two men, and I needed to get my bearings.

We stood on the veranda as two plain-clothes officers ambled towards us. Like their unmarked car, they had that unmistakable police air about them. I didn't think they'd make good undercover cops. One carried a large brown envelope, stuffed with something misshapen.

A scowl settled on Jan's face, and she placed her hands on her hips as she addressed the older of the two. "'evening Dax. What brings you to our neck of the woods this time of night? I'm about to watch an old movie so you'd best make this short because I don't want to miss the beginning."

"And a good evening to you too, Jan," said the one named Dax, a bemused smile on his face. "You can likely tell this isn't a social call."

My curiosity ramped into high gear. Was officer Dax a relative, or had Jan dealt with him before?

They stopped short of the first step, deferring to Jan for an invitation up, although I'm sure they didn't need to. Maybe because one of them knew Jan that they toned down their manner. Questioning eyes focused on me.

Jan relaxed a little and the frown on her face faded. "Sorry, where are my manners. This is Alysha Grant, the new owner of Leven Lodge. She is, you know, the Grants' granddaughter, and Dalton's great niece. Alysha, this is Detective Constable Dakotah Young, and for better or worse, my nephew. His partner is Detective Constable Steven.... I've forgotten your last name."

"It's Dubois, Ma'am," he said, never taking his eyes off me.

"Right, Dubois. And I guess you're both still with the Crime Unit? Unless something's changed?"

"I don't think I've missed out on a promotion, Jan. Have you, Steve?"

Jan may have been his aunt, but I picked up on an undercurrent of the policemen trying to balance a familial connection with official business.

She'd changed out of the beautiful outfit she'd worn earlier but I still wore my shorts and a halter top. I've been told, when my curls decide to take on a life of their own, I can pass for a teenager. Now was one of those times and in this light I probably looked sixteen. No wonder they were staring. "Nice to meet you both."

Standing to full attention, I determined to be all business. "How can we help you? You're obviously here on a police matter."

Jan put herself back in charge. "Dakotah Young, speak up. Have we been breaking any by-laws or have the alpacas been seen wandering in town?"

No smile now, all business. "That would be Detective Constable to you, Janelle, while I'm on duty. You'll be undermining my authority with young Dubois here. Actually, we're here to see the McTaggarts."

Young was serious but his partner had a smile tugging at the corner of his mouth.

Jan could be serious as well. "Is this absolutely necessary? It's late for older folks, and they've been through the wringer lately."

Dax Young tapped his notebook. "Unfortunately, yes, it is necessary. We're in the middle of an investigation, so if you could let them know we'd like to speak to them."

A disembodied voice from overhead said, "I hear you, officer. Have Jan show you and your partner to our room." We heard the door to Jock's balcony close. All thoughts of Jan's old movie were forgotten. I wondered what they could possibly need to see Jock and Bea about that couldn't have waited until morning.

Our attention shifted when Dianne and Ty came around the corner. I thought her eyes would bug out of her head. "What are the cops doing here? No more sudden illnesses I hope?"

Her concern competed with gossipy need to

know, and I didn't care for it. "They're here to see the McTaggarts. Not sure why."

Ty stayed quiet and took a seat beside Dianne.

She carried on. "It's too bad they can't leave them be. At their age this must be so upsetting for them."

Then Jeff arrived, also full of questions, so I filled him in. We sat silently speculating on the reason for the police visit.

Just then the two detectives returned. They nodded at the newcomers and Jan's nephew spoke. "Can I have a word Ms. Grant?" said the dark-haired officer. "In private."

I swallowed. "Of course."

He followed me inside while his partner stayed with the others. I shut the French doors to the sitting room for some privacy. No doubt I'd have plenty to write about in my journal later.

### 

### Dianne

As Alysha and the older officer disappeared into the house, I watched Jeff's reaction. Given the slightest encouragement I think he'd have followed right behind her. Instead, he joined Ty and me, but he was fidgety. No one spoke, and I hate dead air, so I decided to go for broke and test the waters.

"So, officer, what's going on? What can we do to help?" With icy blue eyes and full, dark hair he put me in mind of a young Aidan Quinn. Probably a good thing he wasn't in an official uniform. Deadly combination in my books. Oh, where was I?

Before the officer could answer, Jeff turned to me. "Do you think I should be with Alysha?"

"She'll be alright. I think she can manage Jan's nephew by herself. And if DC Dubois isn't at liberty to divulge the reason for their visit, I'm sure she'll be able to give us the rundown." I deliberately sent a charming smile, in the direction of DC Dubois.

"You've assessed the situation correctly, Mrs...?"

"Oh, silly me." I held out my hand and enjoyed a warm, firm handshake. "I'm Dianne Mitchell, and this is Jeff Iverson. Over here is my good friend, Ty Rogers."

"Thank you, ma'am. But, yes, you are correct. I'm not at liberty to reveal the nature of our call." He reached into his jacket pocket for a small note pad, "But perhaps you, or your friends, could answer one or two questions. In fact, if any of the other residents are available, I'd like to speak with them, as well."

Call me Miss Congeniality. "Whatever we can do to help. Right, Ty?"

He gave a slight nod of his head, but never took his eyes off Dubois.

The porch door flew open to reveal Rose and Lily, both wide-eyed. I thought Rose must have dragged Lily along to see what was happening. Rose had curlers in her hair and both women wore housecoats. Lily's had seen better days, but Rose's looked like she'd just bought it off the rack, not a wrinkle or spot to be seen. Yet she still made as if she were smoothing it out and checking for buttons not done up. Twins, but opposites in so many ways.

Rose, as usual led off. "Jeopardy had just finished when we heard all the chatter and commotion. You're not another reporter, are you?" She gave Dubois a thorough once over. "No, I'd say you were police, right? So what's going on?"

Lily pulled a tissue from her pocket as if preparing for bad news. She glanced at the officer, "It's not Phillip is it?"

Rose seized the moment. "Oh Phillip, poor man. Is he alright? I've been so worried about him, and…"

Rose's growing agitation surprised me. Jeff came to the rescue and put a hand on her shoulder. "No ladies, it's not Phillip, you can rest easy." He let her settle a bit and then went on. "It's Jock and Bea they're here about. We're not sure why though. And Detective Constable Dubois would like to ask us a few questions. So come and have a seat, okay?"

Lily clung to Rose's arm while they seated themselves near Jeff. Dubois seemed to be enjoying the dramatics, and he confirmed our names in his little book.

"Right. Is there anyone else in residence tonight who could join us?"

I didn't miss a beat to offer information. "There's Minnie Parker. And Cassie DeSouza, our cook."

Those blue eyes bore right into me and I knew I'd cave if he asked me to fetch Minnie—or run across the lawn in my birthday suit. Over time, I'd learned to put those feelings behind me, although I still appreciated the effect a fine specimen could have on me. But before he could ask, Jeff volunteered to round up Minnie and Cassie. I think he saw it as a perfect excuse to detach himself from the twins.

We waited in awkward silence while Jeff ran his mission. Within a few minutes Cassie strolled onto the veranda. She didn't seem at all fazed to be summoned by the police. Which was odd because as she passed by me, I detected the unmistakable aroma of hash and the detective must have caught it as well. Perhaps he had bigger fish to fry because there he made no comment.

"Hey guys, what's up? Someone getting arrested?" She giggled and I reminded myself not to partake of any of her homemade brownies in the future.

Ty reached out an arm and pulled her down beside him. "Not the time for jokes, Cassie dear."

She giggled again and then put on a sober face. "Sorry. I'll behave."

And then the piece de resistance arrived. Oh my, I'd never seen Minnie in her, ah, night attire until that moment. Looked like she'd stepped right off the pages of Little House on the Prairie. Ankle length nightgown, which might have been white a long time ago. A shawl about her shoulders and a nightcap, which couldn't quite contain her wiry hair. No wonder she kept it in a bun all the time. Her attitude bordered on combative, and Jeff had to practically push her forward.

I tried to placate her. "Sorry to have disturbed

you Minnie, but this nice Detective would like to ask us some questions. They're here to see Jock and Bea. The other detective is Jan's nephew, Dax. You remember him? He's been here before."

I rambled and couldn't stop. If looks could kill I'd have been dead on the spot. Those eyes of hers were like death rays on me. "Why don't you have a seat?"

"Thank you, no. I prefer to stand so this better not take long."

I hoped the officer would start with her so she could go back to her cave, I mean room.

Dubois cleared his throat. "So, this is everyone then? I'll try to be brief so you can return to your evening activities. We appreciate your cooperation and I want to assure all of you, no one is in trouble, we're merely information seeking. Now, then, who here knows Janet McTaggart?"

What? Janet McTaggart, she'd be gone from the scene for years, certainly long before I'd come to Leven Lodge.

Quizzical looks and head shakes greeted his question. I'd already established a helpful rapport with him, so provided what we knew. "Detective, I think I can speak for all here when I say, we all know *about* Janet, but none of us ever met her, or lived here when she might have visited. We only know what we've heard from her parents over the years. As far as I know she's never even been in contact with Jock or Bea in all that time."

"Thank you, Ms. Mitchell. Can anyone add to this?"

Each in turn confirmed they'd never met Janet, and only knew of her from what they'd heard. He continued to scribble away, and I wondered what the other officer had to tell Alysha about, that couldn't be said out here.

# CHAPTER TWENTY-TWO

*Alysha*

When I'd settled into an easy chair in the living room, I looked into the eyes of DC Young. He'd appraised me in a way which unnerved me. Then his face relaxed, and his lips twitched. "I'd heard all about you but didn't quite expect anyone quite as young, or as pretty."

I offered him a seat and chose not to respond to his assessment of me. "If I'm not in any trouble, can you tell me why you're here to see the McTaggarts?"

He kept his eyes on me and I wished Jeff had followed me for this interview, or inquisition. The blatant flirting left me unsettled. If police tactics were meant to rattle a person, he had this down pat.

"Of course. Yes, down to business." He stopped staring and took out his notebook. He was dressed in pressed black chinos and a lightweight blazer with coordinating tie. He didn't look like any cop I'd met before, especially wearing tasseled loafers. Stylish, with slicked back dark hair he'd fit in better with the city's fashion crowd, not as a detective in a small town like Grant's Crossing.

"I'm here on serious business to do with the McTaggarts. It's unfortunate you've just arrived and have to deal with these problems."

I gave a deep sigh. It seemed I'd never lose the ingénue look. Even the police couldn't take me seriously, same as former employers. "Detective Young, you will find me quite capable of dealing with whatever you have to say. As the new owner of Leven Lodge, the McTaggarts are my responsibility, and their well-being is equally important to all who live here."

"I'm sure you're most capable Ms. Grant. It's a sensitive matter, you see. We've uncovered evidence we needed to share with the McTaggarts."

"And why did you feel it necessary to tell me this away from the others?" I couldn't understand why he'd separated me from the others, and it made me nervous, that guilty feeling even though you've done nothing wrong.

"I'm getting to it, Ms. Grant. The group outside," he inclined his head toward the front entrance, "have been together for some time, correct?"

"Yes, but…"

"You, on the other hand are a recent arrival and don't share the same history, without preconceived ideas regarding the McTaggarts and their daughter."

"Yes, and I believe I've only heard one or two references to her since I arrived, but I still don't understand."

The detective made no comment but appeared to be weighing his words before he spoke. "You've stated you are now responsible for the residents here, and so what I'm about to tell you is not to be repeated outside this room. Am I clear?"

Guess he took me seriously after all. But I had to

ask. "How about Jeff, my boyfriend?"

Dax Young tightened his lips. "We'd prefer you share with no one at this point. So, unless you can agree, this conversation is ended."

Damn! My curiosity needed satisfaction, but I didn't want to keep secrets from Jeff. Then I reasoned with myself as owner of Leven Lodge, I should be able to distance myself from the residents enough to take into consideration whatever information was being dangled before me. Besides, Jeff was so wrapped up with the alpacas and getting friendly with Jock, perhaps it would be better if I didn't share this info with him, for now.

My spidey-senses were tingling. "I can agree, and I also think we're talking murder here. Jock was right about Bradley? Is someone here involved?"

"Hold on. Let's not jump to conclusions."

I wanted to shout at him that he'd started it but held myself in check. "Sorry. Tell me what you have to say, and how I can help."

"As far as you know, have the McTaggarts had any contact with their daughter recently?"

"No. As I said I've heard it mentioned that she left after a dispute with her father years ago, and I believe at one point they were expecting her to return but it never happened." I waited while he made notes.

He moved on to his next question. "Do you know if anyone here has had any recent contact with Bradley McTaggart prior to his death?"

"Sorry, I can't answer that. I assume he'd visit the McTaggarts at times. Jan would probably confirm any visits. But surely you've asked them already?"

"Yes, we have." He didn't elaborate.

"Can I ask what was in the envelope?"

He didn't answer directly, but said, "We have evidence to show Janet McTaggart was in Grant's Crossing as recently as the day prior to Bradley McTaggart's death."

"She was? Where is she now?"

The sober look reappeared. "Before I say more, I need your assurance you'll not repeat any of this information. To do so would seriously hamper our investigation or even risk the dismissal of any possible charges."

"I'm beginning to feel like one of those informants police shows are so fond of."

He managed a small smile. "Not quite, however, we hope any information you might come across in the coming days would be shared with us immediately."

I found that I'd been sitting, literally, on the edge of the chair and now leaned forward in a conspiratorial fashion to hear what he'd say next. "I promise I'll keep this all to myself. So?"

"The envelope contained a knitted scarf. Bea McTaggart identified it as belonging to her daughter. That in itself didn't prove she was in town. It could have been with Bradley for some time. What is more relevant is a second item. An address book, and a notebook belonging to Janet McTaggart. We found them during a search of the apartment. Her entries were consistently dated, and the most recent entry was two days before Bradley's death."

My mind whirled. Where was she now? If Bradley had been murdered, maybe she knew the murderer, and had gone into hiding—unless she was the murderer. But why? More questions for the police. "What did the entry say?"

He stared straight into my eyes and without blinking, recapped her notes, giving me the gist of her observations. Apparently, she'd been concerned at how upset Bradley became after meeting with his employer. Harrison had brought someone from the lodge to the apartment with him, and a heated argument ensued. She stayed out of it but noted she didn't care for either Harrison or the unintroduced visitor.

"So, you can see Ms. Grant, we are anxious to establish who this unnamed person is, and as the entry pre-dates your arrival, we are able to rule you out."

"I can take some comfort there, I suppose. Have you not asked Harrison about this unknown person, or do you want me to find out who this person is?"

He shook his head, "We are still trying to connect with Reid Harrison—he's not been easy to find. And no, you are not required to do any investigating. We just want to be updated if you hear anything suspicious—anything at all—even if it seems trivial."

My mind whirled. How could I not share this with Jan or Dianne? As if reading my thoughts, DC Young concluded. "I remind you once again, Ms. Grant, should any of this information be leaked, and it jeopardizes our investigation, you yourself could face charges."

A bucket of cold water would have the same effect on me. I'd be sure to say nothing. He closed his notebook and stood. Handing me his card, the discussion concluded. "Anything at all, call us. We'll decide if it's pertinent." He reached for my hand to shake. "Thank you for your time and assistance. I'll wait outside. You may want to see the McTaggarts now."

# CHAPTER TWENTY-THREE

### *Dianne*

I'd had a restless night and couldn't wait to grab the first cup of coffee out of the pot. Other than Jan and Cassie busy with breakfast preparations, there was no sign of any of my housemates.

With the early morning air too cool to sit outside, I wandered to the living room where Alysha and Jan's nephew had had their little conference the previous evening. I couldn't wait to hear what they'd been discussing.

Once the detectives had left, Minnie had flown back to her room, Jeff had gone looking for Alysha and the twins announced they were done for the evening. Ty had shown remarkable restraint when the police were there. He made no comments and seemed relieved when they'd gone.

Well, I was relieved too. But now it felt like we were waiting for the other shoe to drop. He'd gone straight to his room, declining my invite to have a nightcap and enjoy the rest of the evening. No doubt he'd want to find out what Alysha had learned, but maybe his change of opinion about Harrison had him in a funk. I wouldn't be disappointed if Dr. Death never showed his face around here again.

I heard footsteps on the stairs. Then voices.

Sounded like everyone arriving at the same time. I drained the last of the coffee and headed towards the dining room and a refill.

Cassie placed the morning meal selections on the side table, and it reminded me of a continental type breakfast found in better hotels. Lots of muffins, bagels, cream cheeses and jam. Fresh fruit, and a chafing dish with creamy oatmeal meant we'd be eating well.

I saw the reason for the oatmeal—a favourite of Jock and Bea's, and now they were back in their rightful places. He seemed uncomfortable with the attention he drew from the others, but Bea had a serene quality about her. Maybe a new prescription was the reason.

"Nice to see you with us, Jock," I said and touched his shoulder. He grunted a response and made busy adding milk to his oatmeal. I had to wait my turn to give Bea a hug. Then all were settled, and conversations ceased as we ate.

Alysha and Jeff made quick work of their meal. I had the impression they'd be out of there once they'd finished.

"We've missed having our meals down here, haven't we, Jock," said Bea. "And we're both so sorry our family business has caused such an upset for everyone."

"And we've all been so concerned about you two as well. Can we help in any way?" I offered.

"It would be a help not to be disturbed at bedtime," muttered Minnie, carefully scooping up the last smear of cream cheese on her plate with her finger. That woman would test the patience of a saint, and I certainly didn't qualify.

Ty's observation came to the fore. "You're a poster child for compassion as usual."

Bea looked contrite, "I apologize, Minnie, but I can't promise there won't be more upheavals before this is all done."

Rose chimed in. "Before what's all done?"

Bea twisted her wedding rings and responded. "I wish we could tell you more, but the police detective has asked us not to talk about their investigation."

Which didn't satisfy Rose. "Did they give you any more news on Bradley? Did you know they asked all of us about Janet?"

Sheesh, people don't listen. "Bea can't comment, Rose, just like she said. We'll have to wait, won't we?" I glanced at Alysha when I said this, trying to catch her eye. I knew she'd have information. She met my eye but looked away. What? Something was going on. The meal ended and while some lingered to talk more with Jock and Bea, mostly Bea, I hurried after Alysha.

"Got a sec?"

She turned. "Um, I have some paperwork I need to get done, why?"

I lowered my voice, "What happened last night when you came inside with the other detective? What did you talk about?"

She squirmed. "Sorry, Dianne, but I'm in the same situation as Bea. I've been asked not to talk about it."

"Oh come on, "I said. "You can tell me. I mean, you, Jan and I are working together to keep the McTaggarts safe from Harrison, right? We should all be on the same page. I only want to help."

"I'd like to Dianne, really. But I can't even talk to Jeff about any of it, or..."

"Or what? You'll get thrown in jail?" The more uncomfortable she looked, the more it annoyed me.

"Enough, Dianne! You heard her, now please respect her wishes and stop putting her in an awkward position." Jan had come up behind me, and I saw relief in Alysha's eyes.

Indignation took hold and I turned on Jan, "Right, and I bet you know everything because of your nephew. You probably know more than any of us. Easy for you to say I should butt out, but who went with you to the hospital with Jock and Bea? And who agreed with you two Harrison should be kept away from them? This is the thanks I get?"

That's the problem with getting angry, uncontrolled emotion takes over. I had to have the last word.

"Fine. Hope the both of you have fun sharing secrets. I'm sorry I offered to help."

Stupid tears blurred my vision. I had a hard time seeing which way to go. I opted for the front door and didn't care when it banged behind me.

I marched down the steps and started walking. Not sure where I was headed, but I needed some space away from the house and those—conspirators.

I found myself heading towards the alpacas' domain. By then I'd started to calm down—a little. I fumbled in my pocket for a tissue. Then a hand on my shoulder offered a pristine linen handkerchief. "Here, pet. Whatever has you so upset? Let's find a spot to sit and you can tell me all about it."

My faithful friend led me to a garden bench and we sat. I resolved not to sob like a schoolgirl even though that's exactly what I wanted to do.

"Thanks for the hankie," I sniffled. "Hope the makeup will come off in the wash."

"I should hope so, pet. Those are definitely not in my colour palette."

I couldn't stop the snide response. "You've got that right." I took another swipe at my eyes and drew a deep breath. "I'm sorry. I don't know what got into me, maybe it was the sleepless night."

He held my hand and let me ramble on, probably the best thing for me. Had I really said those things to Jan and Alysha? Once the anger left, I began to feel horrible. The tears threatened again. "I was awfully mean to Jan. I'll have to apologize."

"You can do it later. Right now you need to tell me what happened to bring this all on."

"You didn't hear me asking Alysha about the police?"

His hand on mine grew tighter. "What about the police? From last night?"

"I thought Alysha would fill me in on her private conversation with the officer. He obviously took her aside for a specific reason, don't you think?"

Yes, I wondered. Would love to know what they told the McTaggarts, and what was in the package for them."

I'd forgotten about the package, but it didn't seem like I'd be able to find out about that either.

"Well, my friend, apparently you and I are suffering in the dark together. Alysha told me she's not allowed to say anything. And Jan backed her on it."

He pulled his hand away. "So, you don't know anything. Do you think Alysha will change her mind and give you any information? Anything at all?"

I looked at him. "You're still worried for Dr. Harrison, aren't you?"

He glanced down; his voice barely audible when he spoke. "Of course."

"You know, if he is in trouble with the police, or being investigated, it's probably not a bad thing you're distancing yourself from him."

"Guilty by association is what you're saying."

Now, who was getting testy. And I had no energy to backpedal. "No, no. Oh, maybe. I don't know. I'm still upset and hurt. And I need another coffee. But I don't need you upset with me. I've had about enough for one day, and it's not even ten o'clock."

I sighed and got to my feet. "I'm going to see if there's fresh coffee. Coming?"

"Not right now. I need to do some thinking."

"Okay, catch you later." I headed back to the house and wondered who else I could upset. The aroma of fresh coffee greeted me as I opened the door. But my momentary emotional lift disappeared when I entered the kitchen and saw Jan and Alysha deep in conversation.

Their voices stilled when they saw me. I had to make amends, because holding a grudge is not my style. But seeing them together brought the green-eyed monster to life again, and he wanted to jab at me some more. I deliberately shut him down and refused to utter another snotty comment. "Fresh coffee I see?"

"Help yourself," said Jan. "Listen, I'm sorry about earlier..."

"No, Jan. I'm the one to say sorry. To both of you."

Alysha stood and came over to me, her expression said it all. "I wish I could tell you, and Jan, what I've been told. But I've promised not to, sorry. Please try to understand?"

I allowed a small smile," So, what you're saying is we're one big sorry bunch?"

She smiled back. "It would seem that way. Come on, sit down with us and have your coffee."

We made small talk until the back door slammed.

Ty glared at us. "And now I suppose you're all talking about me? Well, I know where I'm not wanted Thanks so much, Dianne!"

Like a whirlwind he rushed away, leaving the three of us with mouths agape. What on earth had he been thinking about out there?

# CHAPTER TWENTY-FOUR

*Alysha*

Considering all the recent events, some down time with Jeff would be welcome. But not right now

I slipped off to our apartment after the confrontation with Dianne, and Ty's temper tantrum. What on earth had that been about?

I settled on the balcony in what had become my favourite chair and looked out over the meadow where the alpacas grazed. I waved at Jeff as he closed the gate behind him and headed toward his pick-up. A visit to his new friend's farm, making plans and seeking advice for adding a few more alpacas to our three should take a few hours. As much as I needed Jeff-time I planned on getting my thoughts in order about the latest goings on here. Making notes in my journal would help me assess the situation better.

Clouds started to roll in and the sky grew ominous. The kind of day I liked for thinking and writing. Before I recorded in my journal the police visit, Dianne's strange behaviour, and Ty's even stranger outburst, I picked up the Gazette Jan had dropped off. I wondered if what I'd learned from the cops had been reported.

There it was on page three. Keeping a low profile, I noted.

## Grant's Crossing Gazette

### Police Update - Murder Confirmed

New evidence has come to light in the death of local man, Bradley McTaggart, and the death is now being treated as murder. When asked if they were close to making an arrest OPP Liaison Officer DC Marg Trainer declined to elaborate. She stated the police still have some persons of interest to interview. The investigation is continuing.

I put the paper aside and took out my notebook. Would my list of questions ever be done?

Who are the 'persons of interest'? Surely it couldn't be anyone from Leven Lodge. I made more notes. The McTaggarts? In their eighties—scratch them. Who else here could be involved. Cassie? Janet McTaggart? Why would she be in town and not visit her parents? Why wouldn't Bradley tell them she was here? Were he and Jock really that close?

The next question I scribbled down had to do with Harrison as I recalled what the police had found in her notebook.

Janet didn't like Harrison; Brad had met an unnamed someone from Leven Lodge—who? If I had the chance I'd come right out and ask Harrison whether he knew Janet, or where she was. Although if the police can't seem to find Harrison, not much chance I would either.

I itemized the residents. Why would any of them be visiting Harrison unless they needed some of his fountain of youth pills. Could have been Phillip, or Rose. Or even someone pretending to be from the lodge, as a cover. Couldn't have been either of the McTaggarts. But Harrison seemed quite tame according to my new lawyer friend. He may be a fraud, but a murderer?

I read over my notes since I'd arrived. Perhaps if I concentrated, I could make sense of this puzzle.

Just as I became comfy the rain started in earnest and I could hear distant thunder, so I moved inside and sat at Uncle Dalton's old roll top desk. I took great comfort from the desk of the man who had made my new life possible. I continued to list the residents and their foibles.

Phillip of course was out of the picture, literally. Rose and Lily, different as chalk and cheese for twins but as harmless as they come—or are they? Who's next? Ah, the strange one. Minnie Parker. Certainly different. But it's not a crime to have a bad odour about you although I don't think Dianne would agree.

That left Dianne and Ty. Dianne and I were becoming good friends and I liked her personality, but what had happened after breakfast seemed out of character. At least we were talking again. She doesn't like Harrison so I couldn't imagine her being the unknown visitor Janet saw.

And the resident prima donna? I liked Ty, but he'd certainly had a bee in his bonnet earlier. He used

Harrison's potions but according to Dianne they've had a falling out. What caused the falling out?

A knock at the door interrupted my musings.

"Alysha, it's Jan. May I come in?"

I opened the door, happy to see her. "Of course. Come in and take a load off. Can I get you something to drink?"

"Hey, that's usually my job but yes, I'd love a coffee if you're making one. I'm glad to see you at Dalton's desk. It's a beautiful piece and meant to be used."

"It's certainly an antique. Perfect for my journal entries."

"Am I interrupting anything important?"

We sat with our coffees.

"No. Just making a few notes. Trying to make sense of the residents." I shared some of my thoughts and questions over recent events. "They sure are a mixed bunch."

"Never a truer word. Having said that, do you feel comfortable by yourself this weekend? I came to remind you I'm leaving shortly for home. This is my weekend off."

"You deserve your time away. Don't worry. Jeff and I'll be fine. We'll survive Cassie's cooking, if she stays off the weed." Jan frowned when I mentioned Cassie. "I'll have a word with her before I leave. She's on her last legs with me. I've warned her before about her smoking."

"Your call, but I'll back you on it. Now if the weather holds, Jeff plans on a barbecue for the twins' birthday. It'll be a great diversion."

"Excellent idea, Alysha." She finished her coffee. "You're the right person to run Leven Lodge. There should be enough meat in the freezer for a barbecue or call the deli in town. They'll deliver anything else you need."

Jan stood up, gave me a hug and smiled. "My nephew took quite a fancy to you. It's just as well you're with Jeff or he'd be putting moves on you."

"Hmm, he certainly is full of himself. I'm sure I'll be seeing more of him, but in a police capacity, of course."

"He knew I'd be going home this weekend when he spoke with me last night. He's a good cop even if he does fly by his own rules at times. Not always wise in a cop, but I'm sure you're more than capable of handling whatever he asks of you.

"One more word before I go. Over the years, I've become fond of the residents. However, what we witnessed this morning from both Dianne and Ty is not their normal behaviour. Don't be browbeaten by either of them. They just love to gossip. Something, I can't put my finger on, is up. We'll talk on Monday."

Jan left me to my scribblings but now I'd lost my train of thought. The rain had cleared up and I wandered to the balcony where I saw Jan whisked away by her niece, Fern.

My request to Jan for summer part-time help had brought Fern Young to my attention. I'd been impressed with her maturity and agreed she'd be a welcome addition. She'd be starting next week.

It'll be nice to have a younger face around here.

Better keep her away from Cassie and her special brownies though.

I left my garret and decided I'd find Dianne. It wouldn't be easy deflecting her questions but maybe she knew what caused Ty's outburst. She's not the only one who loves a good story.

# CHAPTER TWENTY-FIVE

### *Dianne*

I heard Alysha calling my name, but I kept going and hoped she wouldn't see me duck out the side door. I'd no desire for chit chat and I had a feeling she'd be wondering what caused Ty's eruption earlier. Nuts, I didn't have the answer, she should just go and talk to him herself.

My car keys were in hand and once I headed down the driveway, I began to feel my spirits lift. I had no particular destination in mind and took a turn leading me along the river's edge. In spots, there was a clear view of the water. Being shallow in places made it a favourite of canoeists and kayakers. But for the most part trees and bushes crowded the river's edge along the stretch of road I travelled. I passed the old mill, where the river began to widen. I knew about the bend in the road ahead and eased off the gas.

As I neared the bend, my foot went to the brakes. Not far up the road were emergency vehicles. An ambulance parked front and centre. Traffic had slowed in both directions, and gawkers got their fill as they passed the scene. I drove by and pulled off to the side of the road, away from the area. But not so far away I couldn't see. If you're going to gawk, get out of the car and do it properly—especially if it's a chance to watch healthy men in uniform at work.

The activity centred at the river's edge. The paramedics didn't seem to be rushing anywhere and I had a gut feeling there was no hurry for whoever they were trying to rescue.

Ropes knotted on a fire truck's bumper were taut, the business end out of sight down the bank of the river. Not much conversation going on and I stood too far away to hear anything audible from radios.

A couple more cars with occupants who had the same idea as me pulled up, and my observation area soon grew crowded. Rumours and guesses began flowing. Morbid curiosity was the drawing card. I imagined each person already formulating how they'd relay the scene to friends and family later. I deflected attempts to draw me into their speculations as curiosity seekers came and went.

I perked up as a ripple of excitement spread among the emergency response personnel and all eyes focused on the rope being drawn back up. Hands reached down and a gurney appeared.

I'd been right. The body bag on the stretcher confirmed a death, which sobered me somewhat and erased my grumpy mood. I started to think of who the police would have to notify and whose lives would be changed forever. Feeling a little shamefaced that I'd been a gawker, I got back in my car and decided to head to town. I'd grab some coffees and bring them back to the Lodge.

Seemed word of the body had spread fast. I'd never known the coffee shop to have so few customers, the servers behind the counter were already discussing theories and identities. Even the main street had lighter traffic than usual. In hindsight I was glad I'd left the grisly scene when I did. It would soon become a circus.

I left the coffee shop with a tray full of extra-large javas and a bag of sugar and creamers. Plenty to go around. I'd had to juggle the tray with one hand and open the door with the other. One of the coffees started to tip and my attention went to the cup and not to where I walked.

"Ms. Mitchell, let me help you."

Mentally swearing is not quite as satisfying as saying it out loud. Of all people, why did I have to run into Dr. Harrison. "Thanks."

"My pleasure. It doesn't seem to be busy in here today?"

"No, I think everyone's gone to the river to see the body."

That wiped the smarmy smile from his face, pronto. "Body? Where?"

"Up river, past the old sawmill. I saw them pulling it from the water's edge about fifteen minutes ago."

"Do they know who it is?"

"No idea. Oh," I said, "Isn't that the police in front of your office?"

"What? Oh no. Damn."

Kind of a panicked reaction, I thought. But he forgot all about me, as he turned tail and headed away from his office. Seemed to me he did not want to be seen by the police. Because of guilt?

DC Young knocked again at the entrance to Harrison's office. Gave him credit for being patient, but he soon gave it up. Good, I'd have something to share besides the coffee when I got back to the house.

When I pulled up to the house and parked, the McTaggarts were making their way to sit on the veranda. It was good to see them starting to get back to normal, whatever their normal had become these days. I decided not to share my recent news with them. They'd read about it in the paper soon enough.

I headed up the steps. "Coffee anyone?"

They declined so I moved inside. Voices came from the kitchen, but I stopped in the doorway to the front room where I saw Ty. He sat leafing through one of his favourite interior design magazines but looked up when I offered a coffee.

"Perfect, yes thank you. But not from those paper cups please."

I laughed. "Of course, your highness. Come to the kitchen with me. I think we can find something ceramic, or maybe fine English bone china would suit?"

We headed down the hall to the kitchen. The voices belonged to Alysha and Cassie. They were discussing recipes. I was anxious to share what I'd just seen in town but felt reluctant to involve Cassie. Alysha looked up as we entered. "Dianne, there you are. I looked for you earlier."

Alysha spied the coffees. "So that's the reason you disappeared."

I laughed. "Yes, and now Ty here would like a real mug to enjoy his brew from instead of these."

Cassie closed the recipe book in front of her. She pulled down a mug from the cupboard for Ty. "Anyone else want a mug?"

Alysha and I shook our heads.

"You're welcome to a coffee too, Cassie. There's lots here."

"Thanks, but I'm going to run into town. Need a few extra ingredients for my new recipe."

I didn't miss the small groan Ty emitted as I transferred his coffee into a mug. If Cassie was out of the way I could share what I'd seen at the river.

"You said you were looking for me?" When I asked Alysha, she glanced at Ty, but said it wasn't important and could wait.

"Then how about some juicy news from town?"

Two pairs of eyes focused on me; Ty's positively gleamed. "What do you mean by juicy, pet?"

"Perhaps juicy is not the right word. In fact, gruesome would be better."

"Oh, oh," said Alysha. "What happened?"

"I was driving along River Road, just upriver from the mill. You know the bend where the river widens? Emergency crews were there pulling a body from the river."

I casually sipped at my coffee and enjoyed their reactions.

"Not again," said Alysha. "So soon after the McTaggart's nephew. I wonder who it is."

"Probably a hiker who got too close to the edge

farther up. It can be a treacherous walk. Wouldn't be the first victim." Ty made it sound like an everyday occurrence.

"But there's more, "I teased.

"What?" asked Alysha.

"I ran into Reid Harrison after I bought the coffee, but we couldn't chat because Detective Young was knocking at his door. And guess what? Harrison took off in the opposite direction! I'd say he was avoiding the police, big time."

"I bet there's a connection," said Ty, a smug smile on his face. Boy, he really didn't want anything to do with him.

"What kind of connection?" asked Alysha.

The sly edge on his face disturbed me. "Oh, I don't know, I'm just saying. First it was Bradley and he worked for Harrison, and now the police are calling on him at the same time another body is found? Sounds like more than a coincidence to me."

Damn, but I felt cheated. I should have made the connection first, but maybe Ty's relationship with Harrison gave him an inside track.

Alysha chewed on her bottom lip. "Let's change the subject. It's too nice a day to be dwelling on something we know little about. Jeff thought we'd have a barbecue tomorrow. It's the twins' birthday and might be a good excuse to have some fun with everyone. Will you both be here?"

Ty said he might be heading into Toronto later in the day, but I promised to be on hand and offered my help. Valiant effort, but the topic came right back on track with Alysha's next question. "Do you honestly feel Harrison could be involved? I've a good mind to run into town and see what I can find out."

"Leave it to the police, pet." The tension in his voice seemed harsh considering the advice.

"I'll think about it," she responded.

"So about the barbecue," I said. "Please tell me Cassie's not baking a cake for Rose and Lily."

Alysha laughed. "We're on the same page there. Because the weather's warm, I told her I'd pick up a cake tomorrow from *Sweet Things.* Eliminates the need to heat up the kitchen. Jeff will do the grilling; all Cassie has to do is put together a salad or two."

A barbecue sounded perfect. I thought Ty would think so as well, but he had other fish to fry. "Alysha, I've been thinking."

"About?"

"Do you remember we talked about the possibility of my working on a piece of art specifically for the lodge?"

"Yes, I do. And?"

"I've been tossing one or two ideas around and may have a suggestion to run by you. When you have some free time could we take a run up to the old sawmill. I know a perfect place to paint the mill and wheel before it's demolished for the casino—if it ever materializes. I've seen the angle to paint, but you could give me a different perspective."

"You never offered to paint me, Picasso." I teased but felt a pang of jealousy. What the heck was wrong with me. I couldn't be jealous of Alysha, could I? Truth be told I wouldn't even want a portrait done.

One eyebrow raised ever so slightly, but he didn't respond to my barb. Probably just as well.

Alysha looked from Ty to me, and back to Ty. "Let's talk soon. Maybe we can grab a few minutes during the barbecue, in case you don't stay for the whole thing."

"Perfect." He tipped back his coffee and then placed the empty mug on the counter. "Well, speaking of painting, I have a bit of organizing to do. You may not see me until dinner time."

"Have fun," I said. "I think I'm ready to get back into my book and have a lazy afternoon."

We went our separate ways and my reading time turned into nap time. When I awoke and made my way downstairs, I sensed a commotion at the front of the house.

No, not the police again. My curiosity won out over etiquette and I went to the doorway of the front room. Voices stilled, but heart-wrenching sobs allowed no silence. Alysha sat on a couch beside Bea, her arm around her shoulder. Where was Jock?

Alysha caught my eye. "Dianne. Jan's not here. Can I ask you to go up to see if Jock is alright? They've had dreadful news and he said absolutely not a word but headed straight upstairs. I need to stay here with Bea. And if you see any of the others ask them to stay away for now. Please?"

I'd never seen Bea so ashen and wan. Alysha, on guard near her, upset but in control. DC Young stood off to one side. He nodded at me as if to encourage me to do as Alysha asked. "Of course. Do you want me to bring him back down here?"

"If you can, yes. The police need them to go into town..."

Bea's soft wails gave me chills. Alysha whispered, "They think it's Janet's body."

# CHAPTER TWENTY-SIX

*Alysha*

As I struggled to console a heartbroken Bea, a flood of memories came rushing in of my own encounter with the police when they told me my parents had been killed. The pain had never left me so I couldn't imagine what this might do to the McTaggarts. First a nephew murdered and now their beloved daughter found in the same river.

"I'm afraid one or both of them need to make a formal identification of the body," said the DC.

This guy needed sensitivity training. As soon as he mentioned identification Bea began to shake and started a wail like I'd never heard before. The keening blocked out the sound of Jock's entrance. Stooped, with red and raw eyes, he came into the room leaning heavily on Dianne's arm.

Thank goodness the others had kept to their rooms. Except Cassie. I could see her hovering at the kitchen door with eyes as big as saucers. I'd have to speak to her later, along with the rest of the residents.

DC Young softened his tone and spoke with utmost respect, I'd give him points there. "Mr. McTaggart, you've had a terrible shock, and I'm truly sorry to ask this, but I'll need you or your wife to come with me to identify the body. After the autopsy the body will be moved to Donaldson's funeral home." He paused, as if to ensure the request had registered. "Are you ready to go now?"

Jock ignored him and went to Bea. They held each other and Jock spoke to his grieving wife. "Darlin, I'll be a short while and then we can make some arrangements. You stay here with Dianne and Alysha, love." He spoke so tenderly to her I had to fight back the tears, especially when he looked my way. I could only nod at him.

Bea's wailing had ceased, and she stood up shakily. "No, Jock. I'm going with you. I want to see with my own eyes that this is our wee lass. They could have made a mistake you know," she said, eyes pleading.

Jock was beyond gentle with her and took her hand and led her out the door. He turned to Dianne. "You've been more than kind; would you mind coming with us. We need a good friend right now."

Dianne paled, and suggested I go instead. No idea how I looked but going with them for this task was not something I thought I could handle. Thankfully, for me, Jock would not take no for an answer. "Please, Dianne. Bea and I would appreciate it if you were with us."

In that moment, Bea reminded me of Gran, and my heart ached. "I'll stay here while you're gone and inform the rest." I stood in front of her. "You can do this, and you'll be back before you know it." I gave her a hug and patted Jock on the arm, but both seemed to have settled into shock. My words appeared not to register with them.

Facing Dianne, I said "I'll go if you really want me to but Bea and Jock are more familiar with you and Jan has gone for the weekend."

"No, no, I'll call if I need you. Perhaps you'd better let Jan know anyway."

I stood watching from the veranda as they disappeared into DC Young's car and drove out of sight. I sank into the nearest chair, thinking on this turn of events. If it was Janet, and the same fate happened to her as her cousin, then who had it in for the old folks to such an extent they killed their only family? Or merely a tragic coincidence? I turned when I heard footsteps and saw Jeff, fresh from feeding the alpacas, with a puzzled smile on his face.

"You're deep in thought. Am I imagining I heard a car and commotion? Where is everyone?"

When I didn't answer he kept talking. "I need a fix of a decent thriller movie. Let's go for a drink at the pub, check out what's playing and take in a movie if there's a good one. We could be back in time to put the boys to bed."

Hated to burst his bubble, but... "Bad news, we're not going anywhere. The worst has happened." I proceeded to tell him about the body and the McTaggarts and Dianne going with them to confirm the identity."

We stared at each other and I'm sure his thoughts were similar to mine.

*Are we in over our heads or can we handle this new situation?*

"Wow, babe. Never a dull moment. Are you going to be alright?"

I jumped to my feet. "You know, this is where I want to live, and together we can handle anything. Now, I need to talk to everyone and let them know what's happening. I'll give Jan a call as well. Can I leave you to round them up, and we'll meet in the dining room. Oh, and ask Cassie to make a large pot of tea. I think it's called for."

We soon congregated in the dining room and a sombre bunch we were. I explained what had happened and we had to listen to Lily's sobbing. Rose as usual came to the rescue. She assured us it didn't matter whether they knew Janet (if the body was Janet) or not, one and all felt truly bad for Jock and Bea.

Minnie, being Minnie, had caustic words along the lines of "she must have had it coming, whoever she is." I noticed the rest paid her no attention when she spat out her nastiness. Ty said not a word. Most unusual. Perhaps his nose gets out of joint when he doesn't have Dianne to banter with. Cassie poured us copious amounts of tea and joined us for a cup.

Finally, Ty spoke up. "May I suggest we keep things as normal as possible around here. It might be easier on Jock and Bea when they return. Jeff has offered one of his famous barbecues for tomorrow, which we hear is his specialty." He beamed. "Perfect for our special occasion tomorrow, right?"

Rose had the grace to blush. "'Perhaps we should cancel. We can have a birthday party any old day."

Mentally I thanked Ty for keeping up the banter. "I think Ty is right. Business as usual. So, who's older? Rose or Lily?"

Lily's tears had dried, and she coquettishly informed us, "Rose is older by ten minutes. So I'm the baby of the family."

Minnie, in predictable fashion, criticized. "Bah! Birthdays! You two are old. Why are you still celebrating at your age?"

Thankfully she was ignored, and Jeff took over. "The party tomorrow will start at four. We may be down in numbers but I'm sure we can have a pleasant time. Frank will help me set up some trestle tables in the shade garden." He snapped his fingers. "Would anyone like to play garden skittles? It's a bit like croquet."

Skittles and croquet? My guy had talents yet undiscovered, but he did a super job distracting them from what had been happening. The decision was made to meet back for a light supper. Cassie smiled in relief, off the hook for another meal, and she had the presence of mind to say she'd cancel the Friday night sing-along with her boyfriend, Dale.

Happier faces all around. Ty left first and the rest trickled out of the dining room. Jeff and I sat longer, relieved we had managed to handle yet another crisis at Leven Lodge.

Two hours had passed, and I still hadn't heard from Dianne. I wondered what kept them. I told Jeff about my conversation with Jan as we sat having a beer on the balcony. Of course, she had wanted to turn right around and be here for the McTaggarts.

"She is very fond of Bea and has a soft spot for Jock. She kept saying 'Oh the poor souls, the poor souls. How will they cope?' I finally convinced her to stay with her parents as long as I promised one of us would definitely call her if we couldn't manage."

"Babe, this is really not what I'd expected would happen today. But I'm impressed with how you're handling things. I'm beginning to think you were meant to be here."

That warranted a hug and after I kissed him said I'd be at my desk waiting to hear from Dianne.

I sat at Uncle Dalton's desk and wrote in my journal the latest events.

> *Janet McTaggart's body found! McTaggarts to identify her. Dianne with them...not sure they can handle this. Must talk to Ty about a landscape of the old mill. I put the idea in his head about some artwork for the lodge. Had the impression he wants to paint me, with the mill in the background. Maybe Jeff and I should take a run out there when things settle. Plans for the birthday party ...play it by ear.*

I get such satisfaction after I put everything away neat and tidy in my journal.

We'd just decided to join the others for supper when Dianne finally called. I put the call on speaker for Jeff's benefit. Her voice strained as she explained what had happened to keep her away this long. She was trying not to cry. I had a hard time understanding her between her sniffles and needed her to repeat what she'd said.

"Bea didn't even make it to the morgue. She collapsed on arrival at the hospital and Jock, well I thought he was going to collapse as well."

"Breathe, Dianne. What's happening with them now?"

She emitted a sound between a hiccup and a sob as she worked to compose herself. "It was just awful, Alysha. Just awful. I've never experienced anything like it. Bea, they sedated her in the ER, and they hooked her up to monitors. Oh, I hate these things. I wanted to stay with her, but Jock insisted—demanded —I go with him to the morgue. Said he couldn't handle it on his own."

She took a deep breath. She sounded close to crumpling herself. I thought she must be in a waiting room, probably emergency, as I could hear calls over the intercom in the background.

I prodded her for more information. "Did the police let you go with him? It's usually only next of kin I think in these situations."

"They said it was unusual, but Jock insisted and as they wanted the body identified they allowed me. I didn't look at first, and then I did, and now I wish I hadn't."

I closed my eyes. "And was it Janet?"

"Jock made the identification and fainted dead away. Oh, I don't mean dead, but they had to cart him out on a stretcher and now they're both sedated. Old dears. This happening at their age. She wasn't in good shape, Janet I mean. Ugh, it was horrible. She'd been in the water for some time."

"You were brave to accompany Jock. I'm sure when he comes to, he'll thank you. Do the police have anything new?"

"Jan's nephew is here; said he'll drive me home as soon as I speak to social services. They're keeping Bea and Jock overnight."

"Would you like me to come and talk with them? I can be there in about twenty minutes."

"Thanks, but I feel better now after talking to you. This has been, so, well something one never wants to do. I can speak to them on Jock and Bea's behalf and refer them to you. They'll probably call you later."

'If you're sure."

"I am. How's everything there?"

"All is calm and quiet. I told everyone what happened and there were a few, predictable comments. And a lot of concern. Jeff wants to go ahead with the barbecue and party for the twins tomorrow. Ty suggests we keep things as normal as possible. I hope the McTaggarts can join us but they may not feel like it, or even be home."

"Sounds like you're in control, I knew you had the right stuff. Right, I better go powder my nose before I meet with social services. See you when I get home."

When the call ended, I said to Jeff. "Perhaps we

tell everyone Jock and Bea are being kept in for observation due to shock. No need for details. I'm sure Ty will want the gory stuff, but Dianne can share with him later."

Jeff held my hands. My rock. "We'll see what tomorrow brings and then decide whether to have the party or not. Weather-wise it's to be a beautiful day but moods may be dampened if the McTaggarts aren't around. Or maybe we should cancel, if you think it wouldn't be appropriate in light of their loss?"

"From what I know of the McTaggarts, I feel they'd want us to go ahead."

Jeff agreed and had the last word. "Remember the cake though. I can always eat cake." He ha to be the most uncomplicated man I knew. Thankfully, he's mine.

# CHAPTER TWENTY-SEVEN

### *Dianne*

Beyond exhausted I finally made it back home just after midnight. I couldn't decide whether I needed someone still awake or get to my room unnoticed. I'd seen far too much of our hospital this week and had no desire to return anytime soon.

Someone had left a light on for me. No one was about so I plodded up the stairs. At the top of the landing, I could hear Ty moving about in his room and for a moment I considered knocking on his door for some company. Deciding against it, I turned and went to my room, where I gratefully crawled into bed.

Morning arrived far too early and as much as I'd like to have retreated back into slumber, I knew Alysha would be waiting for details. I found her already downstairs, sharing a coffee with Jeff. From the dark shadows under her eyes, it didn't look like she'd had much sleep either. I grabbed a coffee and sat down with them.

"You must be beat," she said to me. "I thought I heard you come in. After midnight?"

"Yes. Boy, I was glad to get home, but felt badly leaving Jock and Bea. Poor souls. My heart breaks for them. I managed to say goodnight to them and at least they'd found them rooms by the time I left. Jock's aged ten years and Bea, well, it's like the light's gone from her. So unfair for them to have this crap at their age." I put my mug down a little too hard and coffee sloshed over the edge.

Alysha patted my hand, and I mumbled an apology while I dabbed at the spill with a napkin. I couldn't sugarcoat the news, so best to come right out and tell them. "The doctors are concerned about the shock they've had so soon after Bradley's death. They didn't say it, but I got the impression we should be prepared for the worst."

Alysha's shoulders sagged and she gave a big sigh. Jeff wrapped his arm around her. We were in danger of a major crying jag and I wasn't ready for it. Time to change the subject. "Jeff, are you still planning on the birthday feast for the twins?"

He blinked a couple of times, to clear his glistening eyes. "I'm still game if you think it's appropriate. What do you think, Alysha?"

She glanced out the window to a cloudless sky. "It appears the weather will be in our favour. I wish the McTaggarts were here, but I vote yes. Besides I've already ordered the cake."

Her laugh didn't fool me, she was worried about her charges. But I'd get on board with her.

"And we can't have cake going to waste, can we?" I smiled. "When everyone's down for breakfast we can update them on Jock and Bea and confirm the barbecue."

Cassie entered the kitchen, rubbing her eyes. "Oh, sorry I didn't know anyone would be up just yet.

I'll get breakfast started."

"Let's keep it simple this morning," said Alysha. "Maybe cereals and fruit. We'll be having a good meal later this afternoon, so we need to save room."

Cassie started to clap her hands but stopped. "Oh good, we're going to have the birthday party after all? Will the McTaggarts be here?"

"I don't think so," I said. "But knowing Bea, she'd want us to go ahead and have some fun. The doctor will be in touch later and let us know for sure."

Cassie's mouth downturned. "I sure hope they catch whoever is responsible for this."

"So do we, Cassie," said Alysha. "Now we'll get out of your way, unless you need some help?"

"No, go on. This won't take me long."

Others came downstairs. We soon had our breakfast and Alysha shared the latest on the McTaggarts. "And we'd still like to have the birthday barbecue."

Other than Minnie, who's miserable about almost everything, the news of the barbecue made the day brighter. As we were finishing up, the phone rang, and Cassie came to get me. "It's the hospital," she whispered, but yet loud enough for everyone else to hear.

I nodded at Alysha to come with me. I picked up the extension in the front room and put it on speaker. "Dianne Mitchell speaking."

"Good morning Ms. Mitchell. I hope I'm not calling too early. It's Matthew Hall. We met before if you remember?"

"Junior?" mouthed Alysha. I nodded and knew my eyes had rolled.

"Yes, I was with Jan Young. She's not here today, but I have Alysha Grant with me on speaker. She's the owner of the lodge and is as concerned about Jock and Bea as anyone."

"Perfect. I'm glad I can speak with both of you. Obviously, I'm calling about Mr. and Mrs. McTaggart."

I cut to the chase. "How are they this morning?"

"I've been told they slept well, and the doctor was in to see them about an hour ago. Shock is wearing off, but this has been a huge emotional blow for them."

"Mr. Hall. I'm Alysha. When will they be able to come home?"

"Ms. Grant. Yes, well, see that's what I'm calling about. We want them to stay here for a day or two more to assess them again. After their previous hospitalization, they did appear to be doing as well as could be expected, but our fear is this will be a tremendous setback. We feel, if they recover..."

"What do you mean, if they recover?" demanded Alysha. Her cheeks were flushed an angry red.

"They've become quite frail, Ms. Grant and frankly there is concern with their current health issues that this strain may be too much for them. I think you should be prepared for a negative outcome."

Now I was pissed. Negative outcome! What crap these so-called professionals spouted at times. Junior didn't have the balls to state the obvious, so I did. "You mean they could die?"

"Yes. But, in the meantime it may be best if they were moved to a facility where they would receive the care you may not be able to provide."

Alysha's voice faltered. "A nursing home?"

"Correct. I can recommend a few and depending on their finances they do have options."

No waver in her voice now. "Excuse me, but I think I'd like to talk this over with them first before any decisions are made." Alysha's tone put Junior in his place.

"Of course, of course, Ms. Grant. I'm merely advising you of possible outcomes."

"Leave me your number and I'll get back to you after I've spoken with them."

She wrote the information down and ended the call. "Ooooo, he's a pompous little…"

"Prick?" I offered.

She laughed, "I concur with that assessment. "Let's not share this with the others, except Jeff?"

"Agreed." And then the offer flew out of my mouth without thinking. "Why don't we both go see them after the barbecue and discuss their future with them. Then you'll be better able to judge how to handle Junior's suggestions."

"I'd go with or without you, but your company and insight are always welcome."

Circumstances had brought a new edge of maturity to Alysha that hadn't been apparent when she first arrived. It suited her.

The morning went by. I managed to sneak in a

power nap. When I finally showered and felt ready to face the day it was nearly two o'clock

Outside, preparations were well underway for the planned festivities. Tables had been set up, chairs arranged. Frank and Jeff were in charge of landscape tidying.

Ty had just finished adding balloons and ribbons to the birthday girls' chairs. It did look special. I came up to him and tapped him on the shoulder. "Can I help with anything?"

"Thanks, pet, but it's all under control. How do you like my efforts for the twins?" Ty knew he was good, but that never overruled his insecurities.

"I love it, they'll be tickled."

He smiled, briefly. "I hope so. You'll have to let me know."

"What do you mean?"

"Remember I said I'd probably have to head into Toronto today? I got a call earlier, they want to move their meeting up, so I have to leave earlier. Like now."

"Oh, no. What a shame. You'll miss all the fun."

"Can't be helped. I'm going to stay overnight rather than drive back late."

"Makes sense. Does Alysha know?"

He finished gathering up scraps of colour and pins. "Yes, I told her and she's disappointed, too. I feel bad, but business is still business, and a boy has to make a living."

"And without you here, I'm sure the party won't go on for too long. Just as well, though, because she and I plan to go and see the McTaggarts after."

"Give them my best and tell them they need to be back here soon. But now I've got to run. See you tomorrow."

The promise of good weather held true and about an hour later, the party got underway.

Alysha came up to me, keys in hand. "I'm just running into town now for the cake. Are there any last-minute items we need?"

"I think we're good. Don't make any side trips, folks are getting hungry. And we all know Minnie doesn't like to be kept waiting for food."

She laughed. "So true! Okay, just the cake, and I'll be right back. I can't wait to see what *Sweet Treats* has done for the twins."

I watched her drive off and then went back to the gathering. The barbecue smoked and something smelled delicious. My stomach rumbled in anticipation.

Punch and stronger refreshments were set out. I helped Jeff ensure one and all had their share. Cassie had assembled a variety of, for once, appealing salads.

Rose and Lily were the centre of attention and soaked it up.

"Happy Birthday ladies. You two look especially good today." I gave them each a hug.

Minnie scowled in Jeff's direction. "Hope he knows what he's doing. I'm not in the mood for a burnt offering."

I vowed I wouldn't let her get to me. "It will be fine, Minnie."

Jeff was in his element. A beer in one hand and

tongs in the other—king for the day. I felt sad though, when I realized the small size of our group. So much had changed in the last week.

A car pulled up the driveway. No surprise, Jan had come back early. "How could I miss out on this birthday celebration? Now how can I help?"

I was grateful to see her. "It's all under control. Pull up a chair and I'll bring you up to date." I filled her in on the McTaggarts and asked her to come with Alysha and me to see them after the party. "We're just waiting on Alysha to bring the cake and then we'll get started."

Jeff, tongs in hand, came up to me. "Dianne. Should we begin with the salads? The *party animals* are getting restless."

"I think we can wait a few more minutes. Alysha should be back any second."

Hours later, we were still waiting for her.

# CHAPTER TWENTY-EIGHT

*Alysha*

I came to when pain seared across my lips. Heavy tape, covering my mouth, had been ripped away. Moonlight streamed across dusty floorboards and the brick wall was cold and hard at my back.

I'd never seen this coming, and certainly never suspected the agitated man in front of me capable of this. My captor paced back and forth, mumbling to himself.

I had nothing to lose so I tried a gentle approach. "Maybe I can help you…"

"Shut. Up!"

I cringed and fought back the urge to cry. I should have listened to Jeff and stopped prying into things that didn't concern me. No one knew I was here, and I had only myself to count on.

He stopped moving and crouched down to my level where I sat. I could only turn my head away from his cold gaze. My hands were tied behind my back and my feet were tightly shackled to a massive wooden support beam a few inches away. I tried not to think about the ache creeping across my hips from being restrained in such an awkward position.

"This is all your fault, missy. You should never have come back to the lodge. You and your questions and nosey ways. You spoiled all my plans."

The venom in his voice curdled my stomach, his breath hot against my face. "What plans?" I whispered, hoping to buy time and get him talking.

"Stupid cow," he spat.

I couldn't stop the tears now. "I'm sorry. I didn't know. I'll, I'll help you now though."

"Too late, sweet pea. I'm done here. Once I get rid of you, I'm gone. They'll think I've gone away for a few days and by the time they find you I'll be out of the country. That's if the rats leave anything to find."

He giggled. Ty giggled like he normally did, but this was cold and heartless. He stood and began pacing again.

I willed myself to be invisible to him and strained to hear what he said. "This property should've been mine. Just needed the decrepit old folks to die off and then hurry along those who wouldn't cooperate."

Oh, my God. The pieces started to fall into place, but I kept silent and let him ramble.

"At least you helped my plans by heading into town for a birthday cake. Wonder how long it will take anyone to realize I'm missing too? Maybe once they find your car outside the bakery, but it'll be too late by then."

"Too late for what. What have you done?"

He ignored me and began to recite his plan. "First that slut Janet has to return. She stayed with Brad while making up her mind whether to see her parents. Brad lets it slip I've been giving Reid ground chestnut powder for his own experiments."

He kept punching one fist into his other hand as he ranted.

"Janet overheard Reid asking me what I was using on the McTaggarts. She swore she'd tell her folks first thing. If she did, they'd discover the powder I'd been adding to their water. Reacted well with those sleep aids, better than I thought, but not quite good enough. She believed me when I promised her I'd stop. Simple brains must run in the whole family."

He cocked his head to one side as if listening for something, or to someone. It gave me chills. He nodded as if to himself and continued his tirade.

"And Reid. Damn him—Mr. Straight and Narrow —I'll need to take care of him, too."

I couldn't keep up.

"Worked so much better on Phillip, but maybe being off the rails already helped things along. I knew he wouldn't be back. Yes, yes before Philip I had to stop Janet. Didn't want them to know she'd come back to town. She was a piece of cake. You should pardon the pun. I offered to drive her to Leven Lodge, but we took a detour instead. Once she got in the car it was easy to jab her. Harrison's not the only one who can cook up something special."

He held up a syringe. "Poof! Out like a light." He swept his arm out in front of him. I was his audience of one.

"Brought her here, for a short time. Such a little thing, kind of like you, so it was easy to weigh her down and let the river do its work. I hoped her body would stay caught up in the rocks for longer than it did. I drove right back to town and told Bradley that Janet had a big blow-up with her folks and he needed to get there and calm things down. Sucker."

I could barely speak, my mouth had gone dry, but I needed to buy time. "Ty, maybe we could work something out. I...I might be willing to sell the home to you after all?"

"Too little too late. SHUT UP!"

He started pacing again and lowered his voice, speaking to himself. "Couldn't believe how smooth it went the second time. Mind you, he was bigger and obviously the body didn't end up where I planned. River currents meant it showed up earlier than I'd wanted."

He stopped his bragging long enough to wave the syringe in my face. "This stronger dose is for you. Behave, or it'll be sooner rather than later. Serves you right. Wanting to keep the lodge going, breeding those dumb pack animals." He paused, and cocked his head to one side. "Maybe not so dumb. Ever wonder why they avoided part of their yard?"

I shook my head.

"Wouldn't go near the one spot I used to hide my specialty." He took the protective cap off the syringe and tapped the barrel. The wink he gave me turned my stomach. "Guess they smelled something not right, ha!"

Then he returned to his rhetoric. "Do you have any idea the money I could bring in for my investors who are eager to buy the place? They've already drawn up plans for an upscale spa and resort. Once all the legal claimants are out of the way, the place will go on the auction block."

His ego-driven rant was endless. "Tie that in with a casino, the well-heeled from the big cities would flock here."

Keep talking, keep talking. The longer he talked about himself the more chance I had to try and get out of this mess. He had us all fooled, even Dianne.

"I'd have had them all gone within the year, you know. The twins would have been next, and I wanted to save a special treat for that disgusting stink bag. Onto plan B then. But first get rid of you and then I'll be gone."

He picked up a bulky backpack.

"Please, Ty. I won't tell anyone. Why don't you just go, disappear?"

He pulled out a roll of heavy tape from the bag and fixed a fresh piece back over my mouth.

Panic rose and my heart thumped so much it felt like it would explode.

"Nothing you say will change my mind. You'll be number three and I think I'm starting to like this hobby."

He untied my ankles and the blood flowing back into my legs when he yanked me upright nearly made me pass out. "We'll have to drive a little further than where I dumped Janet. I might not even knock you out first. Trying for something different."

I must have been in shock—my mind blanked and didn't want to offer me any solutions, and I knew every step brought me closer to being killed. I tried with all my might to resist being dragged across the floor. If nothing else, I'd leave evidence I'd struggled with him. Dust swirled in the air, my nose clogged with the stuff, and I couldn't breathe. It didn't slow him down. He jerked me along. I glanced around feverishly looking for anything that might help me.

We reached the heavy wooden door. He had to let go of me to lift the old iron latch bar. I dropped to the floor and rolled onto my back. The door groaned open, and he turned back to me with a curse.

As he bent down to grab my arms, I curled my legs and kicked with all I had left and jammed both feet into his groin.

He howled, dropped to his knees, and rolled onto his side. I tried to struggle to a standing position but without hands for leverage I couldn't do it. Tears stung as I saw my momentary victory slip away into defeat.

Just let it be over quick, I prayed. I closed my eyes and thought of Jeff and how much I'd miss him. I concentrated on his face and his voice.

I could imagine his voice. "Alysha!" No, not my imagination, it was Jeff! Lights cut through the darkness and strong hands pulled me to my feet. The tape came off my mouth and I took a deep breath.

I called his name between sobs. "Jeff, Jeff, it was Ty. He'll get away. I tried, but I couldn't..."

He held me tight and stroked my hair. "Shhhh. Shhhh...it's alright, you're safe now."

Then I noticed someone else standing off to the

side, hand resting on his holster. But the gun wasn't drawn. DC Young stood over a crumpled Ty. He wasn't moving. Had I hit him that hard?

"He's not going anywhere," said Young. "See?"

I looked at the silent form. The officer shone his flashlight on Ty's left leg. The syringe he'd threatened me with was now impaled in his leg, barrel empty.

I looked at the officer.

"I'm not the coroner, but I'd say Ty Rogers won't be a problem anymore."

Shudders racked me, and I buried my face in Jeff's chest and rested there for a moment. Then Jeff gently pulled away so he could look at me. He held my face in his hands.

"Aly, oh God I was so afraid I'd lost you. You're not hurt, are you?"

I rubbed at the raw skin on my lips from the tape. He leaned down to place a gentle kiss on the tender spot. Like he was seeing me with new eyes and my heart swelled with thankfulness for him.

"How did you know where to find me?"

"Let's get outside where the air is better, and I'll tell you." He put his arm around me and led me to the fresh air. Police cars and an ambulance greeted me. The reality of what I'd escaped rushed over me and my knees buckled. Jeff held me tighter, and we leaned against one of the cruisers.

"When you didn't come back with the cake, I worried you'd had car trouble."

"And I didn't have my phone because I was only going to be ten minutes, sorry."

Jeff smiled. "My stomach sank when I called your cell and heard it ringing not far from me. I left Jan in charge of the party and drove into town. First place I checked was the bakery where I found your car, with the cake on the back seat. Honestly, I didn't know what to think."

"Jeff, I'm so sorry I made you worry. Ty was parked outside the bakery, waiting for me. Begged me to give him just ten minutes to check out the mill for the landscape painting. Said it would be quick because he had to be on his way to Toronto and he knew I had to get back. I offered to follow in my car, but he said it would be quicker to hop in his. So away we went. Last thing I remember is adjusting my seat belt, then I woke up in the mill."

I remembered what happened and my hand went to the side of my neck, a sore spot. He must have jabbed me, like he did with Janet.

"Oh babe, this was too close of a call."

"But how did you know to look for me at the mill?"

"After I found your car, I went into the bakery. The clerk remembered you picking up the cake but didn't pay any attention after you left the store. So, I raced back home, hoping you'd maybe walked back there. Like I said, I wondered if you'd had car trouble. The look on everyone's face when I arrived without you told me you weren't there."

"Jan was beside herself and got on the phone to her nephew. Even though you technically can't report a person missing after just a couple of hours, he came to see what help he could offer."

"I felt helpless and didn't know what to do." He paused and a guilty look flashed across his face. "Um, I got desperate and read your journal."

I couldn't be angry with him, and besides there really wasn't anything secretive in it. "You're forgiven. Did it help?"

"I didn't think so, but by the time I'd read through it, DC Young had arrived. We shooed everyone but Dianne and Jan back into the house. He revealed he'd finally had an informative chat with Dr. Harrison. Seems he'd been avoiding the cops over guilt that he might have had something to do with the McTaggart's downturn."

A paramedic interrupted Jeff. He wanted to check me over and suggested strongly I should be taken to the hospital for observation.

"Jeff can take me there, is that alright?"

The paramedic glanced at Jeff and back at me. "I'll be checking to make sure."

"I'll get her there right away. Believe me, I don't want anything else to happen to her."

He walked back to the ambulance, and I prodded Jeff to continue.

"Young said the police had Harrison on their radar as the prime suspect in Brad's death, and then with Janet's body surfacing, they were sure they had their man."

"But?"

"But after interrogating him, they realized they were on the wrong track. Especially after comments he made about Ty's actions and threats. And of course, he identified the mystery person from the lodge as being Ty."

His face grew grim. "Dianne heard all this too, and she looked as if she wanted to be sick. Said something to the effect that Ty hadn't been himself lately and she knew something wasn't right. She wanted to know what Ty had said to Harrison."

Jeff stopped talking, and merely stared at me. His eyes welled, but he blinked a couple of times and continued. "Apparently Ty had himself in a right egotistical frame of mind last time they talked. Had plans for opening a prestigious resort facility here. Harrison thought he was only spouting off until he mentioned something about once all the residents were out of the way."

I shook my head. "He must have been planning this for a long time. Ty told me as much when I came to. I don't think Harrison understood what Ty planned. Oh, Jeff, he was evil and none of us saw it."

"Pretty sure Dianne, with hindsight, knows it now."

I hugged Jeff with all my might. "I'm so happy you were inquisitive."

"Yeah. With your scribblings and what DC Young put together, we figured the mill a likely place to start looking for you."

Chuckling, I said, "My hero. I'll have to get you a t-shirt."

He laughed. "But now it's time to get you to the hospital, you may think you're okay, but if Ty injected you with something, the police will want to know what it is, and we need to make sure there are no after-effects."

Jan greeted us at the emergency room doors, worry lines etched across her face. "I leave for five minutes and look what you get up to." She hugged me tightly. "Dax had one of his constables pick me up as I didn't trust myself to drive." Holding me at arm's length, she asked, "How are you, little one? Dalton would never have forgiven me if something had happened to you."

My protector and hero stepped in. "How about we get her inside and then after she's been checked out you two can chat." I had a new appreciation for him now. I gave Jan a smile to reassure her I'd be fine. She had started to mean a great deal to me, as part of my family.

Saturday night in Grants Crossing emergency was busy. A bar fight and a couple of kids with broken limbs. I must have been a special case because I was whisked through to an examining room right away. A check from the doctor in charge, some blood samples taken, and then I was free to go but directed to get lots of rest.

Not quite so fast though. DC Young waited. "Do you feel up to giving your statement now, Alysha? We can take it here and now, and then the Social Services people would like to discuss the McTaggarts with you."

I looked at Jeff and Jan who'd started to protest. "I'm good. I'd rather get it down while it's still fresh in my mind."

We moved to a small room with table and chairs. Tea and coffee were brought in, and I sipped a soothing cup of hot tea while I wrote my statement.

Jan reassured me that Dianne had stayed with the other residents because she couldn't face the hospital another evening. I could relate. "I think she's blaming herself for not seeing what Ty had planned. But of course, she wants to know the outcome as soon as possible."

The door opened and a new face appeared. From Dianne's previous description I immediately recognized Matthew Hall, the social worker. She was right, I felt old in comparison, he barely looked past puberty. He'd come to tell us we could see the McTaggarts but despite our protests, they would be moved to a facility for more care. Jock had slipped into a depression we couldn't possibly handle, and Bea's mind had slipped away, perhaps permanently. They didn't hold out much hope of a recovery.

"Two more victims of Ty Rogers," commented the DC.

Matthew Hall carried on. "I believe Ms. Young that you're the Power of Attorney for their estate and care. Perhaps we could have a word later about how to proceed."

That came as a surprise, and I realized I had much more to learn about Jan. She made her request. "Do you think I could see them now? I know it's late, but I won't disturb them."

He agreed and Jan left with him. DC Young and

his partner remained. They were ready to dismiss us, with Dax Young's instructions. "Why don't you both go home and if I need any more information I know where to find you. I'll bring my aunt home shortly."

You didn't have to ask me twice. I shook their hands. "Thank you, for coming to my rescue today."

His smile belayed the gruff tone to his voice. "Get going both of you."

Jeff took my arm. "Let's go home to Leven Lodge and see to the alpacas. I've been negligent today. Seems I had other things on my mind—like my best girl."

Home yes. What a sweet word. I let him lead the way, but with a question. "Do you think the cake is still salvageable?"

### Grant's Crossing Gazette
### Abduction, Death, Resolution

The abandoned Grant's Sawmill saw more action last night than it has for fifty years. The scene of an abduction and attempted murder ended in the death of the suspect.

Ty Rogers, 63, was found dead at the scene, after an accidental injection of poison during a struggle. He had been holding Alysha Grant, 28, the current owner of Leven Lodge, against her will after allegedly abducting her. Details are not yet available, but police have confirmed Mr. Rogers was their chief suspect in the deaths of both Bradley McTaggart and his cousin, Janet McTaggart.

# ACKNOWLEDGEMENT

We really depend on, and value, our beta readers for feedback and correction!

Thanks to C. Fellman and S. O'Toole for your invaluable assistance with this book.

# ABOUT THE AUTHOR

## Jamie Tremain

Jamie Tremain was 'born' in the summer of 2007. A collaborative effort brought about by two fledgling authors, Pam Blance and Liz Lindsay. Work colleagues who happened to share a love of reading and writing, and the natural next step  was to try their hand at creating a story of their own.

Attending workshops and writing conferences, as well as blogging about their journey, have helped them along the way to hone their craft. Jamie Tremain has also worked hard to be a visible presence in the writing community, where encouragement and support are golden.

They have three books in the Dorothy Dennehy Mystery series and are excited to now present a new series - Grant's Crossing.

# BOOKS BY THIS AUTHOR

## The Silk Shroud

The first abook in the Dorothy Dennehy Mystery Series.

Private Investigator Dorothy Dennehy and her team work to solve the mystery surrounding two over-sized Geisha dolls targeted to Portland, Oregon businessman, Paul Webster.

What secrets do these silent dolls hold?

## Lightning Strike

Second in the series.

Many of the characters introduced with The Silk Shroud return to help Dorothy and her team tackle a heart-wrenching murder.

Family dynamics have deadly consequences.

## Beholden To None

Third in the series.

Dorothy, with Rolin and HB, head to Detroit to solve a long-ago crime which has resurfaced to threaten one of her team.

Former enemies unite for revenge.

# COMING SOON!

Grant's Crossing Book #2 - Resort to Murder

Alysha and Dianne return, with Jan, Jeff and others from Leven Lodge. When a murder, resulting from a botched drug deal, brings fall-out to Leven Lodge, one of it's residents falls under suspicion.

Guilty or innocent?

Made in the USA
Middletown, DE
09 October 2021

49315415R00175